GIRLS
WHO BITE

GIRLS WHO BITE
LESBIAN VAMPIRE EROTICA

EDITED BY
DELILAH DEVLIN

CLEiS
PRESS

Published in the United States by Cleis Press, Inc., 2246 Sixth Street, Berkeley, California 94710.

Printed in the United States.
Cover design: Scott Idleman/Blink
Cover photograph: Piotr Stryjewski/Getty Images
Text design: Frank Wiedemann

First Edition.
10 9 8 7 6 5 4 3 2 1

Trade paper ISBN: 978-1-57344-715-7
E-book ISBN: 978-1-57344-737-9

Contents

INTRODUCTION

Vampire—vagina. A more perfect sensual pairing couldn't be imagined. Dark hungers, shocking thirsts... For blood, for connection... A sharing of nourishment and comfort... Infliction and acceptance of pain...

Whether the story depicts a traditional blood-drinker seducing a meal, a psychic vampire stealing life force from an unknowing host, or a real-life sanguinarian seeking a partner to share a ritual bloodletting to cement a bond, the stories will be varied and unexpected. Writers will be encouraged to investigate vampire myths from around the world, looking for something fresh to add to the pantheon.

That description was included in the call for submissions I sent out when I began this project. This being the first book where I don the editor's hat and make the selections, I wanted stories the likes of which I hadn't read before. I write about vampires and werewolves, demons and succubi, and a dragon here and there. I love to read about them. But in this shorter format, I wanted to spark authors to provide me with something rare: a surprise.

I made hard, excruciating choices, keeping in mind that I wanted the stories to be beyond simply erotic. If they didn't pull at my emotions, if they didn't provide me with a fresh twist and leave me feeling hopeful or haunted, I put them aside. I am at heart a romantic.

Why vampires? Aren't there enough books and movies to bludgeon the genre to death? Maybe. But I'll bet there will be a tale or two here that you've never read before. Or a twist you didn't expect. Add the sensual texture of Sapphic love, and it's a perfect mix. Blood is life. And for a vampire, a blood host is more than food; the relationship is one to be nurtured, and who better to understand that than women?

So, sit astride the dome of St. Peter's Basilica, sail with modern-day pirates, watch a meteor fall to earth and taste the powdery wings of a monarch butterfly. Not things you'd expect in a vampire tale? Then sip O-positive from a femoral artery while tugging at the silky strands of your lover's hair, or scent a fated mate in an ocean breeze. Not so surprising, but eternally delicious.

Delilah Devlin

BLOODY
WICKED

Vivi Anna

A soft, warm breeze tickled the leaves of the grand oak trees as I stepped out of the woods. The sultry night air pressed down. The weather had been unnaturally hot for the end of October, and the dying sun had brought no relief to the day's humidity. Sweat trickled down my back and over the firm swell of my buttocks. My red silk robe clung sinuously to my clammy skin, and my long hair stuck to the back of my neck. The walk from my home to this sacred place was short, but in this heat even that produced enough sweat to slick my skin.

Bright light from the full moon illuminated the small clearing. I could clearly see the large wood stump I had consecrated months ago for my altar. I walked to it slowly, breathing in the sweet scents of the night air. It was a perfectly delectable night for making magic.

I set down the wicker basket I carried on the wooden altar. Stepping alongside it, I shed my robe and slipped off my sandals. I stretched my arms up to the heavens and closed my eyes. The warm breeze caressed my naked body. The only thing I wore was an Egyptian ankh amulet around my neck, a ward against negative energies. I took in one last deep breath, then turned to my basket and the work at hand.

"I call upon the element of air to be present and to bless the work to be done." I raised the candle to the night sky. "Hail and welcome."

The invocations I did intensified the ancient mystical elements that roamed the woods. I could almost see the magic in the night sky. A faint warm glow emanated around me. The spell would be powerful. I had no doubt it would work. I was a commanding witch.

From the basket, I withdrew a small clay bowl and set it on the altar. Next, I took out a brown glass bottle, opened it and dripped oil into the bowl. The sweet warm smell of cinnamon wafted up to my nose. I took out another bottle, a plastic one full of avocado oil, and poured some into the bowl.

Dipping my fingers into the mixture, I rubbed the liquid onto my nipples reveling in the way it made my skin tingle with heat. As I touched my skin, power trickled over me, cutting a lazy trail down my belly to pool in between my legs. Energy crested at my center, making my juices flow.

I slid my hand over the soft folds of my sex. Wet and hot, I rejoiced in the way my flesh heated even more beneath my fingertips. Slowly, I inserted two fingers inside, pumping lazily, in no hurry to find release. I loved to play with myself. The spell would be stronger because of it.

Arching my back and spreading my legs even farther apart, I added my other hand to the play. I swirled my fingers over my clit, flinching as my legs tightened and flexed in response. An orgasm was building like a raging inferno.

Increasing my tempo, I fingered my sex while flicking my

clit. It never failed to get me off, and I needed to come hard for my incantation to be potent. The elementals would hear my cries one way or another.

As I buried my hand to the second knuckle, I pinched my clit sharply. Within seconds, a surge of pleasure crashed through me. Moaning, I clamped my eyes shut and came like a volcano. Hot cream gushed over my fingers.

Panting, I lay there until I had the strength to move. I sat up, being careful not to wipe off the creamy liquid on my fingers. I reached into my basket and gathered my bolline and two pink candles. With my ritual knife, I carved an ancient symbol into one candle and set it on the altar. I dipped my hands into the oil bowl, mixing my cum with the tincture. Again, I anointed the remaining candle and set it with the other on the altar where I lit them both.

The wind picked up and swirled violently around me but miraculously did not extinguish the flames. My magic was strong. This spell, I hoped, would be one of my most effective. The elementals couldn't deny my call.

I raised my arms to the heavens, closed my eyes and bowed my head. "And let it be done."

I rubbed at my temple again. The headache was getting worse, stronger, more centralized. This morning I woke with a dull throb all over my head, but now, late in the day, it was situated in my temples. It was as if someone had pushed pins into the side of my skull.

The bell at my door rang. I looked up as the door opened and Ted, Raven's Bay's deputy, and a woman strolled in. I smiled.

"Hi, Ted. Did you come for some more bath salts? I just made up a new batch."

Ted blushed. "Ah, no, sorry, Anisa. Business today. This is

Sheriff Alexa Branwell." He stepped to the side and waved his hand at the woman commanding the room behind him.

I felt my heart stutter in my chest as I looked her over. She was tall with wide shoulders and a trim waist. Her curly dark hair brushed at her collar and flirted at her brow, overlooking incredibly dark blue eyes. She had an impressive presence. The weight of her aura pressed back on me, circled me and caressed my skin.

There was power there.

"I had no idea Raven's Bay was getting a new sheriff."

She continued to eye me, as if taking measure. I shivered involuntarily at the intensity of her gaze.

"Ah, she just arrived today and needs to talk to you. In private," Ted said softly, his eyes flitting to Poppy, my young employee, who hovered nearby, her dark brown eyes wide with interest.

"Sure. How about we go in the back?" I motioned to the gauzy curtain separating the back rooms.

I led them to the room where there was a small round table and two chairs. I gestured to one of the chairs. "Would you care to sit?"

"No, thank you." The sheriff's electric voice caressed my skin, and I shivered.

"Well, I will, if you don't mind?" I pulled out a chair and sat, crossing my long legs. I hoped she didn't notice them quivering. Being near the woman was intoxicating. I felt light-headed and almost giddy.

Clearing my throat, I tried to sound unaffected. "Was there something you wanted?"

After several long seconds, she pulled her gaze away and glanced around the room. "Did you know Stan Hart?"

I frowned. "Yes, I know him."

"What was your relationship with him?"

"No relationship, thank you."

"Stan's not your favorite person?" Alexa cocked an eyebrow, and I wondered if she could hear the disdain in my voice.

"Not really."

"You've had words over the years? Arguments? Heated arguments?"

"You could say that. Stan has a problem with...me."

"And that made you...angry?"

I sat forward in my chair and put a hand onto the table. "What is this all about?"

Ted sighed. "Stan's dead, Anisa."

I gasped and put a shaky hand to my mouth. Alexa's gaze never left my face. I could tell she was searching for something. Guilt maybe?

The sheriff nodded toward Ted. "Deputy, could you excuse us?"

Ted looked at Alexa, then back to me. "Um..."

"I'd prefer if he stayed, Sheriff Branwell," I managed to say, my breath nearly catching in my throat at the surge in power I sensed. My skin tingled and my muscles clenched. Sweat rolled down my chest to settle inside my navel.

She narrowed her eyes. "Why?"

"Because I don't like the way you're looking at me." I lied. I liked how she regarded me, with equal measures of lust and hostility. The combination made my skin tingle and my muscles melt in desire. An ache, hot, brutal and intense, burned at my core. I pushed back on the heat Alexa aimed at me and wondered if she felt the same delicious quivers through her curvy body.

Ted looked from me to Alexa, unsure of what to do. "Do you want me to take notes, Sheriff?"

Alexa glanced over at him and nodded, her jaw clenched.

Ted took out his notebook and sat down in the chair across the table from me. "Let's start over, shall we?"

I set my hands in my lap trying to hide the quake in them. "I'd really appreciate it if you'd tell me what's going on. I'm feeling very...persecuted right now."

"Persecuted? Interesting word choice. Why would you say that?"

"Well, you're obviously here because Ted told you Stan and I never got along. You're also here because Stan's death was not accidental, and you're here because Ted told you I'm a witch. So yeah, persecuted, I think, is the correct word for the situation, don't you think?"

"You admit to being a witch?"

"Yes. Do you admit to being a bitch?"

Alexa tilted her head and grinned. I swallowed down the moan threatening to erupt. Her smile was more disarming than her intense gaze, and did I detect tips of fangs between her full lips?

Liquid heat pooled between my legs. I didn't know how long I could hang on without anyone noticing my precarious condition. I desperately wanted to spread my legs and satisfy the throb drumming at my sex.

"Where's your crystal ball?"

"I don't have one. You have me confused with a psychic."

"Okay, where's your broomstick?"

"In the corner." I gestured to the right corner behind her.

The back and forth banter did nothing to quell my growing need. In fact, it ignited the flames, urging them higher. Licking my lips, I did a slow, thorough perusal of her body. I smiled when I noticed the stain on the crotch of her snug jeans. She was obviously feeling the heat between us.

"Do you conjure spells?"

"Yes," I said, tearing my gaze from between her legs.

"Can you put spells on people?"

I leaned back in my chair and narrowed my eyes. "No."

I wanted to beg her to move away. Her hot violent aura was pressing down on me—oppressive but delicious. I wanted to reach up and hook my finger in her jeans and pull her closer. The urge to bury my face in her pussy nearly made me choke. "Spells are only suggestions, nothing more."

"So, you could do an evil spell, on say, me...and make a suggestion that I...hmm, that I take a flying leap off a bridge?"

"Magic does no harm."

"What does that mean?"

"It means, Sheriff, that magic itself is only a tool. It's neutral. There is no such thing as an evil spell."

"How about an evil person? Is there such a thing as an evil person?"

"I suppose."

Alexa touched a finger to her mouth as if in thought. "What if this evil person knew magic? What then?"

I uncrossed my legs and sat forward in my chair defiantly looking up at Alexa. I knew what she insinuated, and I couldn't muster the anger to debate her. If only she really knew how wicked I could be. Would she run, or smile in invitation?

Finally, I found my voice. "Then, I suppose, you'd have one hell of a problem on your hands, Sheriff."

"Would I?"

"Oh, yes."

With those words, I released some magic. I didn't care who saw it in my eyes. I couldn't contain the vortex of power swirling inside of me. Alexa did something to me no person had before. And I wasn't quite sure what to do about it.

The candles sparked to life and the table beneath them

trembled as if the earth itself shook.

Ted stood up abruptly from the table and knocked his chair over. The resonating sound bolted Alexa from her trance. Her eyes snapped open, and she took a shaky step back from me.

"Okay, I think we've bothered you enough, Anisa. We'll just get going." Ted stepped up to Alexa and put a hand on her arm.

Alexa shook her head clear and glanced over at Ted. There was worry in her eyes. I could see it. Alexa looked back down. I still sat forward, but my hands were pressed down on the chair between my legs, as if I was about to spring up and attack, like a cat ready to pounce. If we had been alone, I would've.

"I'll be following up with you, Ms. Crowley, so don't think of leaving town."

I nodded that I understood because words wouldn't form. Too tense and on edge, I couldn't do anything else.

I watched as Ted escorted Alexa out of the room and back into my shop. I could sense the nervousness Ted felt. The way he looked at Alexa told me that he feared for the sheriff. Ted was a smart man.

As I opened the doors to my deck, I inhaled the night air. The sweet smell of jasmine, lavender and freesia wafted to my nose from the garden in the backyard. I took in another deep breath, trying to calm my nerves.

Ever since Sheriff Alexa Branwell had entered my shop and befuddled my senses, I'd been on edge, unnerved. I'd never met a person with her energies. It floated off her like heat waves, causing severe short-circuiting in my own high-energy wiring. The woman had no idea what she did to me.

After she left the shop, I had to sit still in my chair for another half-hour before I could trust my legs to support my weight. She had caught me off guard. I hadn't expected to see her so soon. I knew she would have sought me out eventually, having no choice in the matter. Her aura would have recognized mine in time. But coming face-to-face with her, without my shields in place, nearly drained all my powers.

I turned from the open door and drew my attention back to the tincture brewing on the stove. Putting my nose over the pot, I breathed in the scent of jasmine, patchouli and nutmeg. I closed my eyes and felt an immediate tightening deep in my belly. I picked up the pot and set it on the warmer to cool, smiling to myself.

"Trespassing is against the law in this state, Sheriff." I turned around slowly.

She stood in my open door, looking rumpled and brooding, and extremely sexy.

"Would you like some herbal tea? You look like you need some." I grabbed the teapot and filled it up with water. I set it on the stove and turned on the heat.

When I turned back, I noticed she hadn't moved from her spot. It was as if she was rooted there. I leaned back on the counter and regarded her.

"Have you bewitched me?" Her voice was low and rough.

"The tea will be ready in a moment. Why don't you come in and sit down?"

She moved like lightning. I barely had time to lift my hand before she stood in front of me, her hands gripping my upper arms, fingers digging into my flesh.

"Have you bewitched me?" she demanded, her voice shaking with anger.

I raised my head defiantly and stared into the cold blue depths of her eyes. "No more than you have enraptured me."

Alexa bent toward my mouth. I could feel her hot breath on

my face as she neared my lips. Wanting desperately to taste her, I parted them with a sigh.

She swore and pushed away from me. "I can't eat. I can't sleep. Your face occupies my vision. I can smell your scent on my clothes, on my skin. I showered and scrubbed until I was red and raw, but your smell still lingered." She turned on me, fists clenched. "I'm the one that usually overpowers the other."

I turned, facing the counter, and poured the tea. I took two cups and placed them on the table. I handed one to Alexa. "Take your tea. We'll talk."

Alexa swiped at my hand, knocking the teacup from it. It shattered into pieces on the tiled floor. "I don't want your fucking tea!"

The rage pouring out of her surged over me like molten lava. I gasped and felt my knees go weak. I held the table to steady my stance. My breath came in short gasps, and I had trouble swallowing. The ache in my belly slipped lower, centering and intensifying in my sex. My panties moistened and my thighs quivered. "Alexa, you need to calm down."

"I can't, when all I want to do is rip away your dress, push you onto the table and sink my tongue into your cunt."

Her energy crackled around my body. I could feel it biting into my skin, clawing at my flesh, trying desperately to gain entrance. I moaned and looked away from her electrifying gaze, which now glowed from the darkness inside her. Droplets of lust dribbled down my thighs. I could smell my own scent, musky and intoxicating.

Alexa moved closer. She sniffed the air and leered down at me. "I can smell you. Your cunt is hot and wet, dripping for me."

I put out a hand to ward her off. "It's too soon. I can't protect myself. You're moving too fast."

She stepped into my hand, pushing against it. She grabbed my wrist and twisted my arm behind my back. A twinge of pain surged up my arm and I reveled in it.

She moved in close to me, a breath away from my face. "You smell like a whore. A whore ready to be sucked and fucked. Is that what you want from me, witch? You want me to fuck you first then suck your blood from your veins?"

I could no longer think. All I could see was Alexa, her eyes on fire and dangerous, her mouth twisted into a cruel smile, fangs, now distended, protruding between those lips. Those lips I wanted so badly on my skin.

They were the lips I dreamt about. Her face I pictured when I called her to me. She was the vampire lover I needed.

"Yes," I murmured, out of breath, gasping from the power surging from her.

"What? I couldn't hear you." She spoke into my mouth; her lips hovering a whisper away.

"Yes," I said more clearly.

"Yes, what?"

"Yes, I want you to fuck me."

"Say it again."

"I want you to fuck me."

"Again," she growled like an animal.

"I want you to fuck me!" I screamed.

Alexa brought her other hand up to the neckline of my dress. She yanked downward, ripping the material. Buttons popped off. The dress separated, exposing my lace-clad breasts. She growled low in her throat as she moved her hand over them. Grabbing the lace cup, she pulled, freeing one pert breast.

I groaned while she pinched and pulled on my pebbled nipple. I sensed her loss of control. It was almost audible. She bent and feasted on my flesh, sucking hard on my nipple. She yanked down the other cup and moved over to suckle the other nipple. She rolled it between her fangs, then bit down.

I gasped and writhed in her arms. I knew she wanted to hear me scream; to beg her to end my torment, to end the exquisite suffering. But I refused. It wasn't time yet.

She yanked my dress completely down, ripping it to the hem.

I was now quivering before her in only my black lace panties. My sun-kissed skin glowed in contrast. She pushed me onto the table, unable to rein in her raging lust.

I knew she had thought of nothing but me since our first meeting. I had made sure of that. The oils on my skin contained my magic. When she had walked into my shop and first scented me, my magic had filled her nose, implanted my signature inside of her.

The only way to rid me from her was to give in, to slake her lust and ravage me. Maybe then I would give back her mind, her sanity.

But as she looked down at me spread out on the table, my eyes dark with desire, my skin glowing, and the flimsy triangle of fabric covering my sex, I sensed she wasn't so sure she would ever escape, nor if she wanted to.

Alexa rubbed her hands over my taut belly to the swatch of lace between my legs. Without a word, she slipped her fingers underneath and yanked, snapping the thin elastic band. She brought the black lace up to her nose and breathed in my scent. "You smell like cinnamon."

With a growl, she tossed the G-string over her shoulder and leered down at my exposed sex. A thin angry mark bisected my hip bone where she had snapped off my panties. She traced a finger along the line.

I hissed through my teeth as she pressed on it. She watched

my face as she traced a line down to my naked sex. I was shaved except for a small tuft of golden hair on my mound. She twirled her finger in the hair, and then trailed it down, splitting me in half.

Moaning, I closed my eyes as she stroked me slowly with her fingers. I imagined I was like liquefied satin under her touch. She brought her fingers to her mouth and licked them clean. "Damn, you almost taste better than blood."

Alexa grabbed my legs and bent them, pushing them up and apart so I was completely open and displayed to her. She gazed down at my glistening sex and I saw her sanity break.

Bending down, she buried her face in me, licking my slit from anus to clit, then back down again. She did it repeatedly until I whimpered with desperate, clawing need.

While she lapped at my sex, I massaged my breasts, pulling my nipples taut. I gasped as she swirled her tongue over my swollen nub.

My muscles pulled tight in my legs and belly. I could feel the powerful orgasm building deep in my cunt. She probed deep into me, sucking on my juices. If she sucked on my clit like that, allowing her fangs to flick it back and forth, I knew I would explode into a thousand glorious pieces.

I grabbed her head and pushed her toward my aching nub. I needed release. I would go mad without it. My breathing grew labored, and my mind teetered dangerously on the edge. I needed to plunge into the velvet depths.

Alexa pushed my hand away and sat up, looking smug and pleased. "Beg me." She grinned, her lips slick and shiny with my lust. "Beg me to make you come."

I groaned as her words inflamed me more. Her control over me was delicious torture. "Please, make me come, Alexa," I panted.

"How? How should I do it, dirty witch?"

"Fuck me."

"Not good enough. Tell me more." She brought a hand down to my aching sex and flicked her finger over my clit.

I bowed my back and moaned loudly.

"Like this?"

"Ah, yes. More," I whimpered.

"More what?"

"Touch my clit."

"And?" She flicked it again.

"Rub it. Pinch it. Pull it," I panted.

Alexa pressed her thumb against the swollen, purple nub and rubbed it around in circles. "Like this."

"Yes, harder."

She pressed down hard and rubbed faster. "Like this."

I could barely talk as jolts of pleasure surged through my cunt, over the swollen folds, and up my body. "Y-y-yes."

Alexa pinched my clit between her finger and thumb and pulled sharply on it. The orgasm pounded into my belly and radiated up and out to my extremities. My muscles contracted and quivered as waves of pleasure crashed over me and threatened to drown me under their sublime grip.

I kicked out, forcing Alexa to back up. But she still held firm on my clit, rubbing and jiggling it, urging more from me, more than I'd ever given to anyone.

"Ah, no more," I panted. "No more."

Alexa relinquished her hold on my clit, and gazed down, her eyes slitted with desire. "You're fucking beautiful when you come."

Finally, the ripples of orgasm quieted, and I was able to take in a deep breath. I had no words for the sensations surging through me. I had no words for what she did to me.

"That was foreplay. Now for the main course."

I could do no more than obey. Her words, her energies, commanded me. My surrender was complete. She could do what she wanted. I couldn't stop her. My aura had opened up and accepted hers. It swirled around us, intermingled, converged into a powerful, sensual energy. For an eternity we were bound.

"Spread yourself wide."

I hooked my hands around my knees and pulled my legs back and apart. My knees touched my breasts. I could feel myself stretch. Lust dribbled down the crack of my ass. I'd never felt so wanton, so violently lusty. It was as if my cunt had taken on its own personality, demanding satisfaction at all costs.

Alexa leaned down and licked my cunt from anus to clit, then suckled. I jolted at the sensations building there. I was still sensitive but battled back the urge to flinch.

She slid a finger into my pussy, then another, then another, until she was pumping all four of her fingers inside me. My sex stretched glorious inch by glorious inch to accommodate her. I was afraid to move as another orgasm quickened deep within my belly. I feared I wouldn't be able to control the descent if I let go. No one had ever made me feel this vulnerable, this open.

Alexa pressed her tongue down on my clit as she picked up the pace of her strokes. Her other hand was busy at my anus. Gathering cum from my pussy, she slipped a finger into me.

I bolted upward, but her hold on me kept me on top of the table.

I closed my eyes against the assault of intense pleasure sweeping over me. My whole body vibrated, ablaze with delight as I crested the waves of release.

"Open your eyes," Alexa groaned.

I opened them, but only because I could hear the restrained violence in her voice.

"I want you to watch as I bite and suck you."

She moved faster, sliding her hands in and out with quick hard thrusts. I gasped as my muscles tightened around her. I could feel my orgasm quicken and harden. My breath hitched in my throat. It was too much.

Opening her mouth wide, her fangs fully down and glistening with saliva, she positioned over the main pulsating vein in my thigh. Without another word, she bit down on my skin.

I screamed as her teeth sank into my flesh. Pain rushed up my body. But soon it mixed with the pleasure and became one big ball of pure bliss surging through every nerve ending.

I could feel every draw she took on my vein. Blood soon spilled from between her lips and dribbled down her chin to drip onto the floor beneath us. Every suck she took was like one on my clit, in my cunt. It was the most intense experience I'd ever had. I could barely hold on to my sanity.

And as Alexa slipped another finger into my ass and her thumb and whole hand into my pussy, I let myself go. I stopped fighting the jolts and let them ripple over me unhindered. My orgasm slammed into me, taking me over the edge into a free fall.

White spots flared behind my eyes. Ringing sounded in my ears. I thought of nothing but the wave of pleasure that rolled over me, drowning me in its intensity. Her power possessed me completely. I was hers. And she knew it.

Finally, after what seemed like an eternity, Alexa lifted her head and smiled. Blood stained her lips and chin. And I thought she looked like a goddess reborn.

"You taste just as I'd hoped you would."

"Kiss me my lover." I opened my arms.

My blood mixed with our saliva as we kissed. It sealed our destiny. I had called the vampire and she came just when I needed her.

"Did you like my offering?" I asked.

Alexa grinned. "Stan was quite satisfying, thank you."

"It was easy to dispose of the body?"

She nodded. "Being sheriff has its privileges."

"I'd say."

I slid off the table and shed the remnants of my torn dress. I unhooked my bra and let it fall to the floor. I stood before her naked except for my silver amulet, unashamed in my nudity. Putting my hands on my hips, I cocked an eyebrow. A wind blew through the room and rustled my hair around me. Power surged through me and over Alexa, the magic that bound us evident in my face and on my body. I had thought to conquer her with my mind and my body, but instead I had been overcome and mastered.

The elementals had heeded my spell. They had sent me a powerful woman to quench my desires, all of them. But because of my arrogance they had also set out to punish me.

Here was the vampire I had conjured—the woman I had wished to be my slave—and she had enslaved me. Her bite was more powerful than any magic I possessed.

When Alexa took a step toward me and my outstretched hand, I knew that I was a goner, plain and simple. She was as bloody wicked as they came.

AL DENTE

Delphine Dryden

Julia had never liked the furry ones. Not hairy men, and definitely not hairy women.

"Even when I was just fucking them, I always hated that," she admitted to Astrid one night when they were just starting out together. "But especially now."

"The texture?" Astrid had a foible or two of her own about texture.

"No. I just hate getting hair stuck in my teeth."

They had shared a laugh, though it was true and one of the things people never really talked about when they were seducing you into the ranks of the sanguinarian undead. You had to bite deep to break the skin cleanly and get a good flow going. You had to commit, which meant all manner of nastiness between the teeth.

And flossing was a dangerous task when your canines were long and sharp. Even when they retracted—sometimes taking the damn hair with them—they tended to wreak havoc on the floss.

Such were the thoughts that weighed heavily as immortality spun itself out—over years, over centuries. Julia felt the tedium, the ennui more keenly with every passing decade. Even looking out on a timeless and undeniably exquisite vista like the one before her now—Rome just after sunset, sky still ribboned with pink and gold in the west, the mountains in stark silhouette against the horizon—it got to be too much.

"I thought I'd find you here."

Julia smiled but didn't turn. She waited, and was rewarded by the almost shy slip of Astrid's arms around her waist and the press of cool lips at the nape of her neck. She wasn't yet too jaded to enjoy that.

"I like it up here. It's the perfect vantage point." They were perched on the dome of St. Peter's, looking not over the piazza in front, but to the west, over the park-like grounds of the Holy See.

"It's a poor hunting blind, if that's what you have in mind."

"Not particularly. Though I can see several lovely members of the clergy from here. Ripe for the picking."

"A man, then, tonight? Italy is having a strange effect on you, my love. All these boys with their bedroom eyes." Astrid spread her fingers out, spanning Julia's lean waist and brushing her thumbs over the delicate seam between ribs and breasts. "A girl could grow jealous."

Julia laughed, the lyrical sound fading into the fitful wind. It was darkening now. True dark. Nearly time. She let her laugh turn to a delicate sigh as Astrid continued to move her hands upward. Cupping, squeezing gently. It did seem jealous, a little, but in a sweet way. It was a possessive thing to do.

"Don't be jealous of the beautiful Italian boys. I may eat them, but only you get to eat me."

Two flavors of laughter followed, disappearing into the

deepening Roman night. The back side of the basilica was not quite as well observed, quite as well lit or as often photographed, as the front. But it was still time to move, before the night tourists replaced the day tourists. Before the twilight's forgiving ambiguity gave way to revealing floodlights.

Astrid's thrilling alto deepened into a wordless murmur of delight as she plucked at nipples that were already firm and hot in the gathering chill. She pressed her teeth lightly against Julia's neck, scraping at the skin more gently than she would at any other neck.

"Tonight, perhaps I should share both. Would you like that? Everyone eats everyone? With a little something now to take the edge off while we wait?"

Julia groaned and arched back into Astrid's body, into her words. "*Yes...*"

They didn't select a priest. Not for that sort of evening, not even as an appetizer. The decision was wordless and mutual. They flew from the church's dome into the city and found a poor, lost soul near the Pyramid of Cestius. He was walking alone, mumbling to nobody, shaking his head from side to side. Whatever argument he was having with himself, he was clearly losing it.

"Angels or devils?" Astrid asked as they skimmed to a human pace several yards behind him.

"Angels, I think. Devils later tonight. Succubi. But this poor bugger looks like he could use a visit from the angels." Julia nipped in front of the shambling victim-to-be, startling him from his reverie and forcing him to a confused halt there on the narrow walkway. There were few pedestrians, and nobody would notice them if they did not care to be noticed.

Julia spoke in slow but fluid Italian, letting her voice soothe the man as her eyes did their work. It was sometimes harder, sometimes easier, when insanity was involved. In this case, to the relief of both ladies, the craziness made the meal much easier to subdue, much easier to lead into an empty side street, a darkened doorway.

He spoke no English. So he merely looked on in rapt adoration as the fairer of his two new angels pointed out that he reeked like an open sewer. Her fingers were caressing his shaggy cheek even as she said the words, and her eyes held all the secrets of love and happiness and life itself. He smiled, an expression of beautiful incredulity. When was the last time he had beheld such loveliness? When was the last time anybody had stopped to speak a kind word to him?

His dark angel replied, "We'll take him at his wrists, so we don't have to touch him as much."

Astrid flicked her blonde tresses out of the way before lowering her mouth to the man's filthy skin.

He died with a smile on his face, and the marks on his wrists would be long gone by the time anybody found his body.

"Ghastly. Like biting into a piece of withered fruit," Astrid complained with a delicate shudder as they entered the disco in the Testaccio district. Noisy, over-mixed dance beats assaulted their sensitive ears, part of the price they would have to pay to secure a more delectable morsel.

"He was a leathery sack of blood," Julia agreed, and then made a noise of sheer disgust. "And I have a hair caught in my teeth." She picked at the offending souvenir with a scarlet-lacquered fingernail. To her relief, the hair came free easily. But it was still disgusting, especially considering the source.

"So we want something smooth and fresh for the main course," Astrid said thoughtfully as she scanned the thin crowd in the disco. It was barely midnight now, still early.

The music throbbed out the passing seconds like heartbeats,

and Julia felt her own pulse quicken in response to the collective pulse of youthful blood and hormones that soon filled the small bar. Within an hour, they had spotted him. And from that moment, it was easy.

He was young, perhaps eighteen or nineteen at the most. He was far too sure of his own seductive potential. And he thought himself lucky, but deserving, to have caught the interest of the two foreign beauties who invited him back to their suite at one of the finest hotels in the city.

Luca, as the young man called himself, was easy on the eyes and spoke just enough English to ease Astrid's way. Julia was an avid linguist, and always had been, but Astrid spoke only two tongues. She still recalled the language of her birthplace and had later adopted English. In her chosen language, Astrid communicated quite well.

"We're going to have fun together, Luca. You know 'fun'?"

He assured her that he did. His grin widened as Julia's clothes practically melted from her lithe body and Astrid took the opportunity to continue her teasing from earlier in the evening. Holding her lover from behind, Astrid fondled her breasts, knowing that the skin Luca was ogling still held a tantalizing flush from the first meal. Astrid slid one trim knee between Julia's thighs to part them, exposing her pink folds to Luca's lust-darkened gaze. There was no hair to obscure the view.

"She's beautiful, isn't she?" Astrid asked the boy. "And so are you. I want to watch the two of you together."

Luca shucked his clothes almost as quickly as Julia had. Both women were pleased to see that he was no more than reasonably furred.

"You're being unusually pushy," whispered Julia, as they watched him undress.

Astrid continued to stroke and tease, pressing fingertips down in a smooth, even stroke over her exposed clit.

"What's gotten into you this evening?"

"Lust," whispered her lover. "Pure and simple. Now get on the bed and let the beautiful boy eat your pussy. I plan to find it very entertaining."

"Are you going to join in?"

"Oh, yes. Once I'm sufficiently entertained."

Julia smirked at the now-naked young man as she threw back the red and gold coverlet and climbed gracefully onto the bed. She knew the picture she presented, knew her own allure. Confident, amused, she lifted her hands to her breasts and rolled her nipples slowly between her thumbs and forefingers as she spread her legs. She knew enough Italian to tell him what she wanted.

He knew enough English to grasp that the taller, blonde woman with the short black leather skirt and very tall black leather boots was the one calling the shots. He looked to Astrid for confirmation and waited for her curt nod before joining Julia on the high, wide bed and lowering his head to lap at her cunt.

Astrid undressed slowly.

Julia watched, almost as entranced by the visual teasing as by the surprisingly talented ministrations of the doomed young man between her thighs. The short jacket and tank top came off, revealing a burgundy silk bra that was more a confection of lace than a support garment, then the skirt, which Astrid removed with a slow shimmy and a smirk. She knew Julia liked the boots, so she obligingly left those on even as she removed the tantalizing lingerie.

A clever flick of Luca's tongue brought Julia's attention back to him; she gasped and arched into his mouth, and smiled at the twin sounds of appreciation from the boy and the ancient woman joining them on the bed. Not ancient compared to Julia, of course. But after a few hundred years together, the difference seemed to matter less and less. Astrid was powerful and coming into her prime.

"Is it good, my love?" Astrid asked, as if she knew the answer.

"Oh, yes."

"As good as me?"

Julia shook her head. "Nobody is as good as you."

"Luca, would you like her to fuck you?"

The boy lifted his head, batting his dreamy eyes at them and nodding his agreement. His cock was stiff and red already. When Astrid playfully pushed him down onto his back the erection stood straight up like a pole, easily mounted, easily ridden.

Julia groaned as she eased herself down onto him, impaling herself. Even the boy could see that his primary use now was as a sex toy. He didn't seem to mind. He made no protest as Astrid lowered her head to Julia's clit and held her hips nearly still while she sucked her lover until she came, shuddering around the convenient cock.

Nor did young Luca complain when Astrid straddled his lower belly, her back to his face, and embraced Julia as she sought her own pleasure. Julia moved again, hips and fingers and mouth, satisfying Astrid and the boy at the same time.

Astrid was cool and pale, even in the heat of her orgasm. Julia felt the muscles of the younger woman's cunt tighten and spasm around her fingers, but the beautiful face in front of her never darkened with the familiar flush of passion.

She wondered if she was beginning to wear that same white, hungry gleam. She wondered if the young man straining beneath them—coming at last with a moaned word she didn't recognize—would notice or care.

He certainly didn't seem bothered much when his new friends

rolled off him, tumbling to the bed in a postcoital kiss. Luca rolled toward them, watching in clear approval, his youthful penis already twitching back into readiness at the sight.

There was a moment when Julia forgot him, forgot everything but the slide and catch of Astrid's body over hers and the melting together of lips and souls. She was so beautiful, her icy Viking goddess, and still proving daily the merit of Julia's decision to change her. Her only child, her only real lover in all this time.

"Maybe we should keep this one for a little while, as a pet," Astrid suggested. The language she spoke now was her first, not her best. Guttural, with a cadence that did not lend itself to sensuality. But it had become their language for secrets. Julia smiled at the discordance of hearing those harsh tones in bed.

"As a cow? You don't even like him, love." Julia pulled her creation closer and kissed her slowly, letting her tongue linger before speaking again. "Besides, he's a boy. I know how you feel about boys."

Astrid laughed. "This particular one's been very well behaved, though, I must admit."

Julia smiled over at the boy in question, who was still watching them with his head propped on one elbow. He wore a delightfully confused expression as he tried to follow their suddenly incomprehensible conversation. For the first time, he looked as though a hint of doubt or uncertainty had crept into his mind. Not fear yet, but she could see what fear would look like on his face. It would be brief. Even at their cruelest, they were never completely lacking in compassion.

Besides, frightened meals tended to struggle too much, and it made for a lot of cleanup. A few moments of terror, however, acted as a delicious spice. They both liked the taste of fear, the high note of adrenaline.

The women moved as if they had one mind, conducting a final loving assault on their companion. Astrid kissed his mouth, a leisurely exploration, while Julia worked her way down his firm young body to tease his cock back to full firmness—because that too would add to the taste.

She continued, barely touching with her lips, tongue, breath. He reached for her head to encourage her, but Astrid took his hands and moved them back up next to his head on the pillow, giving her partner time to work at her own pace.

Astrid might seem to be in charge, but Julia always took the first bite.

She drew it out, as she sometimes liked to do. Teasing herself until her own pulse points felt as though they throbbed in sympathy with the blood she could sense beneath the skin of her meal. Not quite a smell, not quite a flavor, but a plain and certain knowledge of what it would taste like when the teeth finally broke through the skin and hit the source. A vein, delicate, the elemental qualities of the blood coming to the fore. Or an artery, rich and heady and often a mess, a bloody feast for all the heightened senses.

It was time now. Julia stopped the licking, the scraping, and pressed her teeth firmly and smoothly into the flesh of the boy's upper thigh, holding him steady when he tried to jerk away. Astrid kept his mouth covered with her own, kept his hands pinned down with a strength no woman should possess. No man, either.

After the first few seconds, Julia knew Astrid would mesmerize the boy into an unearthly calm and he would no longer need to be restrained. But for the first bites, the meal would be lucid and terrified.

Perfect. He was perfect. The slight tension at the surface just before the skin broke, then the slide of sharp bone into the meat and the burst of essential fluid. Hot, his blood was hot in Julia's mouth, and it thawed the deep chill inside her as thoroughly as a bonfire in winter warms the hands of a vagrant. Just as delicious, just as fleeting. She didn't suck, but let the ebb and flow of his heartbeat direct the blood into her mouth.

Soon she was whimpering, flexing her hips down into the mattress in a futile attempt to ease the rush of renewed arousal that made her pussy and clit throb in time with that pulse. Against her cheek she could feel the boy's cock, still hard, and just as wanting for stimulation as she was. She considered shifting her position, taking him into her mouth and biting him there as he squirmed and tried to thrust. Tempting. But she didn't like the taste of blood and ejaculate together.

"We should put him back where we found him when we're through," Astrid murmured. She had opted for a shallow bite on the meal's shoulder, avoiding major arteries and the always delectable jugular. She sucked at the raw holes, licking the blood from her lips before she continued. "Take his memory, leave just enough to make him ashamed. Wondering, always. If we're being devils, it would be so much crueler than killing him."

Julia lifted her head a few inches, eyes sleepy with desire as she contemplated her lover over the straining body of the young man. "You've come so far. I remember when you wouldn't have had the control to consider such a thing."

Astrid laughed and licked at the wounds on Luca's shoulder, closing the punctures. His head lolled to the side. He was near the end, now. Julia bent to heal his thigh as well, knowing they could drain him no further if they meant to leave him alive.

"Did you get enough?" Julia asked as the skin began to seal itself.

"If we hunt again tomorrow night."

It was pitifully easy to walk the drowsy Italian back out

of the hotel. They didn't even have to hide it. He just seemed drunk, and they were still euphoric themselves from their hit of rich young blood. A beautiful, giggling, tipsy threesome they appeared to be, heading back out for another round of dancing.

They left him in an empty street near the bar where they'd acquired him, and he started shuffling away as soon as they let him go. The trip back to the hotel was much faster without the added burden.

It was still full dark when Julia slipped between the cool hotel sheets. She watched Astrid undress slowly for the second time that night, although this time the disrobing was more practical than seductive in nature.

The boots came off. But she didn't come to bed immediately. Instead, she stood at the window for long minutes, staring at the sparkling city lights until Julia finally felt compelled to break the silence.

"Why tonight? Why like this, my love? I'm not complaining, mind you. Only it was…unexpected. Different."

Astrid smiled, turning away from the view and drawing the heavy curtain with a sustained yawn. "It's early. And it's been a long night. I'm glad you enjoyed it."

Julia could have left it at that; left it unanswered. But after hundreds of years, she knew it was better not to go to bed with questions like this one hanging in the air.

"Astrid, why?"

With a sigh, Astrid joined her on the bed, climbing up her body and pulling the bedclothes up after her to cocoon them in darkness and warmth. "You looked so beautiful up there in the sunset, you know. Up on the dome of the basilica. There was just enough gold left in the sky to make your hair look like an autumn day in the forest."

"I miss autumn days the most, I think," Julia mused. She combed her fingers through Astrid's tousled blonde locks, enjoying the play of the soft strands over her skin. It was growing harder to fight the pull of sleep.

"You were beautiful," Astrid said again, tightening her grip. "And I don't ever want you to decide that you'd like to see the view from up there in the sunrise instead. I don't care how many pretty Italian boys it takes."

It was as if a valve had been turned somewhere deep in Julia's body, in her soul—*Oh, is that all?*—and she sighed as the tension she hadn't been fully aware of released itself. "Silly thing. Did I really seem suicidal?"

Astrid hesitated just a fraction of a second too long. "You seem very thoughtful lately."

"It will pass," Julia assured her wryly. "Even without an influx of fine young Italian cock."

"But you won't be complaining if I insist, will you?"

Even though she couldn't see Astrid's face, buried as it was in the hollow between her breasts, Julia could feel the soft huff of her laughter.

"Hardly," she admitted. "But no cows. I don't want the responsibility just now."

"No cows," Astrid agreed.

"You're enough for me, you know."

"Even after all this time?"

"Of course. After any amount of time." She had said it before. And Julia knew she would have to say it again every so often. Every few decades or centuries, Astrid needed that reassurance. But she was worth it, always. "I could have found a lovely boy to turn. I didn't. I chose you. Only you."

Astrid nodded, her hair brushing against Julia's chest in a way that felt more sensual now than sexual. The sun was almost up. It was nearly time to sleep whether they wanted to or not. And then wake when the sun slipped down again and take up the hunt once more. Again and again, forever and ever.

Julia yawned and thought of the metal roof of the basilica. It had still held the heat of the day when she perched there in the early evening. How chilly and damp it would be in the morning, slick with dew. How the rising sun's heat might, at first, feel like a blessing to bones that had been cold so long, chilled so thoroughly. She loved Astrid, who was now in the absolute stillness of sleep. And Astrid was still blood-warm against her body. But she knew that she would wake cold, her limbs entwined with Astrid's equally cold ones, and that knowledge took its toll over the years. All knowledge did.

"The equator," she murmured, nudging her companion just hard enough to rouse her. "What do you think about going somewhere along the equator next? Africa, perhaps, or the south of Asia?"

"Wherever you like, love," Astrid mumbled before falling back to sleep.

The equator. Where it would be warm, even hot, for most of the year. Julia drifted into slumber dreaming of night in the jungle. It made for vastly better sleep than her previous night's dream of the dome of St. Peter's Basilica in the fatal light of morning.

DARK ANGEL

Paisley Smith

Berlin, 1934

Evangelina Vogel's gaze connected with the dark-haired woman's again. She inhaled. Decidedly striking, the woman sidled through the smoky cabaret clad in a man's tuxedo.

The woman flashed a knowing, ruby-lipped smile and Evangelina's breath caught.

"Let's go." Her husband, Rudolf, gave her a sharp tug on the arm.

"Go? Why?"

"You think I don't know you're looking at *her*?" Rudolf whispered hotly, cutting his gaze at the woman.

Evangelina didn't have a chance to reply. Instead, she stumbled along as Rudolf squeezed her arm and ushered her through the shoulder-to-shoulder crowd.

The raucous music dropped to a dull thump as he shoved her out the door and into a nearby alley.

"How dare you disgrace me?"

"Disgrace you?" She snorted and fingered the Nazi party pin he wore on the lapel of his black suit. "You've done a good enough job of disgracing yourself."

Rudolf's mouth twitched menacingly. Without warning, he shoved her so hard she skidded on her hands and knees across the cobblestones. Pain seared her palms and one shin, but she had no time to consider that. She scrambled to regain her footing.

His silhouette loomed in the glare of the cabaret lights. Something else glinted in the darkness. A pistol?

A shot reverberated through the alley, echoing in her ears. Before she could register what had happened, a hard, brute force slammed into her chest. He'd shot her! Shocked, she dropped, covering the bleeding wound with her hand.

Her gaze flew to Rudolf's. Trembling, he gaped. "Look what you made me do!"

Evangelina summoned the stamina to glare at him. Determination welled inside her that his last memory of her would not be of her cowering and whimpering. He gulped, and then he turned and ran.

Once he was gone, she curled into a ball on the cold, damp cobblestones. Every breath sent sharp pains stabbing through her chest.

Her senses flickered and the sounds from the cabaret seemed suddenly faraway. Evangelina knew she was dying. She didn't care. Her life—all twenty-two years of it—had been a struggle. She'd been described as different from other girls, a tomboy. *She'll grow out of it,* they said.

But she hadn't. Marriage had not *cured* her.

Unless dying was the cure.

"You're dying."

Evangelina tried to regain her senses but nothing existed except a soft, soothing voice. Yes, she was dying. She'd always thought she would welcome death. Peace. Nothingness. But not now. Not facing it straight on. Sudden terror of the unknown gripped her.

"Do you want to live or die?" a breathy female voice whispered through the night air.

Evangelina's head swam.

"You must tell me. You must make the choice yourself. Do you wish to live or would you rather die?"

"Live," Evangelina heard herself mutter. "Live."

She heard a sharp intake of breath, and then through the haze of pain, she felt the softest, most tender kiss on her lips. She moved her mouth in an attempt to return the sweet kiss, but the feather-touch whispered away, trailing down her cheek and lower still, to where her pulse barely beat in her neck.

The mouth opened and Evangelina tried to yield, to avail herself to the captivating kiss: so soft, so sensual. Intuitively, Evangelina knew she'd seen this woman before but she struggled to remember where. When. She fought to open her eyes, to see the silky limbs moving over and around her, to touch the spicy-sweet locks of hair tickling her neck and shoulders.

What was happening? She was dying and yet the foremost thought in her mind was to surrender to this mesmerizing creature.

The warm tip of a tongue flicked along the vein followed by a soft, guttural moan. "You will feel no more pain. Only pleasure. From this moment forward, you will know only the joys of the flesh, of conceding to and fulfilling your deepest desires."

Yes...

"I will become your mother, your sister, your lover—your

maker," the hypnotic voice promised. "You will be mine."

Evangelina grasped to feel, to touch, to know the identity of her savior. But it was no use. She was too weak. Too near death. "Are you an angel?" she asked.

A soft laugh met her ears. "Hardly."

And then Evangelina cried out as two pricks of white-hot pain seared her throat. The fiery agony, as promised, subsided and transformed until she sensed her very essence being dragged out of her body and into this being. She floated, unaware of anything except the reality of the existence of her soul, the melding of her spirit with this *other's*.

It was pure. It was magical. It was an end and it was also a beginning.

Her heartbeat pounded in her own ears. Fast at first, and then it slowed and slowed even more. Still, Evangelina had no fear. And when it stopped, for a moment, she drifted among the stars. Perfectly at peace. Perfectly secure.

Dead.

"Drink."

Suddenly, she was back on earth. Evangelina's throat muscles worked of their own accord.

"That's it. Drink." This time, the voice sounded louder. Clearer.

An overwhelming thirst claimed her, and Evangelina clutched a wrist to her mouth, sucking life back into her body with animalistic need. Somewhere in her brain, it registered that she was drinking blood. But instead of bearing a metallic and coppery tang, the heady liquid tasted like the sweetest wine.

With astounding speed, strength returned to her body, and she groaned as muscles mended and tissue healed. Her pulse thrummed again, and her heart raced with renewed life.

Evangelina opened her eyes and discovered the most exquisite creature she'd ever seen in her life—the woman she'd seen at the cabaret.

The opposite of Evangelina's fair complexion and long blonde hair, this woman looked like a dark angel. She stared with luminous black eyes. Her crimson lips glistened. Now dressed in a white satin gown, she seemed more like a ghost than a living being.

A slow smile claimed the woman's lips, exhibiting two very sharp, very pointed...fangs? Evangelina stifled a gasp. "What are you?"

Although the smile faded, the intensity never wavered from the woman's gaze. "I am vampyre. As are you."

Evangelina gulped. Instinctively, the tip of her tongue touched her eye teeth. Fangs!

She shot up on her elbows. Her mind reeled as she tried to process everything at once.

She'd been brought to some old house with soaring stone walls decorated with faded tapestries. A castle? The elegant black dress she'd been wearing when Rudolf had taken her to the cabaret earlier evidenced her struggle in the alley. A violent shudder tore through her when her gaze locked on the gaping bloodstained hole in the bodice of her gown.

This was real. She wasn't dreaming. And yet...

Evangelina touched her chest. No wound. No pain. All of it was gone. Her hands trembled as she pressed her fingertips to her teeth. Fangs. Her insides hollowed. "What do you mean, vampyre?" she demanded although her intuition told her she already knew the answer.

She shook, realizing she knew a lot of things she hadn't known before.

The beautiful woman sat back on her knees. The low

neckline of her gown shifted, baring the hollow between two voluptuous breasts.

Evangelina fought to keep her gaze from settling there—to keep her hands from reaching and touching and exploring.

"I am Lenore," the woman said. "I am three thousand years old."

"Vampyre," Evangelina muttered. "Like Nosferatu? Like Dracula?"

"In a sense," Lenore replied.

Evangelina inhaled. "You made me this...*thing*? A vampyre?"

The black eyes never blinked. "You told me you wanted to live."

"But...but vampyre means undead," Evangelina argued. Panic surged.

Lenore shook her head. "No, darling. You are more alive than you ever were. And now, you and I are connected. Bonded." She leaned forward. Her cool fingers encircled Evangelina's arm.

A jolt passed through Evangelina at the vampyre's touch. Rather than experiencing the expected urge to pull away, Evangelina fought the magnetic draw to move closer.

This beautiful woman had rescued her from the point of death, and Evangelina couldn't resist her. She didn't want to resist her. She had watched her, had been drawn to her from the first time she'd seen her, and if this woman was a vampyre, Evangelina wanted to be one too.

Time seemed to stand still as she lifted her gaze to Lenore's eyes once more. The vampyre's lips parted, her intent instantly apparent. All coherent thought fled as she leaned in, as her mouth claimed Evangelina's, stifling a little sound of surprise.

Evangelina dissolved into the kiss as her taste buds exploded with the deep, rich taste of blood and woman and spice. The need to fill herself with it overwhelmed her, and at once, she launched herself into Lenore's embrace.

The vampyre had claimed her and Evangelina felt powerless to resist. She didn't want to resist. She wanted to do some of her own claiming.

Her hands found Lenore's breasts and she squeezed, eliciting a husky moan from the vampyre. Need unfurled like the tainted blood pulsing through Evangelina's veins, and she heard herself growl as she deepened their already impossibly deep kiss. Tongues mated and sparred. Fangs clashed.

Lenore's nipples grew diamond hard as she arched into Evangelina's touch. Emboldened, Evangelina slid her fingers underneath the shoulder straps of Lenore's gown and pushed the garment down to expose the vampyre's beautiful breasts. Evangelina's gaze lingered there momentarily before her lover's fingers threaded into her hair and drew her head down.

Evangelina cupped one breast in her palm and covered the other with her mouth. Liquid desire pooled between her legs, and when inquisitive fingers wriggled under the hem of her dress and inside her panties, it was as if she'd known this woman— this vampyre—all her life, as if they were mated, fused by some unbreakable blood bond.

Lenore's fingers explored Evangelina's creamy folds, and all Evangelina could think about was taking off her clothes and making love to her savior.

Reluctantly, she drew away and wrenched her torn dress over her head. Holding Lenore's gaze, Evangelina wriggled out of her underwear.

The two moved in tandem as Evangelina lay back on the bed and Lenore lowered herself between her fledgling's legs. Evangelina's hands sank into the black locks of hair, her fingertips delighting in the feel of silken waves that tumbled nearly to Lenore's waist.

Evangelina reeled. The vampyre's breath sent flames licking through her inner thighs. She arched as Lenore's mouth sought her nether lips. She spread, eagerly wanting more. "Yes!" she heard herself cry as if the voice belonged to someone else.

All thoughts of what happened earlier—of the implications of what was happening now—evaporated. A tongue speared her, and she bucked. Inhumanly strong but delicate fingers pushed her thighs open impossibly wider.

Evangelina shook in the vise-grip. She'd known it would be like this with this woman. All-consuming. Overwhelming. Intense.

She writhed, aching for her lust to be assuaged and equally never wanting this bliss to end. Lenore's kiss burned white hot and wickedly wonderful. And then Lenore added a finger to her pleasurable assault. Evangelina thought she would die all over again.

Riotous impulses raced through her veins, all stemming from the place where Lenore's mouth tantalized her body. The vampyre's tongue swept and prodded and flicked, torturing Evangelina, making her crazy for more. Taunting strokes inflamed her arousal, and she tensed, teetering on the edge of orgasm.

Holding Lenore's head captive, Evangelina cried out as ecstasy ripped through her body, stemming from sensitive nerve endings she'd never known existed. Until now. Until Lenore.

Lenore sated Evangelina in a way that only a woman could. For the first time in her whole damned existence, she sensed she was free. She closed her eyes, squeezing out tears that streamed down the sides of her face. Finally free.

Free of Rudolf and free of this new order's judgmental eye. Free to love as she pleased.

Her chest shook with a sob, and she released a breath she hadn't realized she'd been holding.

Insistent kisses moved up her body, over the gentle swell of her tummy, between her breasts, across her collarbone and finally to her lips. When Lenore ended their kiss, Evangelina's gaze found her lover's. "Why me?"

"I saw something in you," Lenore purred as she thumbed a strand of Evangelina's hair away from her face.

"What? What did you see?"

"A need. A desire to live and love in spite of what everyone else thinks. In spite of what *he* thought or did to you," Lenore said. Something flashed in her eyes that made Evangelina's blood run cold. "I watched you leave the cabaret tonight. I followed you. I am sorry I did not arrive sooner."

Evangelina's mind grappled to understand, but she didn't want to dwell on the past. She wanted to know what her future entailed. "What does it mean to be...vampyre?"

Lenore's eyes darkened even more. She toyed with Evangelina's nipple, rolling it between her thumb and forefinger until that connection merged between her breast and pussy. "It has been so long for me that I have forgotten what it means to be human."

"Am I...immortal?"

"Yes," Lenore replied with the hint of a smile. "You will never be sick. You will never age. You will never die. But you may never exist in the light again. We vampyres are creatures of darkness and can only exist at night. By day, we must sleep where no light can touch us."

"There are others?" Evangelina asked.

"Many others. You will recognize them on sight."

Evangelina wasn't sure how she felt about never seeing another sunrise, but if the trade was immortality and eternal youth then she supposed she was willing to concede the daylight.

"Do we...do *I* drink...blood?"

Lenore's smile stretched wider. "Yes. You will find there are many people deserving of death whose blood you will enjoy drinking. As I *saw* into your good nature, so will you see the natures of others. Both good and bad."

"You've killed?" Evangelina was incredulous but even as she spoke an innate primal need called to her. Her virgin fangs tingled as thoughts that would have previously horrified her intruded. She longed to kill, to sink those teeth into a ripe vein and drink blood.

"It is the vampyre way to kill only those who do not contribute to society. But that is a lesson for another night," Lenore murmured as she slipped her hand between Evangelina's legs again.

Evangelina's eyes closed as she relented once more to physical sensations unlike any she'd ever known. At the vampyre's touch, images of Lenore played in Evangelina's head. Lenore, elegant in jewels and a powdered wig, listening to a pianist in some European salon. Lenore dressed in rich burgundy Renaissance velvets. The visions raced faster and faster until she appeared in a flowing Grecian gown.

Another woman—another vampyre—with Lenore.

Deep and violent and devastating images accompanied emotions that twisted through Evangelina—images of the other vampyre consumed with flames. She'd been murdered for what she was. A vampyre.

Evangelina trembled, grasping her connection to Lenore. The other woman had been Lenore's maker, the same as Lenore was Evangelina's. They were one now. More strongly linked than if they'd been born twins.

But they weren't twins. They were lovers. From this night until forever.

Lenore's finger found its way inside her channel, and Evangelina sighed her pleasure. The lazy thrusts ignited a slow, smoldering fire. Her senses filled with the spicy scent of her lover, with the sharp taste of blood on her lips and the sounds of wet suction. Evangelina clutched Lenore's shoulders, crying out when she angled her wrist down and pushed another finger inside.

Stretched and filled to capacity, Evangelina moved restlessly, aching to have her need satisfied once more. Lenore's fingers searched slow and deep, moving in and out with diabolical leisure.

"Please," Evangelina pleaded.

Lips nipped the taut bud of one breast.

Erotic need to touch and taste her lover flooded her but at the same time, Evangelina didn't want Lenore to stop her gentle but unrelenting invasion. Clenching her teeth, Evangelina arched her spine off the bed as if she could bring her desire to fruition.

Lenore moved over her, positioning her hand as if she were a man with a cock instead of a woman with two fingers embedded deep inside her. "Do you want me to fuck you harder?" Lenore's voice caressed her like a silken breath.

"Yes," Evangelina cried, spreading her thighs to give her lover complete access. Her hands found Lenore's breasts. She kneaded and squeezed.

The vampyre let out a hiss and then a sensual moan. "Pinch my nipples. Pinch them hard. Harder. Yes."

And all the while, the fingers thrust faster. In. Out. In. Out. Evangelina felt as if she were being ripped in two. Past dalliances with girls who feared their passion, who worried about the consequences or who were merely *practicing* for boys raced through Evangelina's mind.

This was different.

For the first time in her existence, she felt released and unbound. She could love this woman—this vampyre. Consequences be damned.

Evangelina's muscles clenched around Lenore's plunging fingers. "Yes!" Evangelina screamed at the incredible sensations rippling through her. She lifted her hips, pushing to take more.

The fingers retreated and then sank deep once again. Evangelina rode the rising tide of pleasure. *There. Yes. There. Almost there.*

"You are mine," the vampyre declared.

I'm yours. Anything. Just make me come.

"I am your maker, and you belong to me. You will submit to me."

Evangelina balked. She'd submitted to Rudolf. And she hadn't liked it. Instead, she'd suffered for it.

"No," she mewled, afraid.

"You are thinking of the one who abused you, who hurt you," Lenore whispered. "I will never hurt you. I will lead you and I will teach you. I will master you."

"No..."

"Turn over." The harsh command sent a shiver through Evangelina's limbs. She had no time to voice a protest as inhuman hands twisted her onto her stomach, knees up. Head down.

Evangelina's whimper choked in her throat when a flattened palm swatted her ass. Hard. Fire licked through her bottom, vying with her earlier pleasure for the pain of dominance.

She clutched the sheets in her fists.

"Tell me you are mine," the vampyre demanded.

And when those fingers sought her pussy again, Evangelina was tempted. So, so tempted. "Please." She panted.

"Will you submit to me?"

"I can't."

Another sharp slap landed on her bottom. The sweet sting radiated down her legs and up her back, settling where Lenore's fingers prodded her wet folds. But instead of plunging the two fingers back into Evangelina's eager pussy, Lenore coated them with the slippery cream, and then traced around the rim of her anus.

Evangelina's thoughts scrambled as one fingertip probed her there.

She tensed but made no move to retreat from the vampyre's invasion of her most private recess. The mingling of the pleasure of her throbbing clit and the painful fire rimming her anus; the fingers prodding her, stretching her, exploring her; was driving her mad.

One finger drove in all the way to the fist.

Evangelina couldn't believe she was backing up to take more. All.

Hot kisses peppered the curve of her ass. Fangs raked her skin, leaving chill bumps in their wake. Perspiration formed down her spine. Evangelina knew she would give in.

She would do anything to experience this pleasure over and over and over again.

Lenore withdrew the finger, and Evangelina had never ached for the absence of something so acutely in her life. She groaned in frustration. "Please don't stop."

"Tell me you are mine."

Evangelina swallowed thickly. She drew in a ragged breath and pushed her hips back, wanting more.

"Say the words, and I will ease your desire."

Intuitively, Evangelina realized submitting to the vampyre was entirely different from the abuse she'd suffered at Rudolf's hands. "I'm yours. I will always be yours."

Lenore let out a triumphant snarl and then she thrust her finger deep in Evangelina's tight hole.

Evangelina spread her knees, dipping her spine to take more pistoning fingers. Pleasure exploded and she dissolved. Her intense orgasm flung her past any reality she had ever known into a mysterious world of darkness and blood and lust—and Lenore.

Before Evangelina drifted back to the earth, Lenore flipped her over and straddled her face. With animalistic hunger, Evangelina gripped the vampyre's hips and pulled the sweet pussy down to her mouth.

Her nostrils filled with the sultry feminine scent of sex and desire while her lips and tongue explored Lenore's folds. Evangelina latched on to her lover's clitoris and sucked greedily.

Hands burrowed into her hair and Lenore rode her face, grinding so that Evangelina fought to keep hold of the swollen bud she knew was the key to Lenore's pleasure.

Evangelina understood that she would follow this woman anywhere. She would do anything for her, just to be with her, just to know *this* again and again.

"Oh, yes!" the vampyre cried, bucking furiously. "Bite me. Drink from me, my love."

Without thinking, Evangelina's mouth moved from Lenore's pussy to her inner thigh. Her fangs ached to bite. Her tongue bristled to taste, and Evangelina sank her teeth into the pulsating femoral artery there.

Gripping and tugging Evangelina's hair, Lenore growled. She screamed and she moaned in bliss.

Evangelina felt wild. Crazed. Blood filled her mouth, and she drank as if she were dying of thirst.

Lenore's fingers plunged to massage her own clitoris, and after she'd reached orgasm a second time, she gently pulled away from Evangelina.

Evangelina gaped, astounded. The two wounds her fangs

had created on Lenore's thigh healed almost instantly.

Her gaze collided with Lenore's and overwhelming love filled her with such force Evangelina feared she couldn't contain it.

Lenore gathered her into her arms and covered her mouth with her own. Intense passion flared. Love and belonging replaced lust until Evangelina was left breathless and trembling in her maker's embrace.

At that moment, nothing else mattered. Not Rudolf. Not society. Not even life.

She was free. She was soaring.

Evangelina's eyes snapped open, and the previous night's events' rushed back over her in a torrent. She had been made immortal by a three-thousand-year-old vampyre.

After making love time and time again, they'd slept in a casket together, arms and legs entwined, in the dark catacombs of the castle where Lenore lived.

But now, Evangelina burned with a carnal hunger for the blood. Living blood. Human blood.

She shook Lenore's shoulder.

Lenore opened her eyes and smiled as she brushed back an errant lock of Evangelina's hair.

Evangelina resisted the urge to bat her lover's hand away. "I must feed."

"The hunger is always worse at the beginning," Lenore crooned. She sat, pushing the lid of the coffin away. Lenore climbed out. "I anticipated this moment. Come. I have a gift for you."

Shaking, Evangelina took her maker's hand and climbed out of the coffin.

Lenore stole catlike through the dank catacombs with Evangelina at her heels.

Evangelina realized her eyes had adjusted and that she could easily see in the darkness. With impatient curiosity, she watched as Lenore removed a key from a peg on the stone wall and then unlocked a thick steel door.

The door swung open, its rusted hinges groaning in protest. Evangelina smelled *him*—her prey—at once.

"Who's there?" a panicky voice echoed from the shadows.

Chills broke out across Evangelina's scalp and raced down her spine. She salivated, practically able to taste the blood from here. "Hello, Rudolf." A wicked smile played on her lips and her fangs protracted with a snap. "Look what you made me do."

PET DOOR

Angela Caperton

I scratched, just like the bitch I am.

Wet, shivering, hungry, I pawed at her door and salivated, drooled really, a puppy eager to be paddled with a newspaper and scolded.

I'd watched her for several nights; watched how she'd stared down the valets, eloquently subdued jerks who propositioned her after her performance, salivated as she stroked her tempered violin and fingered the bow before she bound them into the velvet-lined case.

After all, how many virtuosi performed in tight-laced corsets and four-inch spiked heels? For her, I could even listen to the same Brahms concerto a thousand times before I stabbed myself in the chest with a broken broom handle.

She was it; she could give me what I wanted, what I needed. One glimpse of her complete and utter control of the bow passing over the strings of the violin and I knew I was lost, or maybe saved.

The rain fell in buckets, the late-night squall a blessing to me. I shook off the excess water before I scratched at her door again, eyes acceptably pitiable, the tremble in my body horribly exaggerated, but I was in the form of a little wolf-dog. Would she discern the difference between real discomfort and play-acted misery?

The front entryway to the antebellum home made me smile. At the base was a large pet door, one meant for a medium-sized dog.

I scratched and whined with delicate distress and, even before I was ready, she answered, her corset loosened, breasts freely bobbing in the cups, her tight black skirt gone, revealing red silken panties, a lacy garter and sleek black stockings. She still wore her high heels. I wanted to lick them, but they stood beyond the invisible barrier of her permission.

I trembled, but this was no act. I wanted her. God, how I wanted her. I whined, unabashed, begging.

She just stared, fresh rain soaking my pelt again. I tilted my head and lowered my lids, going for a look as forlorn as I could manage. I uttered the slightest yip of distress.

"Jesus," she groaned, looking at me as if I were a worm.

I quivered, excited, wanting more of her contempt.

"Come on in, you idiot," she said, and I bloomed inside, my entry blessed. I started forward beyond the threshold.

And the door bruised my nose.

She closed it. She invited me in, but closed the door.

I blinked, stunned. Was she kidding? Was she just being cruel? I knew about cruel; I was born from it. I could be cruel too if provoked.

The narrow plane of the pet door swung open, kicked by her high-heeled foot.

I shivered anew, almost unable to move for the shaking of my four limbs. She knew me. Oh, she knew me so well.

I pushed my nose against the pet door, her blunt welcome freeing me to enter, and I slid between the wet, cold night and the warmth of her house.

She looked at me as though my damp, musky coat was my fault. Disdain, barely restrained tolerance and chastisement shimmered just a breath away.

Saliva pooled behind my canines.

She pointed. "Kitchen. I'll not have that smell in my carpet."

Kitchen. Hard, cold, smooth tiles. I padded across the forest-green carpet to the Spanish-red floor. I wanted to shake, dislodge the excess water from my pelt before it tickled my skin, but the look in her eyes stilled the instinct. I didn't want to anger her, didn't want to have her toss me out into the rain again.

I trembled for the control, ached for the firm grip on the leash. She had it, I knew she did.

I settled down on the tile, the cut of the grout on the sharp points of my legs welcoming.

"Good, girl." She clicked across the tile, filling a bowl with water and setting it on the floor by my head. My tongue lolled as I panted. Was this love?

She left the kitchen for the bowels of the house. I didn't even think to follow. I heard her moving in the hidden chambers—bathroom, bedroom; sometimes there was music, once a curt phone conversation with someone I guessed was her manager. I ached to see her again, sniff her, taste her. Her scent seduced me, weakened me. All I wanted was the grace of her approval.

Okay. Maybe that wasn't *all* I wanted, but for now, for this first meeting, it would be enough.

My ears twitched as she walked toward the kitchen. She wore silk, an ivory sleep shirt that barely covered her ass. She flipped on the light, blinding me for a moment. She ignored me as she poured herself a disciplined glass of wine. She leaned against the counter, her back to the sink, and reached out her hand, never looking at me, her silent permission a gift.

I rose quickly and went to her, my wet nose easing under her neatly trimmed nails. I wanted those fingers to pet me, stroke me, fall across the bridge of my long nose in a testy tap. I looked up at her with wanting eyes, hoping she'd look down. I needed her to see me.

She smoothed the short hair between my eyes, then blessed me with a glance, her lake-blue eyes cool but depthless. I wanted to swim in them forever, to see them change from calm to calculating, to see fire burn within—for me, her pet.

I looked into those amazing eyes, my desire for her tangible, a living thing I willed my gaze to instill in her. She didn't blink, didn't flinch and didn't soften as my animal-black eyes focused completely on her blue. The tile beneath my padded feet disappeared, the walls melted into a haze of desire, the counter she leaned against slid away from the two of us, her fingers drifting off my head to hang before my nose.

I tilted my head and lolled my tongue out, licking the back of her hand, drunk on the taste of her. Spice and heat, the pulsing life in the delicate veins that tempted my teeth and called to my hunger, the musk of her sex just inches away, the scent as alluring as warm, buttery pastry. My tongue reached out again, a long, wide swath of favor, my gaze never leaving hers.

Lightning flashed across the windows and the loud, immediate crack of thunder broke the spell. She tapped my nose twice, a slight admonition for my forward affection. She pointed to the tile where I had been sprawled, and like a good girl, I circled around the spot and fell to the floor, her flavor still rich in my mouth, fueling my need to feed, and my desire for her leash.

She watched me for a few more seconds, not long enough for

a binding stare. Then she smiled and walked out of the kitchen, flipping the switch and taking the light from the room.

The storm continued through the night, shrouding the stars and moon, but I didn't care. Her roof was all the sky I needed, but I felt the darkness fading, the dreaded sun gaining strength in the east. I did not want to leave, but I knew I must return home to safety, utter concealment, apart from any trace of daylight.

I wanted to see her one more time, struggled against my desire and then padded quietly to the front door. I bumped my head against the pet door and slipped into the night, the rain a welcome misery as I raced through the darkness toward the secret place that would keep me safe.

Until night came again.

I waited an hour after the lights faded from the windows of her house. The door was closed, but the barrier to my entry had been removed by her stern welcome the previous night. I'd come to the house as a little wolf again, and very carefully I pushed at the pet door, thrilled when it swung easily on oiled hinges.

Inside the house, I renounced the wolf and stood upright, bare, my long black hair falling over my breasts and back. The shadows of the house clothed me, and I walked into the kitchen, overjoyed to see a bowl of water, and beside it, another bowl, empty, and a neatly folded blanket.

She knew I'd come back, though she could hardly guess the form I would wear.

I followed her scent up the stairs and paused at her bedroom door. Breathless, I peered into the room to stare at her, watch the life rise and fall in her chest, hear her heartbeat. I wanted the taste of her in my mouth and down my throat almost as much as I wanted her control.

She did not sleep restfully. She squirmed and tossed, throwing off the duvet and the sheet to expose her naked body to the air and my hunger. The perfume of her cunt tickled my nose and filled my mouth with saliva. It would be so easy to take her now, sink my teeth into her thigh, drink, charge, get her off on the pain and the erotic spell of the exchange—her blood, her life for my dark, dangerous kiss. I could have her, make her my toy, make her dance for me, force her to do anything I wanted with one sharp kiss: my ragged, knotted sock, shiny with playful use, limp and without will.

He had done that to me. He had claimed my soul eighty-two years ago. He said he'd been enthralled by my youth, my spirit, my natural desire to submit. He'd bound me to him with his steel control, his desire my command. He'd sealed our union with a bite, a kiss, a brand on my inner thigh that showed the dimples of his fangs' eternal penetration. When my heart stopped, my last breath joined the smoky layer of sin in a Boston speakeasy. Three nights later, he allowed me to feed, commanded me to kill, his will a lash on my skin, welcome, but bitter.

Thirty-six years later, his ashes severed the leash and I was free, hungry and anxious for another firm hand. I found Mistress Rika three years later, an escaped Yugoslavian engineer working in St. Paul. Her steel control had me begging for her hand across my ass or holding my head to her pussy until I lapped her to orgasm again and again. She filled my ass with plugs, teased my clit mercilessly until I drooled like a puppy around the ball gag in my mouth. She owned me and I loved it. We were inseparable.

I knelt at her feet, kissed her toes, cooked for her even though I could not eat, and loved pleasing her in every way. She knew my nature although we never spoke openly of it. Maybe it was her eastern European history, but she didn't ask about my daytime absences, didn't question my lack of appetite or my unbeating heart under her ear when we slept entangled. For five years, we loved and lived, moving twice, once to Los Angeles, then again to Atlanta. It had been in Atlanta that my greed broke the spell between us. The humidity of that old Southern city made her sweat when we made love, and there in the golden light of candles and moonlight, I saw two gray strands of hair curling from her temple.

Forever was mine to give.

I drank deep, gave her my bleeding breast as the last breath left her, then pulled her beyond the beat of her heart.

I felt old and wise then, but I was really still a foolish child who knew too little of the rules that shaped my kind. My gift was our doom. Mistress Rika, my beautiful masterful lover, wore a leash when she returned to me, my leash. Always would she answer to me, always would I feel her most intimate thoughts and feelings. Gone like a guttered flame was the intense mystery of what she wanted, lost forever the joyful game of guessing what she needed.

I watched Rika thrive. Six months later, we could no longer pretend. I know she is still out there. I feel her still, but we will never again be lovers.

I stepped past the threshold of my new obsession's room as her duvet fell with a whisper from the bed to the ground. She curled against the chill, tucking one foot under the other. I carefully eased onto the foot of her mattress, retrieving the duvet. I pulled it up around her legs, a plush wall between us. Her sheets held her scent and a ripe lust surged through me from my lips to my nipples to my pussy. Nothing flowery or soft to her; she smelled of nutmeg and ginger, earth and heat.

She turned over, fully exposed, and I maneuvered to accept her feet against my belly. She stretched, a languid arch of back and legs, a sleepy gurgle in her throat. I watched her eyes slit against waking, and her heart tripped as groggy recognition tangled with dreamy disbelief. I didn't move, my head cradled on my elbow, my worshipful gaze penetrating her lashes, my will kissing to calm her fear, chaste and respectful until it slid away to join her illusions in dreams.

She sat up slowly, rising on her elbows, and in the deep shadows of the room, she took three steady breaths and pressed her feet into my belly, pushing me farther back until my butt rested hard against the thick rods of the brass frame.

She settled back, pulled the duvet cover up over her body and kept me pinned beneath her heels. Sensations lived inside me. The still heart that once measured my desire now burned with longing, the acid of my blood on my tongue a reward for staying still. I bit my lip against a whimper or a yearning touch.

I felt the dawn imminent outside, but I didn't move. Her feet, soft yet strong, held me against the brass rods even as she half dreamed. I had wanted this control, this attention for more days than I could count. The agonizing ash of morning's kiss would be worth another second of her French manicure cutting into my belly.

But she knew enough to spare me. Husky-voiced, her command rang sharp. "Go the way you came."

Release. Sweet, understanding release.

She rolled over as if in a huff, her face buried into the pillows, her neck with its thick pulse of life, yanking mercilessly at my hunger. I swiped my arm against the saliva on my lips, took her final loving kick from the bed with glee and left the bedroom.

My pelt never touched the edges of the frame.

I didn't wait the next night. The lights were still on in the kitchen when I slipped through the pet door and into the warm fragrance of her. She stood there, a glass of wine casually cupped in one hand; the slight curve of her full lips and the cool control in her gaze had me on my belly as I crawled to her.

She wore a simple black slip, the scents of the concert hall faint against the spice of her. Her cunt beckoned me to her, to life, to heat and sex. I wanted to feast, and I knew she knew what I wanted.

"Bold, aren't you?" she asked as I reached her feet. I trembled in my wolf's clothing. "I like bold." She reached down and scratched me behind the ears. The churn of lust within my soul tested my form as my vision blurred and my longing struggled against claws and fur. My tongue lolled out to her bare toes, painted blood red, and I tasted heaven, savory, warmly aromatic, true.

My pelt melted away. Naked, on hands and knees, I kissed her feet, laved my tongue over the fine bones of her foot and worshipped her ankles with nibbles and controlled sharp nips.

"Wicked pet," she breathed, her voice heavy, the scent of her pussy washing over me, lush and rich, cream and earth, the very flavor of desire.

I looked up at her, my fingers trembling above her shin. I wanted to touch with my fingers, with my lips, but waited for her permission.

Some women might recoil in horror or reach for a knife from the block on the counter, but she just looked down into my face, exploring my soul, and as the thick moments passed, we bartered our relationship.

She reached out, stroked my unkempt black tresses, wound her fingers into them and yanked my head back. In a single moment, she sealed our fates.

"You like pussy?"

I couldn't nod, couldn't do anything other than salivate and

gurgle my affirmation, my head pulled back, my neck ridicu-
lously strained.

She smiled, a Cheshire-thin slice across her face that shot
lust to my belly.

"Lick it and don't stop until I say."

Heaven in a phrase. She loosened her grip on my hair, but
didn't release me entirely, and I savored my freedom, kissing
up her leg, nipping inside her knee, worshipping her thigh. Her
femoral artery pulsed under my tongue and visceral hunger
gripped my heart, but I pushed it back, savoring instead the
divine scent of her sex and the juices that had already slicked
her thighs.

The edge of her slip rubbed against my nose as the thin lace
lightly tangled in my lashes. I nudged the slip's hem aside and
brushed my lips along the line of trimmed fur above the wet
cleft. I kissed the crown, the faint taste of her sex a drug. When
the tip of my tongue slid between the lips of her pussy and tasted
her exotic essence, all I knew in that precious divine moment
was the sanctity of her dominance.

I buried my face in her sex, gripped her thighs, pulled them
apart to improve my feast and applied my mouth with all the
strength of my convictions, my longing, my endless faith.

My lips and tongue traced every fold, every ridge of her pussy,
and the wet, warm life that coated my face and overwhelmed
my senses electrified me, jolted me into frenzy. I'd savaged and
worshipped so much flesh, gorged myself in blood and jizz, and
nothing, nothing had inspired me like this beautiful woman's
sweet cunt.

I found her clit with the tip of my tongue, closed my lips
around the bud and sucked as my hands caged her ass, the tips of
my index fingers teasing her anus. She moaned musically, a long
bow of pleasure that echoed inside me, like fire feeding fire.

I felt both pleasure and ravenous hunger.

My chin dripped with my efforts. Her hips ground against my lips and nose, her orgasm loomed before us both. I wanted it. I wanted her to scream, to release me from the torment of unfulfilled dreams, to brand me servant again and bind me to her with a chain only her release could provide.

She pulled my head into her pussy, her fingers nearly ripping hair from my head with the intensity of her claim, and I groaned, my pussy dripping as wet as hers, my fangs aching with the hunger to pierce her. The ball in my stomach became a living squirm of snakes, snapping, biting, tearing at me. I wanted and needed her.

My finger slipped into her ass, my relentless tongue tortured her clit, and she screamed, a blended adagio of joy, lust, release and entitlement as she came, shuddering and clutching me to her as if I were the last anchor in a raging sea.

Her legs trembled against my breasts. She bent, curled over me, enfolding me in her arms and scent. She was heat and life, blushing fruit and savory spice. In that moment, I knew love, had tapped into a stream of vibrancy that only she could provide. I needed her order, her strict control, but I lived for this precious moment of unguarded connection. The sweet sting of her sated sigh branded my soul, and I welcomed the burn.

She patted my head, a condescending triple-tap that thrilled me. "Good girl," she breathed as she straightened, pulling her sleep shirt over her hips with a natural stroke of her hands.

I rested on my heels, her juices cool on my chin. I kept my head down, appreciating the captured glow of subservience as she drank deeply from the glass of wine. Light fluttered before my eyes and my limbs eased from solid to sludge. My needs could not be denied much longer.

"Mistress?" I dared.

She set the empty glass on the counter and looked down at me. Maybe I was pale, maybe gaunt, it didn't matter. She knew.

"Hungry?"

"Yes, Mistress. Ravenous."

The silence that filled the house pressed against my shoulders, brought my chin to the tile, obedient and wanting.

"Eat."

One word, one command: it was what I would always wait for from her; that one single, loving word.

She did not see me move; how could she when even I didn't feel the space melt between my tile-touching chin and her warm thigh? There was that precious barrier, flesh to fang, that singular moment of possession as my teeth pierced her skin, and I found the artery and opened her life to me. There is no greater gift, nor greater bond: her blood, my need. Her essence filled me, completed our union and stilled the animal drive of my soul. I drank deep, the scent of her pussy arousing me even more as warm life filled my mouth, quenched my thirst.

She gasped and groaned, the wineglass shoved off the counter in her throes, shattering on the tiles, the shards slicing sweetly into my legs.

I drank of her, gluttonous, pulling her life into my throat, my hands gripping her thighs, kneading the orbs of her ass.

She clutched my head between her legs, pulled my hair with a fevered grip and screamed as a second orgasm blasted from my bite to her cunt, her breasts, her brain.

She yanked, and I released my hold on her thigh, the lush flow of blood from my bite slicking her leg before my drying saliva sealed the wound. "Enough," she growled.

My tongue circled my mouth, claiming every drop of her precious blood. I wanted more, needed more. I could have it too.

One look, one word, and she'd be on the tile beside me, arching her neck or spreading her legs for me to take all I wanted.

"Out," she panted. "The way you came." She slapped my nose and pointed to the door.

I shivered, my pussy pulsing with delight.

I crawled on all fours through the living room and then looked back at her, her blood still warm on my chin. She didn't smile, but the fire in her gaze promised me her lifetime.

I gathered the wolf, slid into the pelted skin and crossed through the pet door knowing I'd return through the same portal again and again at her command.

Her dog.

My Mistress.

My pelt never touched the edges of the frame.

DARK GUARD

Karis Walsh

S tecker, the chief wants to see you," Lieutenant Cohen said,
as Lisa Stecker was leaving turnout with the other officers.
"What's up?" she asked.

Cohen just shrugged. "Duty roster says you're on special
assignment tonight. That's all I know."

Lisa turned left at the end of the hallway instead of following
the rest of the graveyard shift out to the parking lot. She paused
outside of Chief Bannert's office, making sure her duty belt was
centered and her uniform was neat. She didn't have to worry
since her crew routinely teased her about always looking spit-
shined and ready for inspection, but it had become a habit to
recheck her appearance. She knocked and entered at the chief's
command.

Bannert and the woman sitting across from his desk rose as
she came into the room. Her greeting died on her lips when the
overpowering aura of a Marginal rippled over her like a wave.
Her nostrils flared as she identified the woman as a vampire and

she fought the urge to step back. Her hand automatically traveled to the weapon on her hip.

"Are you planning to shoot me?" the vampire asked calmly.

"Stand down, Sergeant," Bannert warned her. Lisa dropped her hand, but every muscle was tense and ready to respond to the danger she sensed. "Stecker, this is Aurica Nelson. She's a Dark Guard. And your new partner."

Lisa's gaze whipped away from the vampire and onto her boss. "No," she said simply.

"Actually, yes," he said, returning to his seat and gesturing for the two women to do so as well. They didn't. "This is the Council's decision."

He hesitated, expecting them to take a seat, but they remained where they were, Lisa eyeing Aurica warily, and the vampire returning her stare with a casual half smile. "You know about the serial killer we have loose in the city?" he asked finally.

"The Marginal who's been murdering citizens," Lisa clarified.

"Alleged," Bannert amended. "Anyway, the Council and the Dark Guard decided we should join forces to take care of this quickly. Until the killer is caught, you two are together and on the case."

"But, sir..."

"Dismissed," he said with a wave of his hand, as he opened a newspaper and started to read.

Lisa pushed his office door open with more force than necessary and Aurica barely saved it from slamming. Once outside Lisa turned to face her.

"I don't like this," she said.

"You don't like me," Aurica corrected her.

Of course I do, Lisa wanted to say, *and that's why you're so dangerous.* Even through her anger, she found it difficult to resist the scent of the woman in front of her. Her eyes traveled over her, from the coppery blonde hair that reminded Lisa of an ornate, gilded frame to her face that had the perfect features and proportions of a fine painting. And her body…dressed in the simple black of a Guard with no insignia or rank markings so there was nothing to detract the eye from her beauty. Lisa shook her head as if trying to physically shake the image of Aurica out of her mind. The vampires survived because citizens found them so irresistible. Citizens survived only if they could fight the call.

Aurica was watching Lisa while she tried to control her responses, and Lisa knew exactly what the vampire would notice about her. Not her brown hair pulled back in a ponytail, her hazel eyes or her tall body that had been carefully toned in the gym. No, Aurica, like everyone else, would only see the four scarred lines that made deep etchings from Lisa's left cheek to her throat. As if to prove Lisa's guess, Aurica stepped forward and gently trailed a slender finger down one of the scars.

"They say your mother did this," she said, in that voice designed to break a citizen's will.

"Yes, she did," Lisa answered softly, caught for a moment by Aurica's golden eyes. She reached up and grabbed the vampire's wrist in a tight hold. "Stop doing that."

Aurica frowned in confusion. "Stop doing what?"

"Stop calling to me. If we're expected to work together, I can't worry that I'm about to be your lunch."

"I'm not calling you," Aurica said with a tilt of her head and that maddeningly superior smile.

"But I feel…" Lisa stopped, not wanting to admit to the desire that coursed through her at Aurica's touch.

The vampire laughed. "Darling, if you're feeling anything for me, it's simply lust. I already fed today."

Lisa's grimace of disgust was interrupted by the emergency tone coming from her radio. She cocked her head and listened to the dispatcher's emotionless voice announce the location of a murder scene.

"We have another body," she said unnecessarily. She was almost glad to have this interrupt their conversation. "Come on, Nelson. And keep your claws to yourself."

"Call me Rica," the vampire answered, as they hurried to Lisa's patrol car. "And it's my teeth that should worry you, not my claws."

They arrived at the scene and were immediately ushered to the body that lay at the end of an alley. Apparently word was out that Lisa and her Guard were taking point on any new victim of the city's serial killer. This was the fourth body in less than a week, but the first that Lisa had seen. She was momentarily shocked by the gruesome way the man had been gutted, but she swallowed her disgust and maintained a coolly professional expression, she hoped.

"Were-cat?" she asked Rica in a quiet voice when they were alone next to the body. The victim, a citizen in his thirties, was wearing a business suit that had been ripped to shreds, along with most of his midsection. His lacerations were eerily similar to the ones that marked her own face.

"Looks like it," Rica said, carefully avoiding the large bloodstains as she squatted on her heels near the body. "But the claw marks are closer together than yours. Was your mom a werepanther?" At Lisa's hesitant nod, Rica turned back to the body. "Probably a were-lynx then."

Lisa heard the thickening of Rica's voice and she stepped closer, putting a hand on the vampire's shoulder. "Can you handle this?"

"Like I said, I fed today," Rica assured her.

"Good. Try not to lick any of the evidence," Lisa joked,

attempting to cover up her momentary concern for the vampire.

Rica rolled her eyes, but she nevertheless got up and moved a few feet from the body. "Do you smell anything?" she asked.

Lisa frowned. "Blood, urine, garbage. Nothing unusual."

"Get closer, really close, and smell him," Rica insisted.

Lisa glanced over her shoulder to make sure that the other officers weren't paying attention to her. She leaned over the body and sniffed, feeling foolish.

"What am I supposed to smell?" she asked Rica when she sat up again. The coroner's arrival interrupted, and the two women moved a few feet away to let him work.

"Well?" she prompted.

"You're supposed to smell the killer," Rica said. "You have the affinity. That's why I was assigned to work with you."

"The what?"

"It's common among hybrids that you can sense Marginals by smell or sight. It's in your records, I'm surprised you didn't know."

"I thought everyone could do that," Lisa said with a shrug. "I just grew up that way."

"In the ghetto." It was a statement, not a question, since Rica had obviously read Lisa's file. Lisa had spent her childhood in the ghetto with the were-animals, vampires, and their human children and spouses. She had been happy there, knowing no other way of life until the War started and the Marginals won their right to live in society, in an uneasy peace with the citizens. Lisa's mother had been one of the earliest rebels, and once the War started Lisa's human father had turned his wife in to the military. They arrived at the house in time to rescue Lisa from her mother's deadly claws, and they eventually recruited her into the fight.

"Well, with your affinity and my tracking ability we should

catch this killer before the week is out," Rica continued, breaking into Lisa's memories.

"Thank god," Lisa muttered. Getting this vampire out of her car had become her top priority.

Lisa kicked off her covers as she slept fitfully the next day. The city radiated heat on the late summer afternoon, and the sheets tangled around her sweaty legs as she struggled in her sleep to break free. The vampire stalked her dreams, running a hand that was so soothingly cool down Lisa's bare back. The hand was replaced by lips and a tongue that trailed an icy path down her spine and calmed her restless movements. She arched her back, the uncomfortable heat forgotten as that tongue moved across her hips. As if her movement was an invitation, a hand slipped under her, cupping her, teasing closer to the wetness that suddenly rushed from deep within.

Lisa moaned and ground down onto the fingers that flexed below her belly. She felt golden hair cascading across her back as the enticing scent of vampire filled her nostrils and lungs. Somehow the smell triggered Lisa's internal alarms even when her other instincts failed her, and she suddenly snapped awake. She heard Rica's cry of surprise as she lunged quickly upward, throwing the vampire off her back.

"Jesus," she shouted, sliding closer to her headboard so she could put as much distance as possible between her and the vampire who was now sitting at the end of her bed. "What the fuck are you doing in my room? In my house?"

"You overslept," Rica said calmly even though her golden eyes glowed with desire. "I came to get you for work and I guess I got carried away." She raised her hand to her face and inhaled deeply. "You smell so good. I'll need to feed before we go out tomorrow."

"Just don't pack a lunch," Lisa said, pulling the sheet up to cover her bare breasts. "I don't want to drive some poor girl around until you get hungry."

Rica smiled at the tentative return of Lisa's humor. "I eat at the feeding grounds. I don't get my meals to go."

Lisa had, of course, heard stories about the areas where Marginals could legally feed, but she had never seen them. Most of the were-animals could eat regular food as well, but the vampires relied on the grounds for their blood. As in the ghetto, there were always people willing to allow the vampires to feed off them, even though there was a possibility the bite would be fatal. The feeding grounds were stocked with citizens who voluntarily offered themselves to the vampires in exchange for the thrill, the sexual climax, of the experience.

"It disgusts you," Rica observed without emotion.

Lisa shrugged. "I eat meat, so I can't totally condemn the way you have to feed. But I can't imagine..."

"It's not what people think," the vampire said quietly. "There's very little screaming or panic, except among first-bloods. And no one is there without consent."

"But some of your victims die."

"It happens. We try to be careful, but it happens." They sat in silence, aware of the gulf between them. Finally Rica changed the subject.

"I have the photos and coroner's reports from the four murders. Why don't you take a shower and then we can look through them."

Lisa waited until Rica had left the room before she got up and headed to the shower. She felt a little silly locking the bath-room door since that apparently wouldn't stop the vampire, but it gave her some sense of security. Unfortunately the cold water running down her overheated body only reminded her of Rica's touch, and her body's willing response to it.

She hurried through the shower and came out to find Rica settled at her kitchen table. She had photos spread across its surface and she flipped through the pages of autopsy reports as she sipped a cup of coffee. Lisa poured a mug for herself and settled into a chair, pulling some of the photos closer.

"Looks like the same animal," she said casually as she compared the victims' wounds. Rica's head snapped up and her golden eyes flashed with anger.

"Were-cat, not animal," she said. Lisa gestured with her hand as a form of apology.

"Or someone with a weapon trying to imitate a were-cat. How can I be sure *you* aren't the killer?" Lisa asked in an attempt to lighten the mood.

"None of them are smiling," Rica purred.

Lisa cleared her throat and changed the subject. "Any connections between them?" she asked as she inventoried the victims. The two females were an unemployed woman in her twenties and a thirty-one-year-old army captain. A male college student and last night's businessman were the most recent bodies.

"Only one that I can see," Rica said, her eyes not leaving Lisa's face as she spoke. "They were all raised in a ghetto and fought against the Marginals in the War."

"Like me," Lisa said, meeting Rica's gaze steadily and hating the compassion she saw there. They were enemies, and she resented having to work so closely with a vampire.

"Look, I know seeing these wounds must bring up difficult memories for you. The War separated a lot of families, but to have your own mother..."

"Don't," Lisa said sharply, slamming her mug on the table. "You don't know anything about my mother, so spare me your pity."

She went to the window and stared at the city with unseeing eyes, jumping when a cool hand brushed her shoulder. "Tell me how this happened," Rica whispered in her ear, reaching around to brush the scars on Lisa's throat.

Lisa couldn't help but lean back into Rica's arms, feeling the vampire's breasts press against her back. "Are you doing that vampire thing now?" she asked suspiciously.

"Well, a little," Rica admitted with a laugh that sent vibrations through Lisa's body. "But only because I want to know, not because I want to eat you. Well, maybe a little..."

"You're dangerous," Lisa said even as she arched into Rica's embrace. The memory of her touch was still too fresh.

"Yes, I am. But you're safe with me, I promise."

"She saved my life," Lisa said, lured by Rica's soft voice, her scent that wrapped around Lisa as snugly as her arms. "My dad betrayed her, betrayed us. When the military came to get her, she pretended to attack me so they would believe I was forced to be with her. She clawed me, and they shot her."

Rica's arms tightened. "Your file says she tried to kill you because you wanted to leave her."

"She gave her life for me, to give me a chance outside of the ghetto."

"So you wouldn't have to live like I do," Rica whispered. Lisa pulled out of her arms and stepped away.

"So I could live like a citizen because I am one."

Lisa drove out of the city the following afternoon, glancing occasionally at the directions she had scribbled on a napkin during Chief Bannert's call. She and Rica had spent a fruitless shift last night trying literally to sniff out the killer in a city teeming with Marginals. Their conversation seemed stilted after the intimacy of their talk in Lisa's apartment, and Lisa had to admit she felt mostly relief when Bannert told her that they had a break in the case and the Dark Guard was no longer needed. She was on her way to meet him now, and she hoped they'd be finished in time for her to return to normal duty. The sooner she got back to her regular routine, the easier it would be to forget the feel of Rica's arms around her.

She pulled off the highway and almost missed her turn onto a dirt road. Her cell phone beeped as she bumped her way toward the farmhouse where Bannert and the detectives had found the Marginal responsible for the murders. She picked up the phone, wincing as her patrol car hit a deep rut.

"Stecker here."

"Lisa?" Rica's voice was distorted since cell coverage was unpredictable outside of the city limits. "I was just at your apartment. Where are you?"

"Bannert called," Lisa said loudly, hoping Rica could hear her over the static on the line. "They found the killer. The Guard should have been notified."

"...Not a Marginal...Where...?"

Lisa sighed. She should have called Rica before she left, but she had expected to be back in the city long before their shift was due to start. She wondered why Rica had come over so early, and she cursed at herself for wishing she had been there to see her.

"I'm a couple miles off Highway Sixty-Two," she yelled into the phone, but the signal was gone. She tossed her cell on the seat and soon pulled up next to the old farmhouse. There was only one cruiser parked in the driveway and an uneasy feeling washed over her. Something in Rica's voice, even through the poor connection, had sounded concerned. She saw Bannert waving to her from the porch and she pushed her doubts aside. She was being paranoid, only natural after seeing those crime scene photos and the wounds that matched her own scars.

"Hey, Chief, where's everyone at?" she called out as she got out of her car.

"They're around back," he said, waving toward the wooded area behind the house. "Come on in and I'll show you what we found."

Lisa took a step forward, but her instincts fought to override her movement. Too many things were wrong, from Rica's worried voice to the lone patrol car to the lack of any Marginal scent in the fresh country air. She reached for her door handle when Bannert's first shot rang out. The bullet shattered the front windshield and Lisa slid over broken glass as she dove into the car and grabbed the radio. She keyed the mike, shouting her location in the hope it would have enough signal to transmit, and started the ignition. Bannert's second shot went through the grill and the engine went dead.

"Come on, Stecker, I don't want to shoot you," the chief called to her, his voice getting closer as she slipped her own gun out of its holster. She took a deep breath and lifted her head up enough to see through the shattered window, raising her gun at the same time. She fired at Bannert and winged his shoulder, forcing him to take cover behind his own car.

"What's going on here, Chief?" she called, hoping to delay him long enough for backup to arrive. She edged over to the passenger side of the car and quietly opened the door. Maybe if she could make it to the woods she could outrun him.

"You hate them too, Stecker," Bannert said. "I've seen it in your eyes. I'm only trying to help the citizens by getting the Marginals back in the ghettos where they belong."

"So *you* killed those people? And you're making it look like a Marginal out for revenge?"

"I never meant to include you in this, Stecker, but when the Council sent that vampire bitch to work with you I knew I had to get you two off the case. I read your records and I know you have the affinity. You and the Guard would eventually have figured out it wasn't a Marginal."

And Rica already had, Lisa realized. "It won't help your plan if I'm found shot to death with one of your bullets, Chief. It's over."

"I'll just have to rip the bullets out with my claws," Bannert said in a matter-of-fact tone that was at odds with his words.

Lisa leaned out of the passenger-side door and watched Bannert's feet as he changed positions. He seemed about to make a run for her, so Lisa crouched down, ready to move when he did. As soon as he started toward her she was out of the car, taking a shot at him before sprinting into the woods behind the house. She glanced back one time and saw Bannert following, his hand pressed to a stain of blood on his stomach.

Bannert's footsteps were sounding closer when Lisa tripped over an exposed root. She twisted as she fell, and was bringing her gun up for another shot when a flash of gold erupted from the trees to her right and slammed into Bannert. The bullet he fired at Lisa was deflected into a tree as he and Rica fell to the ground. She had him pinned before he had time to react.

Lisa heard Rica's snarl, and she realized that this was no call, no urge for a victim's surrender. She jumped to her feet and grabbed the vampire's shoulder.

"Don't, Rica. Don't do it," she begged, reaching around to grab Rica's chin and force her to meet her eyes.

"Get away, Lisa," she growled.

"Don't kill him," Lisa raised her voice in a commanding tone. "You know the rules for a Guard. If you kill a suspect, you'll be tried for his crimes. Please."

The last word, delivered in a softer voice, made Rica turn to look at Lisa. "I can't...the blood...I didn't..."

Lisa knelt next to her. "You didn't feed today, did you? You came to see me instead?"

"One of the Dark Guard found a dead were-lynx. She was killed a week ago, and her claws had been severed," Rica said. She seemed to have trouble keeping her eyes from the stain spreading across Bannert's midsection.

"Let her do it, Stecker," he wheezed. "She'll pay for what I did and that makes it all worthwhile."

"No. No sacrifices," Lisa said. She tugged Bannert's wrist from Rica's grasp, snapping her handcuff on it. She did the same with his other hand, pushing Rica back so she could make the chief sit up.

"Wait here," she ordered and Rica nodded reluctantly, her eyes following Bannert closely. Lisa pulled him out of the woods and shoved him in the back of her patrol car. A quick check of his wounds assured her that he would survive without immediate medical attention, so she left him hogtied in her backseat and jogged back to the woods.

Rica was sitting where Lisa had left her, clasping her bent knees as if trying to stop herself from following Bannert's blood trail. Lisa knelt by her again, gently reaching out to stroke her golden hair. Rica leaned into her hand, turning her lips to Lisa's palm.

"I can't," she said in a rasping voice. "I'm too hungry. It's not safe."

Lisa bent over and captured Rica's mouth with her own, biting Rica's lower lip sharply when she fought against the kiss. A low growl sounded in Rica's throat as she sucked Lisa's tongue into her mouth. Lisa felt a brief moment of panic when she wondered if Rica might just bite her tongue off and drink from there, but after a few minutes she no longer cared *how* Rica fed, just that she did.

Lisa tugged the Guard shirt over Rica's head, leaning down to cover a taut nipple with her mouth. She held it firmly between her teeth, flicking it with her tongue, as Rica's breathing grew more ragged and her hands tangled in Lisa's hair. Lisa moved to the other breast, sucking it hard into her mouth.

"Naked...please...I need you," Rica gasped, her thirst overriding her ability to speak clearly. Lisa stood up and quickly stripped off her duty belt and uniform before kneeling again to peel Rica's black pants off her. In a flash, Rica flipped her onto her back and recaptured her mouth. She shifted, trailing kisses over the long scars more tenderly than Lisa would have thought possible, and then moving hungrily to Lisa's small breasts. She consumed them with her mouth, grazing an erect nipple with sharp teeth so she drew a little blood. She gently licked the red drops, the mix of pain and arousal making Lisa cry out and arch wildly underneath her.

"Taste so good," Rica whispered in her ear. "Baby, are you sure?"

"Please," Lisa begged, pulling Rica's cool body hard against her overheated skin. "I need you. Want to taste you, too."

After one brief kiss on the lips, Rica moved away. The absence of her made Lisa moan in protest, but Rica quickly placed a knee on either side of Lisa's head before lowering her own to nuzzle Lisa's damp curls.

Lisa spread her own thighs as she grabbed Rica's hips and pulled her closer. She used her hands to open Rica's lower lips, running her tongue through the wetness she found there. Lisa found the scent of Rica intoxicating, and the intensity of the vampire's arousal made Lisa push her hips toward Rica's mouth, silently pleading for more.

Rica fought for control as Lisa drove her toward an inevitable climax. She turned her head to the side, silky curls damp under her cheek, and drew her tongue across the soft skin of Lisa's groin. She felt Lisa cry out against her at the touch, and she quickly slipped her fingers into Lisa's wetness. She entered her roughly at the same time as she punctured Lisa's delicate skin with sharp teeth. She drank, feeling tears sting her eyes at the sweet taste of her lover.

Lisa had never felt so completely filled, with Rica's teeth embedded in her thigh, sucking on her in the same rhythm as those fingers stroking inside. She felt a desperate need to make Rica come, to have her climax while feeding on her. She closed her lips around Rica's clit, feeling it stiffen in her mouth as she sucked hard, catching Rica's rhythm as they fed together. They came together as well, their hips straining toward each other and stifling their loud cries.

Rica withdrew her fangs, leaving small puncture wounds on Lisa's groin. "Are you still alive?" she whispered, a hint of real fear in her voice.

"I'm not sure yet," Lisa answered weakly. Rica rose to her knees and turned around so she could lie in Lisa's arms.

"Thank you," Rica said, her voice still quiet. "It's never felt like that to feed."

"Mmm, I'm glad," Lisa said as she ran her hands over Rica's back. She sighed. "I suppose we should drive Bannert to the hospital now."

Rica grew still in her arms. "And then?"

"Then we'll need to give statements, file evidence and send someone out to get my car. And then," Lisa paused, cupping Rica's chin and meeting her mouth in a lingering kiss. "Back home for a midnight snack."

LA CAÍDA

Anna Meadows

When I was seven years old, I caught a monarch butterfly off the fruit trees in my grandmother's backyard. It had perched on a pear blossom, its wire tongue probing the center for nectar, and I trapped it in one of the blue mason jars Abuelita had once used to can cactus-flower jam. I watched it flutter against the aqua glass, its wings a flash of marigolds and obsidian.

"Let it go, *m'ija*," my grandmother said, pausing from her work in the herb patch.

"Why?" I asked.

"It's hungry."

"But so am I."

Worry crossed her face. Even after years of watching her granddaughters turn eighteen, when a hunger for salt and iron filled their mouths, she didn't know why I would want to eat the winged creature. My older sisters and cousins craved blood, only blood. *Naguales* never wanted anything else.

"Let it go, *m'ija*," she said again.

"Why?"

"He could be a warrior," she said, reminding me of the legend that said fallen Aztec soldiers were reborn as monarchs. "He could be your ancestor." She picked a handful of marjoram leaves. "And even if he's not, he could be *un ángel caído*."

"A what?" I asked. I knew as little Spanish as my mother; she'd forgotten all but the Lord's Prayer since her family moved to Luna Anaranjada when she was five.

"A fallen one," my grandmother said. "Sometimes God takes pity on them, depending on what they've done. An angel who rebels against Him will see no mercy. He'll be thrown to the Earth and vanish before he hits the ground." She pointed up toward the Milky Way, coming into focus and banding the sky as it darkened. "*Como un meteoro.*" She took the jar in her hands. "But for the lesser sins, he might turn the angel into a monarch on its way down, so it can float to Earth. Its wings turn to limbs only when they touch the ground." She eased the jar back between my palms. "Do you see, *m'ija*?"

I nodded, my eyes down, and unscrewed the lid. The monarch hesitated, crawling along the inside lip, but I shook the jar and it fluttered out.

I didn't hunger for another butterfly until after my eighteenth birthday, when I wanted blood so badly I was ready to bite into my own arm. My sisters waited out their cravings like my family had for generations, eating raw, bloody meat from a cousin's shop, and biding their time until they heard about a man who raped a woman or beat his wife. They would surround him in one of the fallow wheat fields outside town and share the meal like guests at a wedding feast. When a village was rid of such men, we moved on.

They always invited me. I rarely came. The man's screams

and the sound of my sisters' teeth tearing into his muscle turned my stomach.

Carmen made fun of me. "Little sister is hungry, but can't eat. She doesn't want to work for it. She wants to buy it in cartons at the store like orange juice."

I didn't hold it against her. She often led my sisters to their next meal, and because of our family, the talk about our kind, *los naguales*, was changing. Villages used to fear *naguales*. They called us witches, and whispered that at night we turned to cats and wild dogs to commit our crimes. They said we were why children became sick and crops withered. They blamed murders and missing livestock on our taste for blood.

Thanks to my family's penchant for the blood of men so evil no one missed them, wives and mothers now spoke of us as guardians. Good men used us as warnings to their sons and brothers. If they guessed who we were, they did not tell, fearing we would flee before we had rid their village of the kind of men we fed on. If one of those men found us out, he never lived to expose us.

No one ever found the bodies. My mother and Carmen never told me how they managed that. Once I asked them if it was the graveyards; two of my uncles ran a funeral home the next county over, and a few of my cousins worked as undertakers. But my mother only looked horrified and told me they'd never defile good men's tombs with the bodies of the depraved.

Depraved or not, I couldn't feed on them. My sisters had grown tall and lean on their diet. I'd gained ten pounds trying to fill the gnawing in my stomach with the olive oil cookies and *chiles en nogada* that were once my favorites. My breasts had bloomed a full cup size. My thighs had softened and widened, and I carried a little pouch of extra fat below my belly button that strangers mistook for baby fat, thinking I was still thirteen.

I ate and ate because I couldn't stomach what I needed. It wasn't that I objected to what my sisters were doing, to what my family had done for a hundred years. But my body rebelled against the nourishment. Carmen, for all her mocking, had brought me a glass of it once. But I heard the cries of the guilty man and their teeth puncturing his ligaments as surely as if I'd been in that fallow field, and I couldn't keep it down. I was eating myself into the next dress size, and I was still starving.

It shouldn't have surprised me that the next time I saw a monarch butterfly floating past a *pitaya* flower, I imagined its powdered wings on my tongue.

It was the night Hector Salazar stormed onto our front lawn, stinking of cheap mezcal and crushing the *datura* under his boots, and waking the whole neighborhood. "Get out here, *putas*! You filthy, murdering whores! You killed my brother!"

Carmen strolled onto the front porch, our grandmother's pearl-handled pistol tucked into her skirt. "Your brother tried to rape another man's wife." She cleared flakes of dried oregano from under her fingers, and tossed her head at Adriana, Lucia, and me to tell us to stay back. "God brings swift justice sometimes. It's not our place to question His ways."

He spat on our statue of *la virgen*. "I'll kill all of you." He waggled an unsteady finger at Carmen. "The sheriff thinks you're pretty. That's the only reason you're not in the jail. But it doesn't matter. I'll kill all of you myself." He stumbled over the brick planter border.

Lucia, pure soul as she is, stepped forward to keep him from falling, but Adriana held her back, and Hector fell into the weeds.

"Not tonight. I'll let you *putas* wait and wonder when I'll get you." He staggered to his feet, his knees and elbows coated in mud, and out toward the main road.

Adriana fumed. I gripped the porch railing so I didn't tremble. When Lucia caught her breath, she cleaned *la virgen* with her skirt.

"Don't worry," said Carmen. "He knows what his brother did, and he knows he has nothing to threaten us. Go to bed."

Carmen slept like a cat in sunlight, and Adriana and Lucia turned over in their beds until they wore themselves out.

I knew I wouldn't sleep until dawn, so I took a walk in the desert behind our house. That was when I saw the butterfly.

It looked already dead as it was falling. It flapped its wings no more than the wind would have done for it, and it tumbled toward the ground without riding the updraft. I lost sight of it and found it again, its path swirling through the dust that clouded the air.

I knew my grandmother couldn't see me. She'd settled with my mother in Cachcaba, thirty-seven miles away; we brought them blood in blown-glass jars on the weekends. But I searched the dark anyway, just in case. No one would ever know. If it was already dead, it couldn't be one of my Aztec ancestors, so what could be the harm? Birds ate butterflies every day.

A last gust of wind swept it up before its body weighted down its wings and pulled it to the Earth. I tried to follow it, but it vanished in the dull gold of blowing dust.

When the thin dirt settled, the butterfly was gone. In its place, a human body lay curled on its side.

I gasped. I didn't know how I'd missed it or how long it had been there. It looked dead, at first. From the cropped hair and straight hips, I thought it was a boy. Then I noticed the slight curve of her breast. She was naked except for bruising that darkened her back.

She was breathing.

I knelt behind her. I reached out to see if she was really there.

My fingers barely grazed the fine, peach-fuzz hairs on her back, but her shoulder blades pinched, her eyes snapping open. She struggled for breath like I'd just pulled her out of water.

"Shh." I stroked her back.

"Leave me alone," she said, her voice young, but low.

"You're hurt," I whispered.

"I'm all right."

"You need help."

She shivered, though the day's heat had barely faded with the dark; she must have had a fever. "Please leave me alone."

"I won't hurt you," I said. "I'll take you to the doctor. He's not far."

"No," she said. "Please. Don't let anyone see me like this."

I took my shawl from my shoulders.

It was light, just enough to guard against the chill that settled over the desert at night, but I draped it over her waist, using some of the slack to cover her breasts.

I caught another glimpse of the bruising on her back. It wasn't indigo or violet, shadowed in yellow. It was veined in black, and filled in with orange. Two great, bruised wings, like a monarch's, but out of focus, spread across her back.

I wanted to touch them. I didn't.

"Are you a warrior?" I asked, even though I doubted it; her hair was gold as new corn silk, and the tan of her skin looked dirty, not coppery like the raw sienna that ran in my family.

"No," she said.

"Are you one of them?" I asked. "*Un ángel caído?*"

She winced. It was as close to a nod as I'd get.

I took her in my arms. She was light, lighter than she should have been even with how thin she was, but she grew heavier as I came closer to our back door, like she was becoming solid and human. She fell in and out of waking, asking me over and over again to leave her alone, leave her out there. But when I put her in my bed and wrapped her in my grandmother's *ojo* blanket, she slept.

I needed clothes. She might let me touch her if I gave her clothes. The shops in town wouldn't open until morning, and the skirts Carmen, Lucia, and I wore would look strange on the *ángel*'s boyish body, with her short, messy hair. Adriana's dresser was my only choice.

She was the heaviest sleeper of all of us. I eased her door open and snuck toward the heavy dresser. But my foot hit the only board in her room that creaked, and she started awake.

"Little sister?" She sat up in bed, groggy. "What are you doing?"

"Could I borrow some of your clothes?"

"Why would you want to borrow clothes from me? You never wear pants. Besides, they wouldn't fit you."

"Please?" I said. "I'll explain in the morning."

"Is there a man in your room?"

"Of course not."

She got out of bed, pushed past me, and slipped toward my room.

I followed after her, but I had to slow as I passed the hallway mirror and the side table I always ran into if I wasn't careful; my hip hitting its corner would wake my sisters for sure, especially if one of the earthen jars fell to the tile and shattered.

Adriana threw my door open and saw the black and orange bruising on the *ángel*'s back. "You brought home *una caída*?"

I shut the door behind us. "She needed help."

"Carmen will have a fit when she finds out. She doesn't even like me going around with women. If she finds out you have one in your bed…"

"Then don't tell her."

She clicked her tongue all the way down the hallway and came back with trousers and a collared shirt. "These might be a little big and too long." She left them on the dresser and nodded toward the *ángel*. "She's cute. I can see why you like her."

"Adriana."

"Don't worry, little sister." She eased the door shut as she left. "She's not the kind I like."

I dressed the *ángel* in Adriana's trousers while she slept. The shirt I'd let her put on herself. When she woke just after midnight, I heated a *chile relleno* in the oven and tried to get her to eat.

"I'm not hungry," she said, still a little asleep.

I looked over her bony frame. "You look hungry."

"So do you," she said.

"I'm not," I said.

"You still look hungry." She turned over, sucking air in through her teeth at the sudden pain.

"What is it?" I asked.

"Nothing."

"You're hurt. I knew it." I pulled the quilt from her shoulders, freezing when I saw the scrape on her shoulder, the one that had been against the ground. It glistened like liquid garnet, warm and alive, the blood of a living woman, not a dead man.

I caught myself biting my lip.

Even in the dim room, I saw the flicker of understanding in *la caída*'s face. "You're a salt girl," she said.

"What?"

"We call you salt girls, because you want the salt in the blood."

I swallowed to keep from crying. I wanted her warmth, and to run my tongue over that slick of blood so badly it was driving me to sobs. "I don't know why. We've been this way for a hundred years. Maybe more."

"Even we're not told why things are the way they are." She lowered her gaze, like shame was weighting it down. "Why we want what we want."

I pulled a strip of cloth over her wound, both to help it heal and so I wouldn't see it. I wanted to dampen the smell of iron, as sweet as rain-made rust. "Why did you fall?" I asked.

A wry laugh stuck in the back of her throat. "Why do you think?"

"You wanted something."

"Yes."

"What?"

Two shallow breaths wavered in the back of her throat, one, then the other, before she grabbed me and kissed me, her desert-warm mouth searing my lips.

"Soft." She buried her nose in my hair and dug the heels of her hands into my back. "You're so soft." Then she dropped her hands and pulled away. "I'm sorry."

I stopped myself from grabbing her back. "I don't understand." I straightened my posture. "You fell because you wanted someone?"

"No." She dropped her head, letting her hair shadow her face. "That's the worst part. There was no one. I didn't fall in love. I just wanted."

I crawled on top of her, slowly pinning her down, and kissed her. She startled, but then gave her mouth to mine. I let my mouth wander down her neck toward her breasts, but it strayed, and her blood stained my lower lip. She arched her back to press her body into mine, but her blood heated my mouth, like hot sugar on its way to caramel, and I scrambled off her so quickly I fell from the bed. She grabbed my waist and pulled me back.

I licked my lip, blushing and guilty.

"You are hungry," she said.

"I shouldn't be," I said. "I eat all the time. My sister says if I don't stop, I'll get so chubby, I'll look like a little girl forever."

She pushed a piece of hair out of my face. "You don't look like a little girl."

I watched her mouth; her lips parted.

She turned her shoulder toward me. "And you're hungry for this, aren't you?"

I looked away. I didn't want to see the jeweled red again.

She cupped my face in her hands. "Could you live off me?"

I raised my eyes to hers. "What?"

"Could you live off me?"

I tried to wrench away from her. "I couldn't do that."

"Because it's not possible?"

"Because I couldn't do that to you."

"Yes, you could," she said. "I'm no good for anything else."

"You'd be weak whenever I had some of you."

"I don't care."

I snuck a look at the streak of garnet on her shoulder. "Would you let me give you something?"

She narrowed her eyes. "What?"

"What you wanted."

"I couldn't ask you for that," she said. "I'm fallen. I'm dirty."

I slid my hands under the sheet and onto her hands. "And I'm a *nagual*."

She moved my hands back on top of the blanket. "If I could be your nourishment, maybe I'd be something good again."

I got up from the bed.

"Where are you going?" She asked, baring the red jasper of her shoulder.

"I need a cookie." I paced in front of the door. "Do you want a cookie?"

"No. I don't want a cookie."

I put a hand on the doorknob. "Well, I need a cookie."

"Why?"

Because I still thought the food of my former life would fill me. "Because when I get upset, I want cookies."

She laughed a soft laugh. That made me madder, and I left.

I hadn't even closed my bedroom door behind me when the barrel of my grandmother's pearl-handled pistol was in my face.

"Good," said Salazar, his drunken breath pressing me against the wall. "The littlest *puta*. Come on." He gestured with the gun, and I followed the gleam of the handle toward the living room.

Carmen always kept my grandmother's pistol in the armoire in her room. I didn't understand how Salazar could have it until I saw my sisters lined up against the mantle, Carmen with a gash across her right temple. Their bedroom doors were open, and they were in their nightclothes.

"All four *putas*." Salazar shoved me toward them.

"Leave her alone," said Lucia, in a louder voice than anyone but her sisters had ever heard her use.

Salazar pointed the gun toward her. "The Virgin Lucia has something to say?" He twirled the barrel through her curls.

Adriana lunged at him, but Salazar jammed the hilt of the gun into the side of her head, and she reeled back toward the mantel.

Lucia stayed silent, glaring at him.

"Any of you whores have anything to say?" he asked.

Blood from Carmen's wound glistened on her eyelashes, heating her stare. Adriana held the side of her head, but glowered through the hair in her face.

"That's what I thought." He lowered the gun, but held it tight. "I want to hear what you did to him. I want to hear where you hid my brother's body."

La caída's face appeared in the hallway mirror out of the darkness, the steps of her bare feet quiet on the floor. She lifted a terra-cotta vase from the side table.

Salazar turned at the slight sound of dried clay against wood, but *la caída* had already lifted the vase over her head, and brought it down on Salazar's.

The gun went off, shattering the mirror in the hallway. Lucia screamed. Salazar fell to the floor, hitting his head on the ceramic tile.

I searched the dark for *la caída*'s face. She was nowhere.

I stepped over the glass shards. "*Caída*?"

I heard her soft moan and followed the sound. She was on the floor, her wound spattered with blood. I knelt to look at her. I hadn't remembered the wound as that big, that open.

It was on the wrong shoulder.

"He shot her," I said, feeling her forehead and brushing her hair out of her face. "He shot her."

Lucia grabbed her shawl. "I'll go wake Marcus."

"She's going for the doctor," I whispered to *la caída*.

"No," said *la caída*. "Please."

Adriana turned on every light in the hallway. "Get her away from the glass."

Lucia cleared a path with the broom and I pulled *la caída* away from the broken mirror.

La caída tilted her head, sweat dotting her forehead with glass beads. "Take what you need."

"No." I kissed her forehead. "No."

Carmen found the bloody bullet among the glass shards. "It's not in her." She held it up. "It grazed her." She crouched near us, taking in the black and orange wings on *la caída*'s back with a slow nod.

Adriana began boiling water on the stove. Lucia crossed herself and whispered a prayer I couldn't make out.

Carmen held *la caída*'s arm by her elbow, not rough, but no more gentle than she had to be. "It's not deep. But you should see the doctor anyway."

"What will he do to me?"

"Nothing I don't tell him to," she said. "He's my brother." She looked at me. "Where did you find her?"

"Outside," I said.

She set her elbow back down and nodded at Lucia. "Marcus will come here."

"Aren't they going to come take me?" *La caída* asked, pulling her limbs into her chest.

"Who?"

"I killed him," said *la caída*.

"No one will know." Carmen tossed her hands toward Salazar's body. "Who's hungry?"

I couldn't lift *la caída*'s body anymore. She was as heavy as a real woman. Adriana helped me get her back into my bed, where our brother checked her wound, pressing his lips together and nodding at my bandaging. "Not bad, *hermanita*." He gave *la caída* something for the pain, and she slept. "She saved all my sisters, huh?" he asked when he saw the lines of her monarch's wings. "Should be enough to get her back into heaven when she dies."

"What, now you're a priest?" said Carmen, shooing him out of the room when he was done. "Get back to your wife."

As my sisters took their meal in the field outside town, I lay in bed next to *la caída*, tracing my finger along the thin cut where a shard of glass had sliced along the edge of her hip. Marcus had missed it because he was worried about the wound on her arm.

La caída moaned awake.

I pulled my hand away.

"No," she said, almost humming. "It feels good." She reached up, her eyes still half-closed, and rubbed a lock of my hair between her fingers like it was silk ribbon. "You're still hungry." She pulled the sheet back to expose the cut on her hip.

I flushed. "I can't. You're hurt."

"Will you take care of me?" She gave me a lopsided smile in the dark.

"Yes." I curled her hand into a loose fist and kissed her thumb. "Yes."

"Then take what I want to give you." She pressed her palm into her hip to thicken the little thread of blood. "Take what you need." She cradled the back of my neck in her hand and gently guided my mouth toward the cut.

Part of me wanted to drain her; I'd silenced my hunger for the months since my eighteenth birthday. But she was so warm, all salt and no sweetness, that I wanted to savor her like the wine of black Tempranillo grapes or the darkest bittersweet chocolate. I drank slowly, and before she was too weak I stopped and slid my mouth across her thigh to the triangle of soft hair between her legs. I sucked on her labia, one at a time. I touched her as I kissed her, and she shuddered when I felt her wetness, and again when my curious fingers made her wetter. I drank her wetness and tasted the same perfect salt I found in her blood. She pulled me on top of her and traced her hands under my dress. Her palms painted my shape so I no longer felt young and hungry, rounded with baby fat. Her hands and her salt were shaping me into something nourished and womanly. Soft.

Her fingers found me, and she touched me in the way I'd tried to touch myself every night for years. She covered my mouth with hers to keep me from waking my sisters. We mapped each other's bodies with our mouths, and when her touch made me as weak as she was, we slept.

When *la caída* was well enough, she and I joined my sisters on their walks, Carmen and Lucia with the lovers that followed them from town to town, Adriana with her woman of the week. As we passed the town cemetery, a headstone caught my eye. It was too new, too free of weeds and dry lichen, and carved with only the letter *S* and the current year. The grass covering the grave looked new and tenuous.

La caída stopped with me, but couldn't tell what I was looking at. She hadn't passed the cemetery a hundred times.

"Mother told you we would never defile good men's graves," Carmen whispered as she passed. "Instead, we make new ones."

La caída watched Carmen, and her eyes narrowed as she listened. She didn't yet understand the ways our family, how the undertakers and stonecutters, the doctors and butchers, all worked together to shield the desires of the women. She didn't yet understand how we worked, humans or *naguales*. She didn't yet know the million little sins we committed to turn our hunger for salt into the best thing it could be.

Carmen took my hand and *la caída*'s and put mine in hers. "Welcome to Earth, *ángel caída*. You have a lot to learn."

THE CRYSTAL ALTAR

Adele Dubois

I t'll be dusk soon," Morgan Hall said to Rosa Martinez, watching the last van filled with picnic-goers exit the Crystal Cave parking lot. "The others will arrive at sunset for our tour." At the edge of the grassy area she threw sandwich crusts, empty bottles of tea, and organic chip packets in the trash and recycle bins. She brushed her palms down the front of her tank top and the back of her shorts, flaking off bits of crumbs and dried clover.

Katydids, tree crickets, and cicadas chirped and buzzed in the thick grass and dark woods of the surrounding Pennsylvania Dutch countryside.

Rosa shook out their picnic blanket and clicked her tongue. "Only your cousin would celebrate her birthday in a creepy place like this cave." She scrunched up her nose.

Morgan tried not to smile, since Rosa was being serious. If she only knew how cute she looked when she made that face, she might never do it again.

Rosa *hated* the dark and anything remotely otherworldly. She refused to watch fantasy or horror movies and detested Halloween. Rosa liked musicals, TV cooking shows and Christmas. She'd come to Angela's birthday party strictly under protest. Morgan had mollified her with a picnic *she* had prepared. Rosa worked as the chef at the restaurant Morgan managed and rarely got a break from food preparation.

It seemed the novelty had worn off.

"The caves are historic," Morgan said, trying to reason with her. "Natural wonders. People travel from all over the world to visit and they're right in our backyard. We'll see formations like calcite crystal walls, flowstones, and dripstones millennia old."

Rosa stopped folding the blanket and set her mouth in a grim line. Her nostrils flared. "I'd rather wait in the car. You go. She's your cousin. And a freak, if you ask me."

Morgan couldn't argue there. Her cousin Angela had turned a whole new kind of weird since her trip to Europe. She'd left eastern Pennsylvania a skinny geek in glasses that nobody wanted to hang with. She'd returned a curvy Goth with facial piercings, night vision, and an entourage of beautiful women who'd moved into the Lancaster home she shared with her father.

Angela had explained that laser eye surgery in Eastern Europe was light years ahead of procedures in the United States. Her new look was the work of some chick she'd met on the road named Lillith. The transformation, she claimed, had made her popular. Angela seemed perfectly happy.

Which was more than Morgan could say at the moment.

"I know she's odd, but she's family and it's her birthday. What else could I do?" Morgan took the blanket from Rosa's hands and laid it on the grass beneath the cover of an old weeping willow. Rosa followed inside the natural umbrella of leaves and slender branches.

"Let's not argue, 'kay?" Morgan pleaded. "We have at least an hour before the others arrive. We haven't been alone all day." She hoped her voice sounded husky and sexy and not as desperate as she felt.

Secretly, she worried that they were headed for bed death. Rosa had become more distant and less interested in sex than she had been during their first six months together. Morgan had plenty of platonic friendships and the last thing she wanted was for Rosa to drift into that category. She loved her and wanted her as much now as she had in the beginning.

Morgan lay down on her back and reached up from the blanket for Rosa. "Come here."

Rosa avoided eye contact at first, but then her gaze tracked the V between Morgan's legs beneath her skimpy blue shorts. Morgan let her thighs relax. The cooling summer air sent a breeze over her flesh and her braless nipples cinched like ripe raisins beneath her light cotton top. She licked her lips and fanned out her long brown hair on the blanket. Then she rested her arms above her head and waited.

Without a word, Rosa lowered to her knees beside her and ran a palm up the length of her bare thigh. Her fingers hooked the hem of her shorts and her nails scraped the edge of her thong. Morgan shivered at her touch, but didn't move. Sometimes Rosa needed to take control. Morgan sensed this was one of those times.

Her patience was rewarded when Rosa leaned over her, trailing tendrils of jet-black hair across Morgan's shoulder. Her heavy breasts brushed Morgan's arm, causing goose bumps to pepper her skin.

"I'm sorry," Rosa whispered. "You're right. You have a family obligation to meet."

Morgan draped Rosa's hair behind her neck and traced the

curve of her creamy tan shoulder. "Who knows? The night might be fun. We'll see thousand-year-old stalactites and stalagmites."

Rosa sat back on her heels and let Morgan run a hand over her breasts. "Sounds interesting." Her tone said otherwise, but Morgan appreciated Rosa's effort.

She lowered her hand. "It's not just the party that's been bugging you, is it?" Fear trickled up Morgan's spine as she realized she might have opened Pandora's box. Once that happened, there was no going back.

Rosa's expression flashed indecision. She nibbled her lower lip. When Morgan thought she'd scream if Rosa didn't answer soon, she finally spoke. "I know I've been distant lately. It's just...you're the first woman I've had an intimate relationship with. I feel connected to you, and comfortable—and the sex is incredible. There's never been anything like it for me."

"*But*?" The word hovered like a landslide waiting to fall.

"I guess I'm not as sure of myself as you are."

Morgan lowered her lids and held back a sigh. "I want you to be sure, Rosa." She lifted her gaze and met Rosa's fathomless brown eyes. "I know who I am. If you don't, that's okay. I wouldn't dream of trying to force you. But you have to tell me soon—before I get hurt." It was already too late for that, but Morgan kept that sentiment to herself. Adding pressure to the relationship wasn't the answer. Rosa had to come to her without guilt, or not at all.

Rosa leaned down and kissed her, as if offering reassurance. "Thanks for not freaking out."

Morgan wrapped her arms around Rosa's waist and deepened the kiss. She touched her tongue to Rosa's and then slid hers inside her lover's mouth.

Rosa sucked it in greedy little pulls. Then she licked and

nipped Morgan's bottom lip before pressing her mouth again to hers.

Morgan reached beneath Rosa's T-shirt and unhooked her bra. She brought her hands to Rosa's warm breasts, caressed their softness and massaged their fullness. She groaned with pleasure at the silky texture of her skin and the scent of strawberry soap that lingered there. Thrills shot through her at the feel of Rosa's nipples hardening inside her palms while her breathing quickened against her mouth. It was the ultimate turn-on to be wanted.

They broke the kiss and yanked off their tops and shorts, returning to kiss and fondle each other.

The trees rustled around them as a gust of wind shook the leaves. Somewhere in the distance a dog barked. Morgan barely registered the world outside the canopy of the weeping willow, as a moment of inspiration struck.

She lowered her mouth to the pulse beating against Rosa's neck and sucked the spot with deep, hard tugs. Her teeth grazed the delicate skin and nipped until bruises formed. She swirled her tongue over the dappled plum marks and savored the taste of Rosa's sweet flesh as blood pooled just below the surface.

Rosa leaned away and touched her neck. Tiny lines formed between her eyebrows as her eyes flashed with uncertainty. "Why did you do that?"

Morgan cradled Rosa's breasts and lifted them higher, watching her hands squeeze and release. "I was marking you. I want to make sure the freaks at the party know you're taken."

Rosa laughed. "You're jealous? I was worried you'd gone goth on me, like your whacko cousin. She probably drinks blood for sport."

Morgan rolled her eyes. "Wouldn't surprise me. She likes to pretend she's a vampire. She and her entourage go to dungeon clubs in the city." Morgan inspected the love bite on Rosa's neck. "That looks kind of cool, though. I like it."

"You do, huh?" Rosa became playful and tweaked Morgan's ear. Then her expression turned sultry and somber. She leaned forward and took Morgan's left nipple into her mouth and sucked while she stroked her right breast.

Morgan closed her eyes and moaned. The invisible cord between her nipples and clitoris pulled tight, sending the first waves of impending orgasm through her.

"Now it's my turn to bite," Rosa whispered against Morgan's breast. She pressed her lips to a spot above her heart and began to nip and suck.

Morgan gasped at the prickles of pleasure and pain as her skin lifted against Rosa's anxious mouth. Hot breath wafted over her breast while Rosa worked her teeth and lips.

It had brought Morgan deep sensual pleasure to mark Rosa's neck, but receiving the bites surpassed her expectations. Her pulse quickened, and adrenaline pumped through her veins, rushing the sound of blood to her ears.

Rosa slid one hand down the front of Morgan's thong and stroked her swollen clit while her teeth scraped Morgan's skin. She moved her mouth to a fresh spot at the curve between Morgan's neck and shoulder and bit down hard against the underlying muscles. Morgan opened her mouth to shout, but the fingers working her clitoris muted her cries.

One finger, then two, thrust inside her passage and brushed her engorged G-spot. The stimulated erogenous zone sent fire to her core while Rosa's fingers plunged and pulled.

Rosa returned to suck and bite the bruised area above her heart until Morgan felt sure she'd drawn blood. When Rosa nipped the end of her nipple and finger-fucked her faster and harder, Morgan came against her hand in a frenzied rush. She gripped Rosa's shoulders and gasped for air until Rosa's fingers slowed.

Her orgasm faded with the sunlight dipping behind the shadow-lined trees. Morgan tipped her head forward against Rosa's shoulder. "Dear god," she gasped. "What just happened?"

When she looked up, Rosa grinned and smoothed Morgan's hair away from her temple. "Turnabout is fair play. I got into it."

Morgan touched the sore spot at her breast and looked down. Even in the fading light she could see indentations and scarlet bruises. The love bites would definitely show above a V-neck shirt. "I guess those lesbian goths won't hit on me tonight, either."

Rosa smirked. "Damn straight."

"You mean, damn right."

When Rosa burst into hearty belly laughter, hope filled Morgan's heart. For the first time in weeks her confidence in their relationship returned.

Who knew biting could be such a turn-on? Maybe screwball Angela was onto something.

Morgan's gaze tracked the caves looming atop the hill above them, and she shivered with an unexpected sense of foreboding. She turned back to Rosa and pressed her mouth to hers in a lingering kiss for comfort. "Guess what, *mi amor?* I'm not done." Morgan pushed her fingertips against Rosa's shoulders to indicate she should lie on her back.

Gentle breezes filtered through the weeping willow and brushed the tiny hairs on Morgan's arms as dusk turned to dark. Pole lamps flickered on around the perimeter of the parking lot, casting a glow over the picnic lawn. The willow swayed and seemed to whisper, "yes," while she pressed Rosa to the ground and pulled off her panties. Rosa lifted her hips and pointed her toes until the satin slid free.

Wearing only her thong, Morgan stretched out on her stomach to lie between Rosa's legs. Her palms glided over the soft skin inside her thighs and she watched Rosa's labia separate, exposing her delicate pink folds and deep, wet channel.

Morgan nipped the inside of Rosa's thigh where her leg met her groin. Rosa moaned as Morgan's teeth grazed the sensitive skin above the femoral artery and began to suck. She worked her mouth against Rosa's flesh, drawing blood to the surface. Dark purple welts bloomed. Morgan licked the salty skin and tasted the fresh bruises, admiring her handiwork like it was a new tattoo.

She dragged her tongue over Rosa's trimmed mons to seek out her clitoris and then opened Rosa's pussy wider with the pads of her thumbs. The sight of her erect clit as it slid free from its tiny, protective hood aroused her like nothing else in the world could. "You have such a pretty pussy," she murmured. Morgan moistened her lips with the tip of her tongue and lowered her head.

She would offer Rosa what she knew she loved best.

She flicked her tongue over the tip of Rosa's swollen clit and then circled the hard bud with precise, rhythmic motions. Rosa lifted her hips and crooned low in her throat while Morgan lapped and licked. She trailed her tongue along Rosa's tender folds to the entrance of her vagina and thrust her tongue inside as far as it would go. Then Morgan began a slow thrust and release, in and out, tongue-fucking while she stroked Rosa's clit with her thumb.

Morgan pressed her pussy tight against the blanket, found a wide nub of hard earth beneath and rubbed in small, deliberate spirals. Desire shot through her system and she shuddered as orgasm surged near. Her thong dampened between her legs as her juices flowed. She paused, pushing back her need to come, while she licked the furrow between Rosa's vagina and clit.

Rosa gripped the blanket and pulled tiny bunches of cloth into her hands. "Finish me. Please. I can't take any more. It's so good."

Rosa's clit had swollen to its maximum size and she was breathing in fast, hard pants. Her hips had lifted inches off the blanket to allow tighter access to Morgan's mouth. Morgan returned to Rosa's clit and swirled her tongue relentlessly around the tiny bundle of nerves until Rosa shuddered beneath her and emitted wild moans.

Rosa's orgasm rolled on and on, and then she peaked. Morgan continued to lick her clit until she came a second time. Rosa pressed a fist against her mouth to keep from screaming.

When Rosa's breathing leveled off and she had recovered, Morgan tugged off her thong, sat up on her knees and arched her back. Her nipples had tightened to stiff points and her clit throbbed until she ached with the need to climax.

Rosa slid down between Morgan's legs, hoisted herself onto her elbows and thrust her tongue against Morgan's clit. She licked her firm and fast in steady revolutions that tumbled Morgan over the edge. Rosa's flickering tongue against her erect bud and swollen vulva slammed a climax through her that pulled the breath from her lungs. She gasped and pressed tighter against Rosa's lovely mouth while the spasms rolled.

When her orgasm was done, Morgan lay beside Rosa to embrace her. She kissed the crown of her hair. "I love you," she whispered. "And I always will."

"The others will be here any minute," Morgan said. She and Rosa pulled on their shorts and tops, but carried their underwear to the car and dropped it on the backseat. They visited the portable potty, cleaned up and then returned to the car to change their clothes.

They'd just finished dressing for the party when a black SUV roared into the lot, spitting road dust and cinders in its wake. Brakes slammed and the car veered to a stop near the path to the caves.

Angela got out of the driver's seat. Three passengers of varying sizes and shapes followed.

Minutes later, two more black cars filed into the parking lot. Doors slammed. In all, ten women dressed in red, gray or black dresses walked in pairs to the mouth of Crystal Cave.

Morgan and Rosa walked hand in hand behind the ten, the only couple carrying flashlights. "Have they *all* had laser eye surgery?" Rosa whispered.

Morgan chuckled. "I guess they've each been to Europe."

"I think we're underdressed, too. We're the only ones in jeans, pullovers and sneakers." Rosa replied.

Morgan agreed. "Who knew we should dress up?" She'd brought Angela a birthday present, which was all she thought would be required. Inside the decorative bag she clutched with her flashlight was something she thought Angela would like. Her cousin had always loved jewelry, even when she was too skinny and geeky for it to look good on her. Morgan smiled inwardly at the memory. *Meow.*

A massive wooden door covered the entrance to the caverns. Beneath a large sign that said, *Crystal Cave, Discovered 1871,* stood a slightly built young woman with shoulder-length blonde hair. In her hands she held an old-fashioned lantern. The name tag pinned above the pocket of her long-sleeved shirt gave her name: *Janine.*

"Welcome. I'm Jan," she said to the group with a perky lilt in her voice. She pulled an oversized brass key from her pants pocket and unlocked the door blocking the cave. When she turned back to the women she said with a smile, "Will the birthday girl please come forward?"

Angela stepped from the center of the crowd, a bright spot of red in a sea of black. Morgan stood on tiptoes for a better look at her cousin. Only Jan's lantern and the flashlights Morgan and Rosa held shed a spotlight over her slender frame and waist-length black hair. Morgan suspected Angela was wearing a weave, but she'd never be rude enough to say so.

"Will you do the honors?" Jan swept a hand toward the door.

The women stepped back as Angela heaved the door outward. The darkness and silence from the cave's interior was so complete that Morgan caught her breath. Cool air poured from the tunnel like liquid.

Rosa released her hand and gripped her arm, instead. "Did you say this would be fun?"

"I'd hoped so." Her stomach had gone queasy.

The group of women formed a single line at the mouth of the cave. The tour guide stood behind Angela at the threshold, where Angela greeted each guest. She wore blood-red lipstick to match her dress, and black braided leather bands around her wrist and neck.

When Rosa reached out to shake hands, Angela shot Morgan an appreciative look. "I see you've brought me a present." Morgan held out the lavender gift bag sprinkled with glitter and butterflies. Angela laughed. "No." She inclined her head toward Rosa. "I meant her."

Morgan dropped her hand to her side, still holding the lavender bag. She should have chosen a color that matched Angela's heart. "Don't get cute. It doesn't suit you," Morgan replied.

Angela smirked. "You know I always get what I want."

Morgan leaned close. "Fuck off, Angela, or I'll tell your

friends how you wet the bed until you were twelve."

Angela bared her teeth and narrowed her eyes. "You wouldn't dare."

Morgan bared her teeth in return. "Try me."

Rosa looked from one woman to the next. "Do you two even like each other?"

"Our fathers are twin brothers." Angela said.

"We're expected to...cooperate." Morgan added.

Angela frowned at Morgan and looked back at Rosa with a sparkle in her eyes. The glint disappeared when her gaze rested on her neck. "You've been marked."

Morgan lifted her chin. "Fair warning."

Angela sighed. "Guess I'll have to play with my old friends. I was hoping for someone...fresh and new."

"In case your friends are also looking for playmates, tell them we aren't interested."

Rosa turned to Morgan and lifted her brow. "So that explains your sudden desire to bite. You wanted to send a message."

"Angela likes to pretend she's a vampire," Morgan explained. She lowered her voice. "We're competitive, but she wouldn't dare touch you and start a feud. Our fathers would be furious." Morgan grinned. "I thoroughly enjoyed biting you, by the way."

Rosa edged closer and whispered back, "I liked biting you, too."

Angela grimaced. "I can hear you, you know. I have extra-sensory perception."

Morgan rolled her eyes. "Yeah, right."

Angela ignored her and pursed her lips. "Sex with the same old, same old. I'd hoped tonight would be different."

"Hey, it's your event." Morgan retorted. "You wrote the guest list."

The tour guide came up behind them to hurry them inside. "Don't let the bats out." She broke into giggles and her blue eyes crinkled at the corners.

"*Querido Jesús*," Rosa prayed, and then crossed herself. "Are there really bats in here?"

Jan nodded. "Thirty to forty live in the deepest, darkest, coldest section of the caverns. It's called the Devil's Den."

Rosa swayed and caught Morgan's forearm.

"We probably won't see them. They usually exit through holes to the outside world at night."

"Damn." Angela said. "What's the use of touring caves if I don't see any fucking bats?"

Jan opened her mouth in a wide O to reply, and then snapped it shut. She was clearly trying to mollify her client when she added, "We'll look for some."

Angela stalked off.

Jan hurried behind her. "Let's go, ladies. We have lots of territory to cover." She lit lanterns mounted on the walls as they all disappeared inside.

"It's freezing in here," Rosa complained.

Jan nodded. "Crystal Cave maintains a constant temperature of fifty-four degrees Fahrenheit, year round." She waved a hand at the shimmery walls. "This is the Crystal Ball Room. The walls are embedded with calcite crystal that looks like diamonds."

"I think it feels great in here," Angela said. The group behind her murmured agreements. "Hey!" She wiped her face. "Water just landed on my nose."

The tour guide smiled like Angela had just won the door prize. "That's five years' good luck. Those are baby stalactites above us, though they're fifty to one hundred years old. A splash of water on the head means a year's worth of luck."

"What's it mean when water hits your arm?" A full-figured redhead asked, brushing off droplets.

"That you got wet." Jan laughed, but the redhead didn't smile back.

Jan cleared her throat and led them through a tunnel into the next expansive cavern. In the center of the room stood a stalagmite about seven feet tall and thick as a young tree. Water droplets had hardened to form an asymmetrical base.

"This is Altar Rock," Jan said with a tinge of pride. "It's thousands of years old and the centerpiece of Crystal Cave."

"Holy *shit!*" Angela yelled. "That's the biggest strap-on I've ever seen." The others broke into uproarious laughter.

The tour guide seemed momentarily nonplussed. Morgan figured the woman had no idea what Angela meant. It wasn't until Angela dropped her dress to the floor and stood naked before Altar Rock that Jan seemed to get a clue this wasn't your average birthday gathering.

Angela reclined on her back near the bottom of the altar, stretched her arms over her head, and spread her legs. The cold, hard floor didn't seem to bother her in the least. "Anyone want to give me my present?" She stroked her pussy and beckoned them to come forward. The others dropped their dresses and gathered naked around her. The redhead sank to her knees.

Morgan turned to Rosa. "Gee. It's a happy-birthday orgy."

The tour guide watched in fascination as the redhead licked and sucked Angela's clit within the circle of her lantern light. The other women began to kiss and stroke one another. Idly, Jan touched her own breast beneath her blouse, and her breathing turned shallow while her eyes remained fixed on Angela. When Angela shouted out her climax as her spasms hit, Jan moaned.

The redhead pulled Angela to her feet and placed her hands

on her plump breasts. Then she swept her hair aside and offered the column of her neck.

Morgan trained her flashlight on the pair, a horrible realization dawning. Rosa pulled at her sleeve and made little whimpering noises.

Angela turned and hissed at the golden glow, her eyes turning a malevolent red. She opened her jaw and her incisors flashed. When she turned her face away from the light, the points of her teeth came down hard on the redhead's carotid artery. Blood spattered down her naked limbs. Angela began to suck and keen.

A second woman licked the dripping blood off the redhead's arm. Another stroked the halves of her ass, found the entrance to her pussy, and began finger-fucking her from behind. The redhead cried out with pleasure.

Instead of running away, the tour guide set her lantern on the floor and began pulling off her clothes.

Morgan gripped Jan by shoulders. "They're real vampires! This isn't a party game."

Jan shook her off, finished stripping, and took two steps forward, entranced. "I want to know what it feels like." Nude women led her away.

Morgan understood with sudden clarity that the only reason Angela hadn't bitten her was because they were blood relations. There were certain taboos even vampires wouldn't break. Yet she wasn't safe from the others if Angela didn't protect her. Neither was Rosa. In a blind frenzy of bloodlust and sex, Angela might let anything happen.

Then Angela would control her. The vampire would like nothing better.

Morgan dropped to her knees and dumped the contents of her gift bag. She scooped up the necklace inside and held it out.

The antique silver cross glistened, refracting the light from the crystal walls.

"Get behind me, Rosa!" Morgan moved to protect Rosa's body with hers.

Vampires hissed their displeasure. Some lifted their arms to shield their eyes. Others lurched forward as if to attack but then pulled back.

Morgan draped the cross around her neck and fought to pull Jan free from the women licking her breasts and pussy. Jan reached out to Angela, instead, and was swept away. The vampire carried her to the base of Altar Rock, opened her legs, and sank her teeth into her inner thigh. Jan screamed in ecstasy.

Morgan and Rosa turned and ran.

"Good-bye forever, Angela!" Morgan laid rubber out of the parking lot. Miles down the road she pulled the car over and hugged Rosa until she stopped shaking and crying.

"I'm so sorry." Morgan kissed every inch of Rosa's lovely face. "I'm buying you the entire season of *Glee*. Rachel Ray's new cookbook, too. At Christmastime, we'll go to Radio City."

"You were so brave." Rosa offered a forgiving smile and touched her cheek.

"The cross was insurance, in case Angela's weirdness was the real deal."

"You were brilliant. That's another reason why I love you."

"You do?" Morgan's spirits lifted.

Rosa wrapped her in a soothing embrace. "It's time I made that crystal clear."

BELOVED

Shayla Kersten

W orld of the Pharaohs Exhibit:

The warrior goddess Sekhmet was known as the Eye of Ra, raining death and destruction on Ra's enemies. Sekhmet is often depicted with the head of a lioness, the fiercest of desert creatures.

However, Sekhmet's blood lust was so great, it didn't dissipate after the battle was won. With mankind in danger of extinction, Ra tricked Sekhmet by turning the Nile red—except the liquid was not water but beer colored with pomegranate juice. Sekhmet slaked her thirst with the potent liquid. When she aroused from her stupor, she was the gentle goddess Hathor.

Hathor personified love, motherhood and joy and was usually depicted with the horns of a cow framing a sun disk. Some legends show the two as

*a single goddess or aspects of the same one; others
have them as separate entities. However, all indicate
their destinies were intertwined.*

Sekhmet laughed aloud at the plaque explaining the relationship between her and the stupid cow. Irritation at the legends
only added to her increasingly foul mood. She whirled around,
then stalked away.

The thirst grew ever sharper with each step, adding to her
aggravation. Parched like the deserts of her youth, her throat
ached with need for the soothing caress of rich, warm liquid.

The air was thick with delectable scents. *Choices, choices...*
She could almost taste the sweet copper-tinged blood. And the
fear that accompanied it. But something...a hint of something
familiar lingered in the air. A scent, a feeling, too vague for
clear thoughts or words.

Sekhmet paused and let her eyelids droop almost closed. She
gave in to the ancient call and raised her head to sniff the air like
the predator she once was. The short series of snuffles shook the
thick bush of braids on her head, rustling with the memory of
a lion's mane.

Something gold shimmered in the strategic lighting of the
exhibit, reminding her of her nemesis's skin. So far, she thought
she'd escaped the bitch's notice.

She hoped the cow wouldn't find her in a backwater state
like Arkansas, even if the capital city was hosting an Egyptian
exhibit. The irony of stalking prey among the ruins of antiquity
wasn't an accident. Sekhmet rarely did anything by accident.

The familiar hint of myrrh and cinnamon wafted toward her
sensitive nose. A flash of skin appeared in the corner of her eye.
The teasing trill of a familiar laugh caught her hearing.

"How in the name of Ra..." Sekhmet twisted toward the

vision but it was gone. *She* was gone. "Or maybe I'm finally losing my mind."

Others had. Lost their minds...their will to live. Most of the old gods were gone. Wisps in the wind, ending like a sandstorm in the deep desert. No witnesses, no one believing enough to mourn. Not even the pharaohs survived in spite of her role of protector.

Sekhmet wasn't sure how she'd lasted so long. Maybe the bloodlust did more than threaten mere mortals with death and destruction. Could it keep her own demise at bay?

Another flash of gold, a hint of dark hair with brick-red hennaed streaks.

"Damn her. How does she keep finding me?" Sekhmet slipped through the crowd, twisting and turning through the human throng. She regretted her choice of clothes as her long cotton skirt swished around her ankles, distracting her with trivial annoyance.

A few minutes ago, the warm, thrumming scent of blood and low murmur of people enthralled her. Now she wanted them all to leave and make the task of stalking her new prey easier.

Another whiff of cinnamon wafted from behind. A quick twirl on her heel only revealed mere mortals gawking at the remnants of a more glorious time, of her time.

Anger twisted deep in her gut as she wove through the crowd. The bloodlust grew stronger. Heat flushed Sekhmet's skin. Barely suppressing the need to roar like an angry lioness, she stalked through the crowd. The sea of people parted before her, once more giving her the respect deserved by the Eye of Ra.

A low throaty laugh penetrated the haze of red. Myrrh and cinnamon almost overwhelmed the heated musk of her prey. A curtain rustled. A door nearby creaked.

Sekhmet slipped behind the heavy material.

A strong arm caught Sekhmet around the waist; another went around her shoulders. A hand on her mouth kept her from doing more than growling her displeasure. A quick yank pulled her through a doorway. As the door slammed shut, darkness descended.

"Hello, lover." Hathor's breath teased Sekhmet's ear. "Long time, no see." The softness of warm, perfumed breasts pressed against Sekhmet's back.

Arousal combined with the desire for blood. In spite of her anger, Sekhmet's pussy pulsed with need. Only Hathor could inflame and calm all Sekhmet's appetites at once. Even when Sekhmet didn't want her to. "How the fuck do you find me?"

"I can smell your heat rising across time and eternity, babe. I'll always find you." Her mouth nuzzled Sekhmet's earlobe.

Hathor's grip on Sekhmet's waist eased. Her hand slid up to the thin silk shirt covering Sekhmet's flesh. Gentle fingers brushed against an already puckered nipple.

Pleasure shuddered through Sekhmet in spite of her anger. Since the time of Pharaoh, Hathor managed to calm her desire for death and destruction. At first, the bitch just got her too drunk to do anything about it.

The memory of pomegranate beer both nauseated and aroused Sekhmet. Eventually, Hathor lured her into submission by a different kind of drink, and she had found peace in Hathor's arms.

Sekhmet pulled out of Hathor's grip. "Why can't you let me be?"

"You know why." A click preceded a light flickering on. Hathor's dark gaze penetrated Sekhmet's resolve.

"Too bad. I'm not falling for your routine again." The storage room was crowded with furniture—benches, chairs, even a small couch—but Hathor's presence made the room seem even smaller.

Hathor, like Sekhmet, hadn't changed in thousands of years. Her lush almost overripe body befitted the goddess of love and motherhood. The top of her full breasts swelled above the low-cut neckline of the simple linen dress. Buttons down the front threatened to pop in their valiant effort to contain Hathor's ample bust.

"Oh, yeah?" A delicate eyebrow rose as a smile curved Hathor's full lips.

These were the lips that could make Sekhmet scream for more and mercy at the same time... Her willpower weakened as Hathor took a step forward.

"You know you can't resist. Ra made us this way. Part of each other."

"Bullshit." Sekhmet took a step back but found the closed door impeding her escape. "You're finally going senile if you've bought into that old legend. We're not the same. Not one. Never have been."

"Believe what you will. The truth is the truth." Hathor pressed her hands on the door behind Sekhmet, framing her between perfumed arms. Hathor leaned in. Her breath teased Sekhmet's mouth. "I've missed you."

Shivers of desire warmed Sekhmet's skin as she bit her lip. She didn't trust herself to speak. Her answer would reveal too much. Instead, she pressed her back tighter against the wall.

Hathor moved forward until her breasts crowded against Sekhmet.

The simple touch set Sekhmet's blood racing, pulsing heat through her pussy. A groan betrayed her.

"Did you miss me?" Hathor's nose brushed against Sekhmet's then her head tilted, aligning lips to lips.

One hand slid down the solid wood door, coming to rest on Sekhmet's waist.

"I think you did." A soft kiss. "I can smell your arousal." The next kiss pressed a little harder. Hathor's other hand dropped to Sekhmet's breast.

Fingers tweaked a hard nipple. Her hand cupped Sekhmet's flesh.

"I want to taste you." Hathor's arm snaked around Sekhmet's waist, pulling her closer. "Bury my face in your heat and your cream."

Sekhmet's breath caught. Her heart tried to beat a hole through her chest. Need wracked her body from the tips of her toes to her scalp. She couldn't say yes. She wouldn't say no. Instead, she plastered her hands against the door and flattened her back against the solid support as her knees went weak.

"So stubborn, my love." Hathor's chuckle colored her words with her amusement. "Fine. Play the martyr while I have my way with you..." Hathor ran her hands down to the hem of Sekhmet's shirt.

Closing her eyes, Sekhmet savored the warmth of Hathor's hands as they slid up her stomach. Her breath caught in her chest as Hathor cupped her breasts, finger and thumb tweaking sensitive nipples through the thin material of her bra. Before she could catch her lip between her teeth to bite back a groan, Hathor's mouth found hers.

Sekhmet opened to the insistent tongue—the wet heat, the soft hands... Need coursed through her flesh, scattering goose bumps across her skin. A half moan escaped. Then another. Her body betrayed her. Her need outweighed her fears. Her hands left the safe haven against the door. Arms wrapped around Hathor.

Hathor's hands moved away from Sekhmet's breasts. Her

arms mirrored Sekhmet's. Desperation and desire enveloped Sekhmet in a tight embrace. Lips met hard, with teeth clashing before the kiss settled into soul wrenching sweetness.

"Please..." Sekhmet couldn't stop the desire. She'd take what Hathor's embrace offered but not the other. She'd slake *that* thirst elsewhere. After...

A soft sigh of relief followed. Sekhmet wasn't sure if it was hers or Hathor's. Maybe it was both.

Hathor pulled away from the tight hug.

Before Sekhmet could protest, her lover pulled Sekhmet's shirt up and her bra down. Warm, wet sucking pulled one nipple. Finger and thumb worked the other. Once again, Sekhmet's hands found refuge on the cool wood of the door.

Her body flamed with the heat of a thousand desert suns. She wondered how she didn't burst into flames. Desire slicked her pussy and dampened her panties. Trembling weakened her knees. The door at her back helped support her as her legs betrayed her.

"No!" The hot mouth disappeared, leaving her wet nipple chilling in the cool air.

Hathor slid down Sekhmet's body, fluttering kisses down her stomach, until she knelt before her. Pressing her face against Sekhmet's mons, she inhaled a long breath through the lightweight cotton skirt. "I've missed your scent." Her hands cupped Sekhmet's ass. "And your taste." The pressure of her teeth raked across Sekhmet's sensitive flesh through the thin material.

"Oh, yes..." Sekhmet banged the back of her head against the door several times as a futile attempt to distract herself. To keep from saying more, from begging for more.

Hathor's fingers curled into the skirt's elastic waist. Urgent tugging pulled the material down Sekhmet's legs into a puddle of cloth at her feet.

Hathor nuzzled the silk of Sekhmet's boycut panties. An openmouthed kiss teased Sekhmet's clit with hot breath.

Please... It wasn't begging if it wasn't aloud, right? She couldn't stop her feet from sliding apart, opening her thighs for better access.

One finger teased under the leg of her panties, dipping into the crease where thigh meets groin. A second joined the first then both slid closer to Sekhmet's aching nub.

Please. Sekhmet pushed her hips forward just slightly, barely a hint of motion. Need overrode her desire to maintain her aloofness. "Please!"

The single word seemed to release Hathor's restraint. Her mouth pressed hard through Sekhmet's panties putting pressure on her needy flesh.

Sekhmet's palms left the safety of the door. Her fingers twined through the henna-streaked strands of hair. She tugged Hathor's face tighter against her mound.

Her pleas were answered when Hathor pulled away, then yanked Sekhmet's underwear down her legs. Hathor's fingers dug into Sekhmet's thighs as she pried her legs apart.

Soft tongue parted Sekhmet's pussy lips. Fingers slid into her channel. Gentle sucking on her clit sent fire through Sekhmet's groin.

"Oh..." The word deteriorated into a howling moan. Her orgasm roared to life. Ecstasy renewed her soul and her hunger. Her body writhed, hips bucking. *Too much...too quick...too sensitive...*

Hathor persisted. Her mouth held on, sucking Sekhmet's sensitive flesh. Her fingers plunged in and out of Sekhmet's channel.

Sekhmet came again, harder. "Too much!" She pushed Hathor away in a shove more violent than she intended.

A surprised Hathor glanced up from her ignominious sprawl on the floor. She raised her fingers—still slick with Sekhmet's cream—to her mouth. Her tongue ran their length. "Still as tasty as ever."

Sekhmet's legs nearly gave out. Her breath came in short bursts. Her heart beat in rapid, irregular beats. The ancient thirst overrode the aftermath of ecstasy.

Hathor rose slowly from the floor. "But you aren't interested in the taste of come." She stepped toward Sekhmet.

"No." In spite of the burning hunger, Sekhmet wouldn't risk Hathor. Not again...

Another step forward. "But it's what you need..." Hathor slid a small object from a pocket hidden in the folds of her dress. The flash of a sharp edge popped from the switchblade.

Before Sekhmet could stop her, Hathor sliced across her palm. Blood pooled in her hand as she held it up as an irresistible offering to Sekhmet. "I can quench all your thirsts, all your hungers. All your desires. Why do you insist on stalking prey?"

"Because they don't—" Sekhmet stopped before she revealed her deepest secret. *Because they don't strip me bare, leave me vulnerable then threaten to desert me for all of eternity...*

The scent of blood, of Hathor's blood, sent a tremor of need shivering down Sekhmet's spine. Her willpower weakened and desire flamed as hot as the desert sun.

The side of Hathor's hand pressed against Sekhmet's lower lip. "Drink, beloved. Drink and be renewed." Her other hand cupped Sekhmet's sensitive breast. Fingers tweaked her plumped nipple.

Too much... With a long groan, Sekhmet did as she was told. She didn't pause to savor the rich warm liquid. A simple taste added to the bloodlust instead of curing it. The sudden strength of her addiction overwhelmed her.

Hathor took a deep breath as Sekhmet obeyed her whispered plea. If only she'd stay...

The warm tongue lapped at Hathor's bloody palm like a cat's at cream. The tension radiating through Sekhmet's scent lessened but the lingering musk of her sexual release teased Hathor's nose.

She wanted so much more that Sekhmet wouldn't give.

Full lips closed over Hathor's rapidly closing wound. Her nature made healing quick and painless, most of the time.

Sekhmet's frantic sucking softened to gentle kisses, creating an ache in Hathor's loins that only her wayward lover could cure. Many had tried. As the goddess of love, Hathor had been more than free with her charms. It was in her nature, especially when her chosen lover refused to stay by her side.

A soft growl dropped lower to almost a purr. The bushy mass of braids reminded Hathor of Sekhmet's alter ego, the lioness. Sekhmet lifted her gaze to meet Hathor's. Her golden eyes glowed with desire and need.

Hathor had only seconds to prepare as Sekhmet's pent-up yearning pushed her forward.

A fast pounce, and Hathor was on her back on the strategically placed couch. As she hit the hard cushions, she was grateful for having had the forethought to rearrange the room before she lured Sekhmet into her lair.

A hard jerk, and Hathor's linen shift ripped from neck to groin. Buttons popped and rolled around the small room.

Kisses fell across her face, fast pecks of passion until Sekhmet's lips met hers. Deep, hard, Sekhmet's tongue explored Hathor's mouth, probing like a man's cock in a pussy.

Pleasure exploded through Hathor's synapses. Her nipples

tightened under Sekhmet's rough hands. Fingers tugged and pulled. Bodies rubbed together. A hard thigh pressed against her groin, friction and pressure bringing her a little closer to what she needed.

Cream of arousal pulsed through Hathor's channel. "Yes. Take what you need." Her hands caressed Sekhmet's back. "Take me."

Frantic kisses left Hathor's mouth, trailing lower until a nipple was caught in a hard suck.

Hathor arched into the hard pressure. "Yes." Her fingers twisted through Sekhmet's mane, tugging her closer. "Do it."

With a half cry, half growl, Sekhmet did as commanded. As Hathor knew she would. Sekhmet had no choice. Neither did Hathor...

Sharp teeth penetrated the swell of Hathor's breast, just above the nipple. Her heart beat faster, racing to keep up with the loss of blood. Her body tingled with the lack of oxygen as she held her breath.

Deeper her lover drank, pulling the liquid of life from Hathor's body. Sekhmet's hand slid lower, moving past the ripped material, dipping into the barely there underwear. A quick flicker of a touch set Hathor's clit quivering.

"Yes. Oh, yes!" Hathor's hands tightened on Sekhmet's head. "Make me come..." Lightheadedness from blood loss forced Hathor's eyes closed. Weakness made her breathing shallow. The lack of oxygen helped push her body toward satisfaction. "Make. Me..."

Fingers plunged into her wet channel. The palm of Sekhmet's hand pressed hard against Hathor's clit.

Orgasm spiraled out from Hathor's sex, each wave harder than the last. The lights dimmed as Hathor struggled for breath. With no life left to express her victory, Hathor let her laughter echo in her mind as she faded into the darkness. *I win again...*

"Damn you." Sekhmet's lust faded into oblivion, for now. She slid to the floor next to the couch. The thirst that had brought her here was once more a memory. And her lover, her beloved, *habibty...*

Hathor's body sprawled across the small couch, arms akimbo, legs spread wide. An obscene smile graced her parted lips. Her dark eyes had faded to a light brown. Her golden skin had paled in death. The rosy color of her lips was blue. Even her full perfect breasts taunted Sekhmet, the destroyer now having destroyed the goddess of love and music, of motherhood and joy...

Again.

The life energy of her lover flooded Sekhmet's veins. Need had pushed her too far.

But it was all Hathor's fault. It was always Hathor's fault.

"Bitch." Rising on her knees, Sekhmet leaned over the still form. "Why do you do this?"

A soft kiss only proved Hathor's lips were cold and unresponsive.

"*Ya Umri?*" My life... The endearment fell on deaf ears. Panic welled up, clogging Sekhmet's throat.

Another kiss, a little longer, a little harder. Did her chest rise? Sekhmet pressed her hand to the almost-closed wounds next to the faintest of scars. Memories of all the times before.

She pushed a little harder. Not even a drop of blood escaped the tiny puncture marks.

But was that a gasp? However tiny? The faint thump of a heartbeat? She pressed her ear to Hathor's breast.

No, nothing. Not even the slightest sign of life.

"Damn you!" Sekhmet scurried across the room on her

hands and knees. "I knew one day..." She slammed her back against the wall, facing her victim.

Tears stung her eyes, but she forced them into submission with only her will and a tightly clenched jaw. "You had to push me again." Her throat tightened to the point of choking. Sobs forced her airway open.

The dam burst. Tears spilled past her carefully constructed barriers. Grinding the heels of her palms against her eyes did nothing to stop the flood. Gasping sobs ripped through her chest, choking her throat raw. An eternity of fears culminated in an ache so vast Sekhmet didn't think she'd survive.

She'd known from their first encounter, the first time Hathor offered her blood, her body, in salvation of mortals, that someday the task would prove too much even for the goddess of love.

And when it happened, Sekhmet would have no reason left to live.

Unfortunately, she had no idea how to die. The ones who went before didn't leave instructions. "Selfish pigs..." Another sob wracked her body. The room seemed colder without Hathor breathing life into it.

The murmur and shuffle of the museum patrons faded as time marched on. And Sekhmet sat waiting to see if this was the last time her lover would rescue mankind.

An eternity later, a loud gasp penetrated her grief. She jerked her hands away from her face.

Hathor's mouth opened wide as her fingers curled. Her chest rose with a long, moaning breath. She exhaled a low groan.

"You fucking bitch!" Sekhmet scrambled across the hard stone floor and back to Hathor's side in time to catch her before her shaking body slid off the couch. She cradled her lover with a tenderness her tone didn't share. "You stupid fucking cow. How could you do that to me again?" She buried her face in Hathor's neck. "Don't. Ever. Do that. Again."

Hathor mumbled an incoherent word before a coughing fit interrupted.

"I thought you were gone this time. For good."

"If you'd—" Hathor gasped for air. "Do as I ask—" Another ragged breath. "This wouldn't happen."

"How do you know?" Sekhmet couldn't stay with her for eternity. Close contact would only make it worse if something happened. When something happened...

"I've told you..." A short series of coughs interrupted her words. "If you drink before the bloodlust consumes you, controlling your appetite will be easier."

Sekhmet kissed the arch of Hathor's eyebrow, then the bridge of her nose. "You say that, but if I lost you... Better we stay apart." The idea of eternity without Hathor somewhere in the world... A shudder played down her spine. Despair barred her from more words. Instead, she found Hathor's lips.

With soft, sweet kisses Sekhmet drank in Hathor's breath, reveling in the feel of life. Sekhmet's hand rubbed a slow path to the swell of Hathor's breast, to the rapidly fading bite. The faint remnants of blood smeared the golden skin.

"I love you." Sekhmet slid down until she rested her ear against the now-closed wound and the faintest scars of so many before. The reassuring *thump-thump* of Hathor's heart was the most joyous sound in all of eternity.

"If you truly loved me, you'd trust me and do as I ask." Hathor's hand shook as she caressed Sekhmet's face.

Kissing the still-cold fingers, Sekhmet shook her head but with less conviction. "It'd be too dangerous." Dangerous to her sanity.

Hathor rubbed her hand up and down Sekhmet's back. "Stay with me until the next stirring of the bloodlust begins. If you think it is too dangerous after that, then I won't ask again."

"And you'll stay away? Forever? No matter what happens?" As much as Sekhmet said she wanted nothing to do with Hathor, the idea of never seeing her again stung her eyes with more tears.

Then again, the next time the fever took Sekhmet might be years away. She'd never found a pattern, even after all this time. Could she spend so much time with Hathor only to leave in the end?

"Please. Forever isn't all it's cracked up to be..."

Sekhmet raised her head to look at her lover. The soft, plaintive tone wasn't like the self-assured Hathor, but her expression held no guile or subterfuge. "Are you lonely?" Sometimes Sekhmet didn't think she could face another day alone.

"Yes. Aren't you?"

"Yes." Why deny it? Sekhmet lowered her face back to Hathor's chest and the reassuring beat of her heart. "I'd be lonely in a crowd without you." The words sprang free of their own accord. Her fear of losing Hathor weighed heavily against her heart. "I've thought about dying but I don't know how... And if I lost you, I couldn't stand to live."

A soft laugh bubbled through Hathor. "But you wouldn't live. Don't you know we keep each other alive?"

"What?" Sekhmet lifted her head then met Hathor's gaze.

Little crinkles of amusement teased the sides of Hathor's eyes. "We keep each other alive. It's part of Ra's design. We are truly part of each other, although not as the old legends proclaim. From the first fateful bite, the taste of my blood changed you— us." Her fingers traced a line from Sekhmet's temple over her cheekbone then down to her chin. "It's how I always find you. Your lust draws me to you."

Sekhmet's heart raced as the years of wondering seemed at

an end. The words rang with a hidden truth. And if what she said was true... "Then if you died, so would I?"

"Yes. If either of us lost the other we'd eventually fade on the wind, like the others."

"That's the secret to their deaths?" How could she be sure Hathor spoke true?

"Yes, love." Hathor's fingers curled through Sekhmet's braids. "The others lost the will to live not because of an individual but because their followers ceased to believe."

"But we're different?"

"Yes, we live on in each other. And always will. If we had depended on our followers, we'd have gone a long time ago." Hathor's full lips teased Sekhmet's brow. "If you do as I ask and remain at my side, you'll see the truth."

Eternity in Hathor's perfumed arms without fear of loss? "I will." The hunger of a thousand lifetimes engulfed Sekhmet. Need welled up with the ferocity of a rampaging lioness, but fear forced her to gentleness and restraint.

Hathor might have survived, but weakness invariably followed a full blooding.

Planting kisses along the rise of Hathor's breast, Sekhmet made her way up to the long neck, over the chin until their lips met. "Why haven't you explained this before?" she muttered between soft kisses.

"Because I didn't think it needed explanation. I thought you were being your usual stubborn self." Hathor's hand gripped the back of Sekhmet's neck. Warmth had begun to return to her fingers.

"But you are certain I won't live if you die?" Hope wanted to believe, but fear and doubt had always ruled Sekhmet where Hathor was concerned.

"Positive." She pulled Sekhmet closer with surprising

strength. "Now make love to me like when we were young and unafraid."

Sekhmet lowered her mouth to Hathor's, drinking in love instead of blood. Savoring the warmth of living breath instead of the stillness of death. "*Habibty...*"

Eternity in her beloved's arms... Now that legend, she could believe in.

BOUND LOVE

Christine d'Abo

Maili scratched her forearms raw as she paced the decaying hotel room. The stench of grease and rotted food from the Dumpster in the alley outside turned her stomach, but did little to distract her.

She couldn't stop it this time.

Throwing herself against the wall, Maili pressed her fists against her eyes, sucking in deep breaths as if air were hard to come by. Being out of control was something she couldn't afford, not with the bloodlust riding her so close, so hard. She was too old, too tired, and if she let herself slip into the oblivion of the lust, Maili knew it was a pit she wouldn't be able to emerge from. The fine line between feeding her hunger and becoming a ravenous monster was one she dared not cross.

Somewhere below her a door opened. The bass line from the latest dance song pulsed out of the club next door. It was silenced by the bang of the door, only to be replaced by giggles and then the undisguised moans of a couple in the alley. The gasps and the rustle of clothing, and then the sounds of their fucking were amplified by her jacked-up hearing. The scent of alcohol and sex invaded her nostrils, even from this distance. Maili flicked her tongue across the tips of her razor-sharp incisors as her hands fell listlessly to her sides.

It would be so easy to let herself slip.

It's not like anyone would miss her if she did.

It took her several seconds to realize she'd walked away from the wall and was well on her way to the window. The three-story drop wouldn't harm her in the least, and she'd be in the perfect position to surprise them. She could be on the couple, her teeth embedded in their necks, before they even realized she was there. She knew their blood would taste extra sweet with all the endorphins running through their systems.

Her pussy clenched at the thought.

Maili took another step closer, reached up and yanked at the tight neckline of her T-shirt. The reasons to keep fighting the bloodlust were dissolving along with her resolve. It would taste. *So. Good.*

She didn't exactly hear the door to the hotel room open, so much as she sensed another's presence. The monster rising up inside her dismissed the intruder as irrelevant and forced her to step closer to the window. That was certainly the only reason she was caught off guard and the person was able to knock her to the floor without a struggle.

Maili lay flat on her stomach with her arms bent back. She had no leverage with which to push up her body. Thrashing helplessly, Maili growled and snapped her teeth, trying to catch a piece of her assailant's leg.

The person holding her jerked Maili's arms up so high that

one of her limbs nearly popped from its socket. "Now that I have your attention, I want to know what the fuck you think you are doing."

Maili instantly stilled. She knew that voice. It took a hard shake of her head before her mind cleared enough that she recognized her surroundings once more. Below, the scent and sounds of sex were fading. Instead, the spicy musk of perfume and leather took over, jerking her attention to where it needed to be.

Maili licked her lips, tasting her own blood. She managed to find her voice. "Lana?"

The other woman's hold didn't let up. "Do you know how much time I've wasted trying to find you?"

"Lana I didn't—"

"Did I give you permission to speak?"

Maili's entire body tensed. "No."

"Excuse *me*?"

There was something else she was supposed to say. Something important. Lana pressed the heel of her boot into Maili's back and her mind snapped back to reality.

"No, *Mistress*."

"Good girl." Lana flexed her fingers around Maili's wrist. "What the fuck are you doing here? Answer me."

"I'm..." The reasons she'd run away from the woman who had been helping her regain a small measure of her humanity seemed weak now with her face pressed into the floor. Lana was the strongest human she'd ever met; more than able to help her gain control and stop the bloodlust from consuming her. "I don't know. I was scared."

Lana's snort accompanied her relaxed grip on Maili's wrist. "You're a vampire. What were you scared of?"

Hurting you. "Losing control."

"You know better. When you're with me you don't have to worry about that. I take care of you."

"But I—"

"No more. No talking."

Maili snapped her mouth shut. Her lips couldn't contain her vampire overbite and her teeth cut into the sensitive flesh of her lips.

"Don't you dare move." Lana shifted her foot to the floor, but kept Maili's arms high. "This is the worst place for a scene, but you haven't left me any other choice. I'm going to have to improvise."

The metal of the handcuffs was surprisingly warm when Lana snapped the rings around her wrists. They must have been in a pocket, up against Lana's body. Maili fought the urge to squirm as her pussy grew damp from the unexpected arousal. Even if the bloodlust hadn't been upon her, just being this close to her domme was enough to make Maili's body sing. It had been a long time since Lana had let her come, even longer ago than the last time Maili had fed. She would need both tonight if she was going to keep from turning into the very thing she'd feared becoming for over a century.

Maili didn't fight her mistress as her hands were secured and her boots were pulled from her feet. Lana was an expert at controlling Maili's needs, almost psychic. She didn't stop Lana when she rolled her onto her side, giving her access to the fly of her jeans.

"Too much clothing." Lana jerked the denim over Maili's hips. "I should add this to the list of transgressions I need to punish you for."

Maili could almost taste Lana's disappointment. "I'm sorry. I promise I'll do better."

"Of course you will. I'll see to it."

Maili shivered as her shirt was ripped from her shoulders. Her nipples stiffened in response to the air-conditioned chill in the room. With her body bound and open to Lana, there was nothing she could do to hide her arousal.

Lana finally pulled away, leaving Maili on the floor.

"Get up and stand with your face to the wall." Despite the harshness of the words, there was no cruelty in Lana's tone. Firm directives helped Maili focus on what she needed to do, acting as a buoy against the turmoil rising within her own body.

With her hands secured behind her back, Maili was forced to wiggle to her knees. She was about to lift her head up, when she felt a soft touch at the small of her back.

"On second thought, stay there."

The sting of Lana's hand on her ass after that initial gentleness was all the more painful because Maili hadn't expected it. After the fourth slap, the pain had begun to bleed into the heat of her wet pussy. The taste of blood filled Maili's mouth. Her fangs had scraped her lips, splitting them and giving her an added rush. She hadn't realized she'd been moaning until Lana jerked her head up off the floor so she could stare Maili in the eyes.

"You're so turned on right now I'm surprised you haven't broken through those cuffs yet."

"Please."

Lana dropped to her knees in front of Maili, helping her to a kneeling position. "Please what?"

"I need..." Closing her eyes, Maili was overwhelmed with the scent of Lana's arousal, the awareness that she'd cut her leg shaving earlier that morning and the blood, while long dried, was still present on her skin.

Stronger than when the couple had been fucking in the alley, Maili's urge to feed and rut slammed into her hard. "I need you."

"Baby, I know." Lana cupped her cheek and placed a gentle kiss on Maili's forehead. "I'm going to make sure everything is okay. But I need to do this right. What was the one thing you told me you didn't want to happen when you first came to me?"

Closing her eyes, Maili sucked in a quick breath. "I didn't want to become a monster."

"That's right. You need me to help you focus so that creature living inside you can't come out to play. And I will, but I need you to do something for me? Do you know what that is?"

"Trust you."

"Good girl. See, you are so smart and beautiful. You know we're going to make this better. Together." Lana bent forward, pausing for a moment, her lips a hair's breadth away from Maili's. She licked a drying trail of blood from her mouth. "You went and hurt yourself. That's not good."

The flush of shame at having disappointed Lana proved stronger than the bloodlust. Dropping her chin to her chest, Maili muttered a soft, "Sorry."

"Don't be sorry. I'm going to get you up and secure you to the desk so I can punish you properly. You'll make it all up to me by being a good girl and taking everything I give you. Once that's done we'll look after your other needs. Okay?"

"Yes."

Lana gripped Maili's chin between her forefinger and thumb, lifting it up. "Pardon?"

"Yes, Mistress."

The knot of dread in her chest melted slightly as Lana smiled at her. "Good girl. See? You remembered, even though that monster is trying to take you over. You're better than *it* is. Now get up."

Lana released her and moved away. It would have been faster

if she'd helped Maili up and over to the wall, but that wasn't really the point.

Maili's balance was off and her head spun as she tried to get her foot under her without toppling over. She could use her vampire reflexes, but not without giving in to the lust.

Sweat covered her naked body by the time she struggled to her feet. The burn on her skin from Lana's slaps had now faded into a dull ache, but it was enough to keep her grounded in the present. Once she'd finally succeeded in standing, Maili looked over to Lana, who was smiling. It was enough.

The short distance across the room proved to be a challenge. Her body shook with unfulfilled needs, making it hard to focus. When she reached the small desk, Maili didn't wait to be told what to do. This was familiar, safe, the one constant in the three years she'd been coming to Lana.

Keeping her back as straight as possible, Maili leaned over the wood, letting it take her full weight. With her ass on display, she spread her legs wide and waited silently for what was to come.

The sound of Lana moving around the room helped drive Maili's focus, while increasing her anticipation. This wasn't their usual room with the normal equipment and safety measures. There'd been times in the past when Lana had pushed Maili hard and her vampire side had taken over. Without the chains and leather bindings, she would have torn out Lana's throat.

Now, with the bloodlust pumping hard in her veins, Maili feared that Lana's life was very much in danger.

"I don't have anything to tie you to the desk. So I want you to stay still, just like that with your legs spread. No matter what happens."

"Yes, Mistress."

"I mean it, Maili. If I think for even a second you're not

listening to me, I'll walk out that door and you won't see me again."

"No!" She drove her fangs into her bottom lip, hard. The pain helped her focus and the taste of blood gave her strength. "I won't move."

Long fingers caressed the back of her head, tangling for a moment in her hair. "Prove it."

The air whistled for a split second before something landed hard and heavy against her ass. The thin stripe of pain across both buttocks had Maili thinking it was either a ruler or long piece of wood Lana had found god only knew where. She didn't look back—the instrument being used really wasn't the point.

If she was going to survive the night, Maili knew she needed to get through the next few minutes.

With unerring precision, Lana landed blow after blow, never quite in the same place twice. The sting of pain quickly dissolved into the burn of desire. Maili's pussy dripped, and she fought the urge to squirm against the desk, searching for relief. What she couldn't stop were the moans slipping from her, mixed with surprised gasps and muffled sobs.

"One more, darling. One more and you'll have paid me back. Then I think you've earned yourself a treat."

"Please." Though what Maili was begging for she no longer knew.

The final blow landed low across the tops of her thighs, kissing her cunt with a sharp sting. The contact thrust her hard against the desk, forcing a groan from her.

Lana grabbed her by the hips and pulled until Maili fell in a heap on the floor. Looking up, Maili was struck by how beautiful the younger woman was—black hair loose from its ponytail, the long tendrils caressing Lana's bare arms. Her mistress's eyes were wide and she was panting. It didn't matter to Maili if it was from the exertion of the blows Lana had administered or from arousal. The only important thing was that Maili had pleased her mistress.

Lana reached out and carded her fingers through Maili's hair. "Such a good girl. I promised you a treat, didn't I?"

"Yes. *Please.*"

With her free hand, Lana popped open the button of her pants. "You told me once that arousal makes the blood taste sweeter."

Maili's eyes locked on to Lana's hand, watching intently as she pulled open the barrier preventing Maili from getting to the warmth of Lana's cunt. She licked her lips. "It does. Especially if the person has had a recent orgasm."

Lana cocked an eyebrow as a small smirk played on her mouth. "Then you better get to work."

Maili didn't wait for further permission. With a jerk of her arms she broke free of the handcuffs, the metal chain dangling impotently from her wrists. Maili hardly noticed as she yanked open Lana's pants, tearing the material in her frantic efforts to get close to her mistress.

"Careful!" Lana slapped the back of her head. "Treat my clothing with respect."

"Sorry. I'm sorry," Maili muttered as she continued at a slower pace, pulling the denim down Lana's long legs. "Sorry."

The boots Lana normally wore were not present. Thankfully, her sneakers came off easily as Maili pulled the jeans free, leaving the domme bare from the waist down. The smell of Lana's arousal hit her like a blow. While sex was rarely the end goal between them in their sessions, Maili had always known of Lana's desire for her. Lana responded enthusiastically to the danger that Maili represented—her domme loved life on the edge.

The chaos in Maili's head suddenly stopped as she looked

up from her position on the floor. Lana stood before her, clad only in a tight black T-shirt, mouth open and eyes lust-blown. Without breaking that visual contact, Lana slowly moved to the desk where Maili had been splayed out only moments earlier, and slid back so her ass rested near the edge. She lifted one foot, opening herself up completely and giving Maili full access to her pussy.

The stretch of her incisors over her bottom lip would have been painful if it wasn't for the rush of adrenaline coursing through her. Crawling to close the short distance between them, Maili needed every second to ensure she had herself under control. She rose to her knees so her face was in line with Lana's cunt, but didn't move in immediately to the one spot she wanted to taste more than anything. Instead, Maili licked a long swipe up along the inside of Lana's inner thigh. The taste of sweat and the subtle scent of Lana's pheromones dragged a low growl from her.

"Behave." Lana let her leg fall to the side, exposing herself even more. "I don't want so much as a scratch from those teeth of yours. Not until I say."

"Of course, Mistress."

Maili slid her hands across the tops of Lana's thighs, enjoying the contrast of her too-pale skin against Lana's tan. She didn't stop until her thumbs brushed the dark curls of her pubic hair, eliciting a shiver from her domme.

"That's it. Show me you're better than the monster. You can control your impulses and do what you want, when you want."

The angle was painful as the edge of the desk cut across the tops of Maili's breasts, not that it mattered. Leaning in, Maili pressed her nose into the crease between Lana's bent leg and her body. She ran her tongue over the heated skin, soaking in as much of the warmth as she could. When Lana's fingers threaded through her hair, the gentle gesture was enough to push Maili farther.

The first taste of Lana's cunt on her tongue ripped another groan from Maili's throat. She teased Lana with the tip of her tongue, tracing a line down one side of her pussy, flicking across her wet hole and up the other side. Lana's grip tightened in her hair when Maili came close to her clit, only to skip over it.

"Bitch," Lana muttered, stroking her thumb across Maili's temple. "Don't tease."

Even though it wasn't a direct command, Maili couldn't deny Lana anything. On her second pass, she stopped and flicked the tip of her tongue gently across the engorged flesh of Lana's clit. The tang of Lana's juices filled Maili's mouth. The pounding of Lana's heartbeat increased with every teasing flick against her clit. It drove the blood so fast through her body, Maili could almost hear it surging through her domme's veins.

Not wanting to tease anymore, Maili latched on to Lana's clit, sucking it into her mouth. Careful of her fangs, Maili licked and sucked Lana's pussy, losing herself in the scent and taste of the woman who grounded her.

Lana moaned, bucking her hips as best she could given the angle. "Fuck. So good."

Reaching up, Maili drove two fingers into Lana's pussy, twisting and driving them deep, pressing up against her cunt wall. She timed each flick of her tongue with the thrust of her fingers. Maili knew it wouldn't take long now for Lana to come. She slowed the pace and tilted her head so the blunt edges of her fangs couched either side of Lana's clit, spreading her pussy lips.

"I can see your ass, Maili. It's so red from where I slapped you. I bet you're just as wet as I am right now. Aren't you?"

Maili moaned, but refused to move away from her prize.

"Finger-fuck yourself, but I don't want you to come. Not until I tell you to."

She moved without thinking, letting her free hand fall to tease her own clit before sliding lower. Maili pushed her middle finger deep into her pussy, mirroring the pace of the hand thrusting into Lana.

The bloodlust had passed, leaving a carnal need in its stead. Maili ground her swollen clit into the palm of her hand, knowing it would be a challenge to keep her orgasm at bay for long.

Whether Lana could sense Maili's struggle, or she simply knew her well enough, the domme didn't prolong her agony.

"Faster, baby. Hurry now and make me scream."

Maili sucked hard, only too late realizing the tip of her fangs had pierced the skin around Lana's clit. It didn't stop her orgasm. Long fingers pulled Maili's hair as Lana came hard. She held her face in place, grinding her cunt against Maili's mouth as she screamed. The mix of cum and blood set Maili on fire. It was only a taste, not even an appetizer to the feast she wanted so desperately to gorge on.

She didn't stop. Maili slammed her fingers into Lana, driving her hand into her as deep as she could go, needing to wrench everything she could from the other woman. Cum rolled down Maili's fingers, pooling in her palm and then continuing down her forearm. It was only when Lana jerked her head up by her hair that Maili realized how far gone she was.

"Come up here." Lana helped Maili to her feet, supporting her weight before she collapsed against the desk and Lana's overheated body.

They'd rarely kissed in the past. Their relationship wasn't one of love—Maili was too old and Lana too jaded. But somehow something had changed. The brush of Lana's soft lips against hers brought tears to Maili's eyes with the realization that along the way this human had become precious to her.

Maili opened her cursed soul and her mouth to let Lana explore. The brush of Lana's tongue against one of her fangs sent a shiver through her body.

"I'm going to make you come," Lana whispered against her mouth. "And when I do, I want you to feed from me."

The monster inside threatened to roar to life, clawing madly deep within her gut, but Maili sucked in a deep breath and nodded once.

The feel of Lana's fingers on her clit was so different from her own explorations. Lana was hot where Maili was cool. The shiver of pleasure radiated from her pussy and heated every inch of her long dead body, inside and out. Shifting so her mouth rested gently against Lana's throat, Maili closed her eyes and let the sensations take over.

"You're beautiful. So strong and smart. But stupid too. I know you could never hurt me. Not really." Lana pressed her thumb hard against Maili's clit and slipped a finger into her pussy. "I lie in bed at night thinking about you. A fucking vampire who needs me. I promised I would look after you and help keep you strong. You need to believe that. God, you're so wet right now."

Maili whimpered. The ability to speak was beyond her. She could hear the beating of Lana's heart like a gong in her head. Her mouth watered at the temptation of tasting her sweet blood, even as the rest of her strained toward orgasm. A heat she rarely felt anymore flushed through her body and Maili knew the end was close.

"Lana," she whispered.

"That's okay, I'm here. Go on and do what you need to."

The scream ripped from Maili as the first pulse of her orgasm ripped through her. It was only when she sucked in a breath that she clamped her mouth to the juncture of Lana's neck and shoulder.

Blood flowed into her mouth and Maili swallowed without thinking. Lana's life force was heavy with the sweet taste of her orgasm and it rushed through Maili's body as she drank. As if responding to a drug she'd been too long without, Maili shook as she absorbed the nutrients. It was too much. The taste of Lana in her mouth, of the woman's blood and cum, the heat of her body, all of it sent another surge of release through Maili.

Whether it was minutes or forever, the pleasure of the sex and the feeding slowly faded. Unable to sustain her weight, Maili felt Lana go limp beneath her and the two slid from the weakened old desk to the floor. Their bodies tangled together, Maili shifted until she could rest her head on Lana's chest, an ear over the other woman's heart.

Lana's fingers found their way back to Maili's hair, where they once more resumed a soothing caress. "Are you okay now?"

"Yeah." Maili licked her lips. "Did I hurt you too badly?"

"I'm...I feel a bit light-headed. Nothing I will die from."

"Sorry."

Lana reached down and slapped Maili's ass. "Did I ask for an apology?"

"No, Mistress."

"That's right. If I say I'm fine, then I am. And next time I expect you to come to me before things get this bad. I made you a promise that I'd help you for as long as you needed me."

"You did."

Maili fought back the unwelcome tears, closing her eyes so Lana wouldn't see. Lana wasn't the first to try and help her. Maili knew that sooner or later, Lana would be dead and she'd be on her own, once more battling the monster. Every time that happened, it got harder to resist the pull into madness. Sooner or later, Maili knew she'd lose.

For now she would keep fighting as long as she could.

Pressing her nose close so she could inhale her scent, Maili placed a kiss on Lana's naked breast.

"I promise."

THE GIFT
OF LILITH

Myla Jackson

M usic thrummed, vibrating against the soles of my shoes, the beat fast and steady, like the heart thumping against my rib cage. The moon rose high above the Chicago skyline; it was a perfect night for anything to happen.

Normally, I avoided parties, preferring my solitude. When you lived to be over two hundred years old, parties lost their appeal. I'd never liked social engagements, never felt comfortable with idle chatter, flirting and inane conversation. I feared I'd say too much, reveal the truth and expose myself to those who would think me crazy. By distancing myself, I'd gained little experience in the art of mingling.

Tonight, however, was different. Tonight Molly would be there.

I wondered yet again if I should have stayed at home reading a book. But the image of Molly standing there in her very short, tight black dress, her red hair gathered loosely up on her head, flashed in my mind and I couldn't sit still. The desperate excitement flashing in Molly's green eyes worried me. Ever since her visit to her doctor, she'd been acting strange and secretive.

She'd spent the evening primping in the apartment over mine. I could smell her perfume through the walls as I lounged on my sofa, imagining her standing in a black lace bra and thong panties, adding blush to her cheeks and eyeliner to frame her emerald eyes.

Then her bare feet had pattered down the wood stair steps and she'd entered without knocking, holding two dresses in front of her, wearing nothing but the skimpy black lace panties and a strapless bra that pushed her ample bosom up and out.

"Need your help, Katherine." Molly shook a red dress, then the black dress. "Which one?"

"What's the occasion?"

Her eyebrows rose into the fiery red of the hair swinging down over her forehead. "I want to party like there's no tomorrow. Get dressed and come with me."

"Sorry, I'm not into parties."

Molly's brows twisted. "Sometimes I don't get you." She planted a hand on the sweet swell of her hip. "How long have we known each other?"

I frowned. "Two years."

"Long enough to know me." Molly's eyelids drooped. "I've been watching you." She tossed the dresses over the back of the sofa as if she'd made a decision. She crossed to where I sat and perched her pert little ass on the sofa's arm, her naked knees touching my silk-pajama-clad legs.

I could feel the warmth of her skin through the thin fabric and my heartbeat stuttered. "So, you've been watching me."

Molly's pale fingers stroked my long, straight black hair. "I know more than you think."

I cleared my throat, every part of me screaming to take her

hand and guide it lower to that aching place between my legs. "What do you know about me?"

"Right now you want to touch me."

I looked up, my eyes wide. "I beg your pardon?"

"Oh, don't go getting all proper on me." She trailed her fingers along the curve of my cheek and down the V of my neckline. "I know you've been watching me too." She tweaked the point of my nipple, standing out against the royal-blue silk shirt.

My hand came up, covering the breast to keep her from touching it again. "Why did you do that?"

"Because I've wanted to for a long time." Molly crossed her arms beneath her breasts. "You liked it, didn't you?"

"No, of course not. I prefer men."

"Then why haven't I seen one come to your apartment in the two years I've lived here?"

"Perhaps I go to theirs." I hadn't been to a man's apartment in several years. They no longer interested me. I found myself more and more interested in the lively redhead living above me. I'd wondered at my change in tastes after all these years. But then everyone who met Molly loved her. Her zest for life, the happiness that shone from every particle of her being was like a beacon tempting the lonely into her light.

Molly's leg slid along mine, her knees parting, displaying a wide swath of her peaches-and-cream thigh. "See? You're looking now."

"How can I not when you practically planted yourself in my lap?" Oh, indeed, I was looking, more than I'd ever thought possible at any woman. But then Molly wasn't any woman. She was...Molly.

"I got a bikini wax just for tonight." Molly grabbed my hand and ran my fingers beside the triangle of black lace. "Smooth, isn't it?"

I couldn't resist. She was smooth and as silky as my lounging pajamas. I swallowed hard, wanting to slide my fingers beneath the lace of her panties, but proper ladies of the early eighteen hundreds didn't contemplate such deviancies. I removed my hand from her crotch. "Do you always prance around in your unmentionables?"

"Only for the people I want to do the unmentionable with." She leaned close and whispered in my ear, "Ever do it with a girl?"

Shock skittered across my skin with the warmth of her breath. "Once." A very long time ago. The event might have been over two hundred years past, yet I could recall it as though it was yesterday. Life changing barely began to describe the experience.

Molly curved her hand around my cheek and turned my face to hers. "Honey, life is incredibly short, you have to make the most of moments like this." Her lips descended on mine.

I sat motionless, unable to stop her, not really wanting to. For two years, I'd lusted after the young woman living above me. I'd denied my hunger, telling myself it wasn't natural and bad things always came to those who went against nature. My situation was a prime example.

When her tender lips touched mine, a sigh escaped me. I'd wanted this for so long, fighting instinct with every fiber of my being. The last time I'd been tempted by a woman, I'd taken on more than I'd ever dreamed. She'd made me immortal.

It all began with Lilith when she refused to be subservient to Adam in the Garden of Eden. She'd been cursed with the gift of immortality until she chose to pass the gift on to another woman equally resistant to man's dominance.

Ultimately I'd been chosen as the vessel to contain the memories of those who'd come before me. A burden no twenty-year-

old could begin to comprehend until she'd been twenty for
several lifetimes.

As Molly settled into my lap, all I could think of was her
soft curves pressing against me, her breasts within reach of my
tongue. All the thousands of years of memories fled my mind as I
surrendered to the red-haired beauty. My arms came up around
her; my fingers pressing into pale, creamy skin; my hand curving
along her waistline to the swell of her hips, dragging her closer.

Her tongue darted past my teeth, thrusting in and out in a
steady age-old rhythm. Slim, supple fingers found my nipples,
plucking at them through the silk fabric, bringing them to
turgid, quivering peaks.

She leaned away, a smile curving her lips. "Wow. I knew it
would be good, but...wow." She reached for the buttons at the
V of my blouse and flicked them open, one at a time, her fingers
brushing against my skin. "Katherine, you are so beautiful, like
a dark, English rose, so perfect."

I shook my head. "Anything but perfect."

"What are you talking about?" Molly's brows rose into the
bright hair falling over her forehead. "You have it all."

"I'm neither rich, nor famous," I argued.

"You have your health."

A very unladylike snort escaped me. "If you want to seduce
me, you'll have to try harder than that."

Molly rubbed her thumb over my cheek, the gesture gentle
and almost innocent. "I never see you sick."

"There are a lot more elements to happiness than perfect
health." Outliving your friends and loved ones made for a lonely
existence.

Molly's fingers resumed their work unbuttoning my blouse.
"I don't know. Good health gives you more choices." Her fingers
paused.

I held my breath, praying she'd continue. The heat building low in my belly flared. "What's wrong, Molly? I've never seen you so quiet and introspective."

She sighed and smiled. Not her usual, sunshine smile, but a sad, wistful smile. "Have you ever been in love?" She released the last button from the hole and spread my shirt lapels wide, her smile widening.

"Yes," I replied. On more than one occasion. When you lived as long as I had, you had ample opportunity to fall in and out of love. And you outlived the ones you loved.

"With a man?" Her hand reached out to cup my breast.

I sucked in a sharp breath, my chest rising into her palm. "Yes." Memories flittered in and out of my consciousness. In my life, I'd been in love three times. "At least I thought I was in love. I guess I'm not cut out to love men. They always wanted to dominate me."

Molly sat up straighter, her breasts rising. "Exactly. I've tried finding the right man, but I never felt they valued me as an equal. They'd tell me I was too silly or aggressive." Molly plumped my breasts in her palms and touched the tip of one with her tongue. "Do you think I'm too aggressive?"

"No." I had to remember to breathe, drawing in a long steadying breath. "There's nothing wrong with going after what you want."

"I'm glad you think that, because I've decided to go after you." Molly sucked more of my breast into her mouth and drew on it hard, her tongue swirling around the tip, flicking it until I squirmed beneath her.

"Why me?" My pussy ached, moisture pooling low, dribbling into my panties.

"Because you understand me." She reached behind her back and unclipped the hooks on her bra. "You don't judge me or try to make me something I'm not."

I slipped the straps from her arms, not really registering the movements, they seemed so natural, caught up as I was in this wonderful woman I'd only dreamed of touching. "Who would want to change you, Molly? You're so happy, vibrant and alive."

"Looks can be deceiving." She kissed me and slid off the ends of my knees. "I can't tell you how many times I've imagined you naked. I knew your skin would be as perfect beneath your clothes." She slid her fingers under the elastic band of my pajama bottoms and tugged them down my legs, taking my panties with them.

Cool night air did nothing to chill the heated wetness between my legs.

I let her undress me, anxious to be naked, while my mind kept screaming *Don't get involved.*

"Are you sure about this?" Logic forced me to give her an out, when all I wanted was for her to touch me, love me and make me forget all the memories crowding my head. I wanted to be alone with Molly, just me and her, writhing naked together.

Molly slid out of her lacy panties and stood before me, the picture of youth and beauty, her skin pale and dusted with freckles, her red hair falling down below her waist, eyes as brilliant as the finest emeralds. "I want to love you, Katherine." She nudged my legs apart and kneeled on the floor between them.

"I can't fall in love, Molly."

"Why not?"

"It hurts to love and lose and the pain lasts a long time."

"Then love me for a moment. I won't be around forever."

"That's what I'm afraid of." I leaned forward and captured her face in my hands. "I'm afraid I'll remember for a lifetime." To Molly, that wouldn't be very long. To me, it was forever. I couldn't add another lover to my memories. I'd lost enough for several lifetimes.

Molly caught my hand in hers. "Love me, Katherine." She pressed my hand to her breasts. "No strings attached, no promises of tomorrow. Love me for now."

The plea in her voice captured me. Her eyes shone, misty with moisture. Molly wanted this as much as I did. The difference being, she wasn't afraid of tomorrow. I was.

As I hesitated, her smile faded, a sigh escaping her parted lips. "If you won't love me, let me love you." She leaned into me, capturing one of my nipples between her teeth, tugging gently.

I closed my eyes and tried to resist, but couldn't. My fingers circled the back of her neck and drew her closer.

She suckled my breast, pulling hard, triggering a resulting tug low in my belly.

My legs tightened around her, my pussy throbbing the lower she went. I tangled my fingers in her hair, urging her downward until her mouth kissed the thatch of hair over my mons.

Slender fingers wove into the tight curls, finding and parting the folds beneath.

My bottom rose off the sofa meeting her strokes, urging her on.

Molly brushed feathery kisses along the inside of my thighs as she fingered my clit, the kisses edging closer to the center of my arousal.

I held my breath as her mouth replaced her fingers, her tongue laving my sensitive nubbin. Her tongue swirled and flicked, until the tingling began. It started when the tip of her tongue touched me and spread throughout my body, the sensations intensifying until all my muscles grew rigid and I cried out, "Please!"

"Please what?"

"Please, don't stop." My cry faded into a whisper. Never in

my long life had I begged for release as I did with Molly.

Relentless, she pressed on, her tongue torturing me into submission.

When I could take it no longer, I burst through the heavens, tumbling downward until I landed in front of Molly, spent and utterly amazed.

She grinned up at me. "Like that?"

I shook my head, a smile lifting my lips. "Need you ask?" I raised her chin, forcing her to look at me. "Get up."

Her auburn brows rose. "Are you angry?"

I rose along with her. "No. But we aren't finished."

"No?"

"No." I drew her closer until our breasts touched, then I kissed her, my mouth covering her lips, my tongue pushing past her teeth to taste the minty freshness of her tongue. I tugged her hand, drawing her down to the warmth and thickness of the Persian rug covering the wood flooring.

Molly lay down beside me, her body molding into mine.

My fingers trailed along the curve of her breast. I took one into my mouth, sucking hard, nipping at the pointed tip. My hands skimmed lower, following the contours of her waist and hips, sliding down to the apex of her thighs. The soft curls over her pussy sprang back as I feathered my fingers through them. I smiled at the color, every bit as red as the hair on Molly's head.

"You're beautiful." I stroked her clit. "You should be out dating someone who would make you happy for the rest of your life."

"You make me happy." She kissed me fiercely. "I don't have forever. I want to spend my time with you. What is it going to take to make you see that?" Her voice caught on a sob, and she buried her face in my neck.

My hand rose to push the hair out of her face. "You have me

for now. I just worry that you could find someone better to fill your life."

"You are all I need."

"You have me." I draped her leg over mine and gathered her close. I sought to please her as she'd pleased me, my fingers working their way across smooth skin, so soft and firm, to the curly mass of hair hiding her feminine core. Sliding two fingers between her folds, I found her clit and teased it until she cried out.

Her fingernails dug into my arms.

Scooting lower, I took one of her breasts into my mouth while my fingers dipped inside her, one, then two and three, her entrance damp and ready for more than I could give her.

Her fingers curled around mine and pressed me deeper.

"I can't do what a man does."

"I don't need a man, Katherine. I need you."

Gently, I rolled her to her back. "Wait here."

"Where are you going?"

"To get something."

"Hurry."

I dove into my bedroom, rummaging through my nightstand, searching for the vibrating dildo I'd purchased on impulse a year ago. I'd been too embarrassed to use it, and it had remained in the box until now.

When I returned to the living room, I held up the shiny silver toy.

Molly laughed. "I'd never pictured you as the owner of one of those."

Suddenly unsure, I frowned. "Is it not appropriate?"

"Oh, sweetie, it's more than appropriate." Molly rolled to her side and patted the floor. "Come on, I'll show you how to use it."

Butterflies fluttered in my belly as I strode naked toward Molly. She lay like a siren tempting me to the edge of a cliff, and I went willingly, handing her the device.

She twisted the bottom and the shaft hummed to life.

My pussy quivered in anticipation, but I wanted Molly to be first; the idea of pleasuring her was more tantalizing than that of pleasing myself. I held out my hand. "Let me."

She grinned giving me the dildo. I held it vibrating in my hand, the metal hard and cool against my fingers.

Again, Molly patted the floor beside her. "I'm ready, are you?"

I dropped to my knees and reached out to trail the shaft down over her belly and lower.

Molly rolled to her back, her flat stomach quivering. "Lower. Lubricate the dick. Get it good and wet."

With my empty hand leading the way, I dipped my fingers into her pussy, coating them in her juices and rubbing them over the silvery prick. "Like that?"

"Oh, yes, now use it quickly before it dries."

I climbed between her legs, spreading her knees wide.

Her entrance glistened. Her fingers trailed in the moisture seeping out.

Before I plunged the dildo into her, I wanted to taste her like she'd tasted me. I wanted my tongue to flicker over her clit and make her writhe with passion.

Parting her folds, I bent and flicked the little nubbin with my tongue.

Molly's ass rose off the floor, urging me to take more.

I sucked her clit into my mouth and bit down gently, swirling and teasing it with my tongue.

Her feet digging into the rug, Molly moaned. "Fuck me with the cock. Fuck me now."

The words should have made me, with my nineteenth-century upbringing, cringe. Instead, they made my nipples pucker tighter and my pussy drip. I positioned the slick metal cock at her entrance.

"Oh, yes, now. Ram it into me. Fuck me fast," Molly said.

Slowly, gently, I thrust the dildo into her pussy, deeper and deeper until only my fingers held the end.

Molly pushed up off the carpet, her eyes squeezed tight, her body rigid. "Faster. Fuck me faster."

I obliged with one hand, my other going to her clit, the rhythm of my strokes in unison. The faster I thrust, the more frenzied Mollie's movements and breathing became.

At last, she screamed out my name, her ass levered off the ground, her body poker straight. Then she fell back to earth, her face flushed, a smile curving her pretty lips.

I held the dildo inside her, the fingers of my other hand parting her folds. I bent to suck her clit into my mouth for one final taste—warm, musky, heady. Then I removed the dildo, laying it to the side.

"That was great." Molly sighed, lying back against the rug, her arm draped over her face.

As she lay there, I ran my finger along her thigh, across her pelvis and up to the tip of her full, rounded nipple. The nipple puckered, jutting out peachy-pink and taut.

I tweaked the tip between my thumb and forefinger.

Molly's body tensed. A grimace crossed her face.

My hand jerked away. "I'm sorry. Did I hurt you?"

"No, no." She pinched the bridge of her nose and bent double, her face and lips blanching. "I get headaches at the most annoying moments."

"Want me to get you something?" I rose, concerned. I'd never seen Molly in this much pain. She always seemed to be happy and carefree.

Molly lay there, her fingers pressing her temples so tightly her knuckles turned white. "No. I'm fine." She sat up and smiled, her teeth clenched, the smile never quite reaching her eyes.

"Maybe you should lie down a little longer." I grabbed a throw pillow from the couch and pushed it behind her.

"No, I have a party to go to at the Brewery, tonight." She lurched to her feet and swayed, reaching out to steady herself.

I grabbed her arm. "I don't think you should go out. You're face is pale. You don't look well."

"I'm fine. I have to go to the party. It's the last time I'll see J.J. and the Jolly Rogers play."

"What are you talking about? They come back every three months. You'll have a chance to see them then. Stay here. Relax and let me take care of you."

"No." Molly scrambled around the living room gathering her bra and panties. "I told you, no strings attached. I don't want any strings, no emotions. Nothing, just the sex. Thanks, by the way. It was better than I could have imagined." She grabbed her two dresses and ran for the door, her feet stumbling as she neared.

"Molly, what's wrong?"

"Nothing, Katherine. I'm fine." Her fingers gripped the door handle and she paused, her shoulders tensing, her back hunching over.

When I ran to her, she pushed me away. "No. Don't pity me. I want you to love me as I am now. I can't stand pity."

"What are you talking about?"

"Nothing." She yanked the door open and paused. Turning back toward me, she cupped my cheek and kissed me. "Don't get involved with me. It won't last."

After she'd gone, I stood in the doorway wondering what I'd done wrong.

That had been over an hour ago. Now I stood with my back to the bar, scanning the Brewery for Molly.

"You're Molly's friend, right?" The bartender placed my glass of wine on the bar.

"Yes. Have you seen her?"

He nodded to the dance floor. "She's been dancing since she got here. Such a shame that one."

"What are you talking about?"

"The brain tumor."

My head reeled and I sank onto a bar stool.

"You didn't know?" The bartender stared across at Molly. "The doc gave her two months to live."

"I didn't know."

"Wow, she should have been the one to break it to you." The man touched my arm. "I'm sorry."

I sat for a long time staring at the beautiful, vibrant redhead, gyrating around the floor like there was no tomorrow. For her, there would be none—for me, an endless procession of tomorrows. Molly had lived only twenty-five years. I'd lived more than two hundred. She was just beginning her life—I was tired of mine. I wanted to grow old and die. Molly wanted to live.

I stood, walked across the floor, knowing exactly what had to happen, should Molly choose. As if on cue, the music ended and the band went on break. Molly stood out in the middle of the floor as everyone else filtered back to their tables and drinks. Someone played a soft lilting song on the jukebox.

I gathered Molly in my arms and swayed with her to the music. "Why didn't you tell me?"

"I didn't want your pity, just your love."

"Honey, you have my love." I hugged her closer, my eyes filling with tears.

"I wanted you in my life, to grow old with and love for a very long time. But I don't have that long."

"You could, if you choose."

Molly shook her head. "The doctor gives me two months. How can I pack a lifetime in two months?"

"I know how you can live longer."

"You do?"

"Do you trust me?"

She nodded. "With my life."

"I can give you more time in your life, if you let me."

Light from the disco globe shone in her eyes. "How?"

"Just one bite." I ran a finger along her neck, stopping at the base of her throat where her carotid artery beat strong.

Molly leaned back in my arms. "Huh?"

"It's a gift, kind of like the myths of the vampire, but not."

"Vampires aren't real."

"No, they aren't, but I am and it will only take one bite from me and you'll be cured."

"I've never seen you drink blood."

"I'm not a vampire, and you won't be either. You won't crave blood or have to stay out of daylight. But you will live forever or until you decide to pass the gift to the next woman." I cupped her cheek. "Only one woman at a time can carry the gift."

"What gift is this?"

"A gift as old as Adam, the gift of Lilith." I chuckled. "Don't look so doubtful. I'm over two hundred years old."

"What?" She tried to pull free of my arms.

I gently hugged her to me, swaying to the music. "The question is, do you want to live?"

"Yes." She sagged against me, the music the only sound for several moments. "I want to live with you forever, Katherine."

I stopped moving. "That can't be. When I pass the gift of

Lilith to you, you will become immortal and I will grow old and die."

"But I don't want you to die. What good would it be for me to be immortal without you?"

"I've had a long life, you haven't. You have much more to experience—I've had enough. I want to grow old and die. Please, let me give you this gift. I want you to have it."

"But—"

"I ask again. Do you want to live?"

She stared into my eyes, her own filling with tears. "Yes."

I smiled and folded her into my arms. "Then dance with me."

As we moved around the floor, Molly relaxed in my arms and I spoke of the women who'd come before us, of the memories that would soon be Molly's. I knew I'd found the person I wanted to spend the rest of my life with, someone who would understand me and stand by me as I grew old. As the music slowed, I sank my teeth into Molly's neck, our lives became intertwined, our pasts joined.

A new song started. Molly looked up and smiled, and I knew she would be all right. I'd given her the gift of Lilith, and in return, she'd given me the gift of her love.

MADELINE

A. E. Grace

I first met Madeline when I was twelve years old. It was at a charity book fair my mother had organized in the summer of 2003, a particularly humid season to be stumbling about a church hall with crates of secondhand paperbacks, in what was a particularly overcrowded village.

Breezing by with an armful of hardback Stephen Kings, my mother had craned her neck and called, "Find Stella and see if she needs a hand or something, will you? You're hanging about like an infant, Lil."

Lil was, as you might've guessed, short for Lilly; I'd never liked that name. A Lilly is a beautiful flower, and, like the frocks my mother had dressed me in as a preteen, the name never seemed to suit me.

The shortened version, Lil, allowed me to assume a kind of non-gender-specific status amongst my peers, and I liked the feel of it very much. It was something that would later aid me in "finding myself," as some people and teachers liked to call it, and made kissing Madeline as a teenager seem like less of an alien thing, despite what the other girls thought of it.

Fanning myself with one of the Kidson notebooks my mother liked so much, I waded through the wandering elderly church people, and found my mother's friend Stella peeling plastic wrap off of various goodies she'd made for the occasion, the light pouring in from the bay window to form a halo-effect around her puff of auburn hair.

Crouched beneath the table, sucking on the oval-shaped remnants of a lollipop, was Madeline. My heart had given its first surge in the presence of a female, as I looked in awe at her long legs and tumbling red hair, approaching her with a slowing pace to allow myself more viewing time. Of course, subsequent to this I had to think of something to say to her too, a nerve-wracking task in itself.

Stella exhaled a gruff breath of air and smoothed down the front of her blouse. Seeing me, she grinned and ushered me over with a flap of her delicate, manicured hands. "Lilly!" she beamed, pacing round to my side of the stall, blissfully unaware of the potentially *fatal* mistake she'd made addressing me by my full name.

"Been helping mum, have we?" Before I'd parted my lips to respond, she turned and called to Madeline, who unfolded her spiderlike limbs and glided dutifully to stand by her mother. "This is my daughter, Maddy; you won't have met her before. She's back from boarding school," Stella breathed, with an air of pride about her raspy, whispering voice.

Nodding to Madeline, I felt myself reddening from the neck up. She acknowledged me with her catlike eyes, green-yellow in the haze of the spore-filled hall. My own eyes were so fixed upon her face that I could count each freckle dotted about her nose.

She stood a good foot taller than I, and I remember the distancing remaining that way until we parted at seventeen years old, after what I now refer to as our "accident."

Folding her thin arms, she said, "Fancy a walk? It's bloody boring in here, ain't it?" And, giddy at the knees and feeling as though my thundering heart would create an echo against the stony walls, I followed her into the glorious sunshine outside.

As I paced the concrete outside a greasy café, a full twenty years since we'd last spoken, my heart thundered once again in the fashion that Madeline had first engendered. The night was chilled and still, ominously lacking any police sirens or screams from streets farther away. Reaching into my pocket, I pulled out a glistening hip flask and took a glug. The blood, more popularly referred to as the Red Stuff on TV commercials, had remained salty and warm in the snug of my trouser leg.

I replayed the scene of our first meeting bitterly in my mind, aching not for the sight of Madeline, but for the golden sunlight that I was now deprived of, and the church of a town, *our* hometown, that we had fled from after our accident occurred. I often wondered about our mothers, picturing them fretting in each other's living rooms, calling the police stations, the hospitals; crying: *Where have our daughters gone?*

Mid-pace, I sensed a change in the atmosphere, a shift, and I knew Madeline had arrived. Moistening my lips with my thin, pointed tongue, I tasted her in every pore. Without having any mentor throughout my adjustment period for my condition, I'd come to recognize certain changes and connections that occurred as a result of becoming—and I hated the word—a vampire.

Once you've mated with a fellow vampire, it seemed, the pair created a bond that allowed them to sense each other's taste, or scent; I felt Madeline's presence as if she were nestled in my mouth.

"Lil?" she whispered. Her voice enveloped me like a velvet curtain, and I shuddered.

Biting my lip, I turned to face her, and ran an anxious hand through my crop of short, mousy brown hair. The sight of her, standing like a delicate porcelain doll, caused my breath to catch in my throat.

"I thought you weren't coming," I croaked eventually, clearing my throat. I pocketed my hands and scuffed my boot on the pavement, suddenly searching for something to look at, anything but her.

Still, a glance was enough; she wore a silk bell-sleeved dress, the color of coal, which stopped just short of her milky knees. A delicate line of cleavage peeked between the sweetheart-shaped cloth, appearing like the entwined necks of two swans. On her feet, she wore a pair of suede Mary Janes in deep red.

"I was worried about the same thing," she replied, smiling meekly. Her almond-shaped eyes glistened in the darkness like shards of reflective glass. "I'm sorry I left it so late."

I nodded, nervously tapping my foot. "Not to worry. Shall we go in?" I gestured to the door of the café, a curl of my hair falling irritatingly onto my forehead.

"Of course," she said, stepping aside and allowing me to open the door for her, then striding in. I used the brief moment it took me to pull the door closed behind me, the little bell ringing, to calm my nerves. I breathed deeply and, wiping my clammy hands on my thighs, joined her at a nearby table.

The place was dead, barring a bearded man in a camouflage jacket, who sat in the far corner by the window nursing a steaming mug of tea. The hanging lights cast deep shadows over Madeline's face, hardening her soft features.

The sound of a waitress clattering about in the kitchen was suffocated by the hiss of the coffee machine. I looked again at Madeline's dress, and suddenly became overly aware of the dirty tiles and torn linoleum floor.

"I'm sorry about the location," I gushed, nervously scratching my head. "I just saw the twenty-four-hour sign and didn't give it enough thought. We can find somewhere else, if you like."

She shook her curls. "No, no, this is fine. Really," she added, seeing my unconvinced face.

"Sorry," I said. "I know it's been a pretty long time, but I should've remembered you liked to dress up."

Twenty years, it turned out, wasn't all that much time where a vampire was concerned. Sure, I'd done a lot in that time; met a few girls, traveled. But it wasn't much, not really. Not when you consider the fact that you've got the whole of eternity to look forward to.

"Please, Lil, I said it's okay."

A short blonde girl in a polka-dot apron approached us then, clutching a little pad—and abruptly pocketed it when she saw us for what we were. Our creamy white skin had an unmistakable glow and, on seeing her bare, youthful neck, our fangs had extended of their own accord.

"You guys want Red?" she asked, her voice cracking slightly.

"Yes, thanks," I said, steering my eyes away from her collar, which seemed to quiver against the pulse of her neck. I glanced at Madeline, who was also gazing fixedly at the girl, unable to draw her eyes away. I reached for her hand and squeezed it.

"Any particular type?" asked the girl, whose badge revealed her name was Wendy.

I shook my head, not taking my eyes off Madeline for a moment, in case she lost control completely. I didn't like to patronize her, but I'd no idea of her temperament—she had been a fierce human, and I dreaded to think how she could be now as a predator.

"Anything you have is fine," I uttered quickly, and she disappeared into the kitchen.

Madeline giggled. "It never gets easier to resist, does it?"

"You have the same problem, huh?" I laughed, leaning back on my chair. It occurred to me seconds later that I still had hold of Madeline's hand, her fingers writhing beneath mine. Pinking slightly, I slid my hand away.

Madeline straightened, wrinkling her nose. "You didn't have to do that," she muttered, her tone sharp.

I blinked. "Do what?"

"I'm not diseased, you know," she snapped, keeping her voice low.

"Maddy! You know I wouldn't—" I hushed quickly as Wendy reappeared with our morsels of blood in two piping hot mugs. Madeline swiped hers from the table immediately, and, unfazed by the heat that would blister a human's skin, drank greedily.

I sighed. I'd quite forgotten how short tempered Madeline used to be, so it shouldn't have surprised me to see that, two minutes into our meeting, we weren't getting along. Once Wendy had left, I leaned over the table and looked Madeline dead in the eyes.

"Tell me you aren't going to be like this, Madds?" I pleaded.

She dotted her plump lips with a napkin, her mouth slightly swollen now. "Like what?"

I huffed. I'd grown tired of her games a long time ago, and knew that it was best to nip this in the bud before the evening got worse.

"I know we've had our disagreements, Maddy." I began, treading delicately. "But please, you *know* me. I would never think that about you."

She looked up from her mug, which she clutched between her long fingers. "You did once," she said coolly.

"No," I urged, helplessly scratching the tabletop with my nails. "I just felt hurt, that's all."

Her eyes fired up, her eyebrows arching. "Hurt? We were both hurt, Lil, but some of us knew how to move *on*."

Despite my best efforts, her sudden rage awoke the anger inside me too. "You call that moving on, Madds? Yielding to those disgusting, loathsome—"

"Men?" she finished for me, her face set as steel. I gritted my teeth.

"Yes, men," I said, my entire body tensing at even the mere utterance of the word.

Allow me to make something perfectly clear: I do *not* hate all men. The thought of Madeline, *my* Madeline, writhing about in the sheets with a man between her thighs does a lot to repulse me, it's true; but I don't hate them, not all of them. Too glamorous for night shifts at some factory, Madeline liked to call her new career as a lady of the evening a "stand" against the male sex. I called it a stab in the back.

"Think about the money, Lil," she'd said, a full twenty years ago. "Besides, not all men are monsters."

The front she'd been putting on, that air of dismissal she had whenever I mentioned our accident, had sickened me to the core.

"*He* was a monster, Maddy! How can you forget it all so easily?" I'd cried, pacing the apartment we'd shared, like a mad woman, in the same fashion I had paced the pavement tonight.

"I'll never forget it, Lil," she'd soothed, pulling me into her arms and planting a delicate kiss on my ear. "I just can't dwell on the attack any more. We've got such a long, wonderful life ahead of us; what does it matter how I make my money? Oh, Lil, please don't be that way."

I'd thrown her arms off and stormed to the window to look at the moon that had been so high in the sky, so bright. But to think that under that very same moon, a vampire had hunted two young women; had fed from them, like an animal, and changed their lives forever: it was more than I could bear.

Contrary to popular belief, being a vampire didn't mean your emotions were drained as quickly as the blood was. I knew this all too well. So well, in fact, that I couldn't stand to look at Maddy's face any longer—and I had left her that same night.

I looked at her now, with her wide eyes and youthful sprinkle of freckles, and knew I'd been a fool to do so. But the knowledge was still within me, still twisting in my gut—and I couldn't suppress it.

"Men pay, Lil," she said now, crossing one leg primly over the other. "That's all. And if anything, I'm coming out trumps," she said, smiling coyly. I narrowed my eyes.

"You can't mean...? Oh, Maddy! You don't—"

"Oh, I do," she grinned, drawing the mug of hot blood to her lips. "Every last drop."

I sat there for what seemed like an age, simply staring at her, my untouched blood bubbling away between us in delicious irony. "Madeline, that's—"

"What? Murder?" she asked, grinning. Her eyes seemed to light up, passionately glinting at the thought of draining her paying customers.

Ever since vampires had come out, or "come out of the coffin" as the media liked to quip, blood had become available for purchase in just about every store and restaurant; even seedy cafés like this, it seemed, had stocked up a good supply. Not only did this make the afterlife a whole lot easier for vamps, but it made hunting humans, even for food, officially illegal.

"That's evil," I finished, making her shriek with laughter. I have to admit, her impish, heartless laughter sparked something within me, something that had been subdued—and I found myself grinning.

"I know, I'm terrible," she said when the laughter subsided, giving me a sly wink.

Was she terrible? I couldn't help but feel, as I drank of my mug of warm, velvety blood, that there was a romantic sense of vendetta about Madeline. I thought of the past, of the night we were preyed upon like kittens in the grip of a cobra. And I realized, with a sickly revelation that tingled in my toes, that in killing the pussycat, he'd unleashed the tiger. One that wouldn't be tamed.

And where had I been all these years? Hidden, that's where—behind the monotony of factory life, my mind flitting to and from the night of the attack like a moth to a bulb.

And now, slithering about with my burnt and useless wings, I sat across from this butterfly, Madeline.

Madeline, who had abandoned the sun and embraced the moon, and was now basking in its glow. I experienced a pang of what I first thought was envy in my gut, but then I realized with a concoction of reluctance and glee that it was lust.

I licked my lips, a drop of blood catching in the corner of my mouth. I cleared my throat.

"And has business been good lately?" I asked casually, glancing at the waitress, who had given up her chores and was nose deep in a book.

"Business is always good," said Madeline, resuming her sharp tone of voice; detached, yet commanding of one's attention all the same. "I don't much like the foreplay, though. Especially with the needy types. Sometimes I'm there all night before I get the opportunity for a taste."

"Why do you wait at all?" I asked, perplexed. "Surely you could get it over with in a matter of moments?"

She grinned, showing her even teeth. "I could, but part of me enjoys the wait. The touching is what really gets on my wick, you know; having to sit there while they fumble about with my breasts, not knowing what to do with them." She rested her chin in her palm, her polished nails becoming lost in the tangle of her hair.

"Besides," she added. "I prefer to wait till they pay up first, rather than just feeding and taking it. I'm a seductress, not a thief."

I smiled, not knowing how to respond to that. We shared a few moments of silence, downing our drinks and enjoying the simple normality of each other's company, before she spoke up once more.

"Let's talk about you, Lil," she said spritely, jabbing me with her long index finger. "What have you been doing with yourself?"

I talked sparingly about the late nights of factory work, about fixing the machines, generally maintaining the place, and so on. She nodded with forced interest, but I could tell by the slight drooping of her eyelids that she wasn't particularly amused by my tales.

Eventually, she grinned and said, "Did you meet any girls, in that lonely warehouse?"

I laughed, but more with a grimace than a smile. "I've had the occasional encounter, yes, but nothing too serious." I spoke delicately, afraid of breaking the fragile shell in which I held our past relationship, happy to leave the uncomfortable acknowledgment of our separation alone.

But that wasn't Madeline's style at all.

"Nobody quite like me, eh?" she said softly, biting her nail. She narrowed her eyes so that the emerald pupils glowed between the fringe of her lashes. My heart gave a surge; I felt a familiar, throbbing sensation in the fork of my knickers; and I moistened under her gaze.

I almost missed it, but I caught the soft twitch of her nostrils, and knew that there was no hiding my longing for her now. Her expression twisted into a kind of anguished, desperate affection, and she plucked my hands from the table to hold them by the hollow of her neck.

"Oh, Lil," she breathed, her eyes gently narrowed and her mouth slightly parted. I felt the drum of her heart beating through the fabric of her dress and suddenly longed to be close to her, entwined with her, enveloped in each other's body like two desperate, clasping hands.

Abandoning any sense of decorum for our audience of two in the café, Madeline lurched upon the table, her knees knocking the cups and spilling the dregs of the glistening juice inside. She clutched me by the hair and pulled me to her, kissing me so hard that I had to anchor us down with my feet, while quivering naively at her touch.

We kissed ravenously, tasting tongue, teeth and lipstick, and I pulled her down to straddle my lap. One of her Mary Jane shoes slipped off and clattered dramatically on the tiled floor. The sound of this, apparently more obvious than our panting breaths, alerted the waitress who, throwing down her book, gasped in shock.

"Stop! Listen, you can't do that in here!" she wailed, her hands poised at her neck as though the sight was sickening. Madeline paused to bite my lip, her own slightly chapped from the cold outside. Caressing my cheek, nose to nose with me, she whispered, "Where can we go?"

Holding her hips and ignoring the wails of the young waitress, I kissed Madeline's freckled neck and felt my fangs extending, inch by inch, with the throbbing in my pants. I thought frantically, unable to picture the ghastly world outside the glow of her emerald eyes.

Leaping from my lap and clutching my hand, she pulled me from the café and out into the cool night air, leaving her shoe behind like some amusing tribute to Cinderella, and the whole frigid affair of fairy tales.

We blundered through the darkness hand in hand, the wind whipping at our faces, until Madeline abruptly turned and dragged me down a dark and narrow alleyway. There was little in the way of romance here, but the cold walls and isolated blackness, away from the glaring streetlights and prying eyes, fueled our passion all the more.

We paused, Madeline pressed against me with her right thigh nudged between my legs. I leaned in to kiss her, softer this time, and we sank into each other's embrace as the mist of our breath caught in the cold night air, and drifted up like spirits.

My hands shaking, I fumbled with the zip at the back of her dress, and she swiftly tugged it over her flame-red curls and tossed the thing aside. She draped herself upon me, bare breasted. She wore white lace knickers that blended almost completely into her complexion, giving the impression of complete nudity.

Softly biting my ear, she whispered, "Your turn." And in my bleary, dazed lustfulness I couldn't articulate what she was asking of me, and so she tore the shirt from me herself, and hurriedly unfastened my bra. As she did this, the widest part of her thigh nestled against my crotch and nudged repeatedly, pleasuring me with each movement.

Soon she was thumbing my nipples, which were erect both from the cold and for the longing of her, as her hips swayed and gyrated in my grasp. Slipping a hand beneath the soft white lace, I felt for her moist folds of skin and slipped a finger in. Madeline groaned into my hair and twisted my nipples all the more.

Our passion grew like wildfire. But somewhere in the depths of my mind, I did wonder how it'd ever come to this; how Madeline and I could part for twenty years and end up here, groping in some dark alley. More shocking was the thought that those two girls, who had met in a crowded church hall, would one day be transformed into predatory creatures of the night.

Madeline hastily delved into my pants and balled her fist, to rub and twist and make me cry in glorious, clitoral pleasure, her knuckles caressing the spot that longed for caressing most, until I was moaning as hard as she was.

"Lil!" she cried, burrowing her face into the swell of my breasts. "Oh, Lil, the blood! The blood, I want it, I—" But I didn't allow her to finish, for I knew what she desired and longed for it just as she did. Grasping her by a handful of hair, I slipped in two more of my eager fingers, and thrust slower, for I knew she was close to climaxing.

I whispered, "I love you, Maddy." And, without further cruel hesitation, I cried with animal hunger and plunged my fangs into her neck. Screaming, Madeline sank her fangs into mine also, and jerked hard against my hand.

As the blood streamed from our veins, we interlocked, our hearts beating unnaturally fast, *supernaturally* fast, and soon Madeline was quivering spasmodically in orgasm. She released her grip on my neck and relaxed softly into my arms.

"Oh, you naughty girl," I breathed, after retracting my fangs and licking the wound. I felt a shudder as Madeline laughed, and soon we were giggling foolishly, like a pair of schoolgirls who'd locked themselves in the storeroom. Madeline wrapped her arms about my neck and we embraced, our mouths swollen and red, engorged with each other's blood.

Madeline inclined her head to look at me, and asked, "Will you leave me again tonight, Lil?"

Smoothing back the hair from her warm, clammy forehead, I wondered how I'd ever *wanted* to leave her at all. It occurred to me now, in the calm, that Madeline had simply been embracing something that I'd been trying too hard to run from.

Madeline straightened and stood a foot taller than me, just as she did when I'd first met her. But this time she didn't intimidate me, and when I looked at her pale, sullen face, I realized that my silence had hurt her.

I shook my head, and awoke a beaming smile upon her face. "Never again, if you'll have me," I said.

We dressed in silence, glancing sheepishly at each other as we did so, the schoolgirl image tickling us both into fits of giggles. We emerged from the alley hand in hand, in time to see Wendy the waitress ending her shift at the little café and walking out to her car.

Madeline squeezed my hand and in a dark voice said, "Fancy a bite to eat?"

A smirk crept onto my face, and I accepted by extending my fangs. We pursued poor unsuspecting Wendy almost gleefully, as if it were the most natural thing in the world.

RED HORIZONS

Victoria Oldham

The heat of the early winter sun left the deck warm, even after dark. The waters of the Mediterranean lapped gently against the side of the 105-foot schooner yacht as the inhabitants woke and started to make their way about the upper deck.

Gas lamps flickered to life everywhere, and eventually the all-female crew were lit well enough that the few mortals on board could see them. Of course, they had no need for it themselves, as each crew member had superb night vision, as do all night predators. And using gas lamps instead of electricity meant they could stay at sea longer, which meant better lead time after a hunt. Modern pirate ships were so much more practical than the originals.

"What port are we closest to?"

Captain Jayne Green looked up into cerulean-blue eyes and grinned. "I thought you might enjoy some Spanish food tonight. We're on the east coast of Spain. Cartagena is twelve miles from here, with a nice port and good night life."

"Nice. I do like the tang of Spanish women." Eleni Demetriou stretched the muscles in her back, which were, thanks to her heavy feed the night before, pulsing like they were still living. Her thick black hair was tied in a ponytail, serving to highlight her high cheekbones and full lips. No Greek woman alive was more beautiful than Eleni, and she knew it. More times than she could count her looks had gotten her an easy dinner and more than a few orgasms for dessert.

"Smells like home." Anna Valencia, affectionately known as Skinner by her friends, leaned over the bow and sniffed before turning to their human captain. "It's been far too long since I enjoyed the flavors of my homeland. What time is it?"

"Twenty past six. You've got a full night ahead of you. And the sunrise will be dimmed by the clouds, so don't get caught out," Jayne said seriously.

"Aye-aye, Captain," Anna pressed her mouth to Jayne's hand, nipping slightly before gliding across the deck, shouting, "Right, crewmates! Let's get to our dinner dates, shall we?"

The rest of the crew joined her on the swimming deck, where they jumped into the small speedboat they kept tied to the side. With a wave, the howling, laughing women sped off into the night, moonlight trailing in their wake as they became nothing but sirens in the dark.

"Not going ashore tonight, Eleni?" Jayne asked, keeping her voice steady.

"Nope. I fed well enough last night to last me a few days. A nice lean one, healthy and active. Her blood was like those energy drinks they sell these days. Imagine—selling something like that in cans to vampires!"

Eleni laughed and Jayne joined in, hoping, in part, that she was kidding.

Jayne watched as Eleni stretched out on the white leather

couch on the foredeck, her olive skin setting the couch aglow like a white nova under her. Jayne loved watching Eleni, no matter what she was doing. Watching the water, sleeping in death, enjoying a bath. She had sailed with the vampire for nearly two years, and every day it got harder to watch Eleni take her beautiful victims to bed, knowing that she wouldn't ever be there herself. When she had been hired by the beautiful Greek vampire, Eleni had made sure she knew her place, and her safety levels: no one would ever use Jayne as a food source, and no one would ever force her to do anything she didn't want to do.

The problem was, that meant Jayne traveled the seas with remarkably, utterly, insanely beautiful women, and never got laid, even though she listened to the sounds of passion all night long when they made port. At least, until the splash indicating that feeding time was over and the remnants were left for the sharks.

Eleni watched as Jayne fought her innermost emotions, the ones she tried to keep hidden, although every woman on board could feel, smell, her arousal and need. Eleni had been alive long enough to have been a pirate the first go-round—she was patient, and could wait as long as it would take for Jayne to break down and ask for what she needed. She raised her eyebrows in surprise when Jayne spun toward her and said, "I'm going to port. No reason for me to stay on board tonight if you're here. And the cook and maid are both here as well. So I'm going."

She stood there, seemingly waiting for Eleni to object, but when no argument issued forth, she nearly ran down the aft stairs, jumping into the smaller motorboat and launching it across the water with no regard for her own safety.

Now what is she doing? Eleni got up and leaned over the bow, watching as the human she cared for more than she wanted to admit made her way to the dark streets of Cartagena.

* * *

Jayne swallowed hard against the flurry of panic that swam through her body as she entered the lesbian bar she had Googled while her vampire crew had slept during the day. Heart-thumping music blared from every corner speaker, and women in all states of dress gyrated on the dance floor, hips thrusting, breasts bouncing, hands caressing. After the quiet, albeit unusual, life she led on open water, it was all nearly too much and she turned to run back out to the street, to the boat. *To Eleni.*

She jumped when a hand clasped her forearm. "Dance with me, *amiga*. I promise it will be fun." The woman's dark skin was smooth, her hair short, her jeans low and her grin cocky. *Exactly what I need.*

Jayne nodded, not bothering to try and outdo the music, and followed the compact woman to the dance floor, where she quickly lost herself in the music and the feel of someone's hands running possessively over her long-neglected body.

When the woman pressed against her, pushing her thigh between Jayne's legs, Jayne pressed back, letting her head fall back as she immediately took pleasure in the feel of the strong thigh against her rigid clit. Three songs later she thought her clit would burst through her jeans.

"Let me take you home and fuck you, *mi amor*," the woman said in her ear.

Once again she just nodded, her wet panties screaming against her hot, throbbing center. She let the woman lead her from the bar, turning quickly when she thought she saw Eleni from the corner of her eye. She wasn't there, of course. She was with the boat, which couldn't be left captain-less.

Jayne shook her head to force Eleni from her mind and concentrated on the heavy biker boots leading her from the bar.

* * *

Eleni crossed her arms over her chest. *What the fuck? She wants* that *instead of me?* She moved silently through the bar and down the street, watching as the little Spanish butch stopped periodically to plant a sloppy kiss on Jayne's lips, hands, chest.

With every move she wanted to rip the woman's head from her shoulders, wanted to swim in the blood that would pump from the gaping wound she would create in the woman's chest after ripping out her heart.

They disappeared up a narrow stairway leading to second-story apartments across from the excavated Roman amphitheater. Eleni struggled with what to do next. Should she follow, watch as the Spaniard made love to *her* Jayne? She knew that if she did, she wouldn't be able to keep from killing her, and Jayne would never be able to come to her if she watched her kill without mercy. She punched the wall, taking a measure of pleasure at the shattering of rock and cement under her fist.

With a leap, she cleared the wall of the amphitheater and made her way back to the yacht. She would wait for Jayne to come home, but she was done waiting for Jayne to make the first move. It was time Jayne understood her place. Eleni would give her this one night in the arms of someone else, because there would never be another.

Jayne moaned as the woman's tongue slid over her neck, her lips chapped and her mouth wet. Suddenly, her stomach recoiled and an image of Eleni, her mouth hot, her hands soft and cold, blew through her mind and body. With a gasp, she pushed the woman away and stumbled to the open window. Leaning her head on the cold glass, she took in great breaths of air, trying to stop the sudden trembling taking over her.

"*Que pasa, amiga?* What's wrong? You sick?" The woman placed a tentative hand on her lower back, but sounded more disgusted than concerned.

"Yes. I...I think I need to go home. Something I ate, maybe." Jayne lied easily, knowing there was no way in hell she could go through with letting someone other than a centuries-old vampire fuck her. *Fuck, damn, shit.*

"Okay, no problem. You want I should walk you home?"

Jayne could hear the reluctance in the woman's voice, and nearly laughed out loud at the idea of her walking her "home." Home. Where she lived with two other mortal women and nine vampires. Right. Sure. Why not?

"No, thanks. I'll be fine. It isn't far. Sorry."

"Yeah, well, another night, eh?" The woman locked the door behind them and nearly flew down the steps toward the bar, still in time to try for another conquest. "You take care." With that, she disappeared, and Jayne found herself alone outside the impressive ancient amphitheater.

Climbing through a gap in the wire fence, she slid inside the theater, and mounting the high stone steps, she found a row she liked. Lying down on a wide stone bench, she placed her hands under her head and stared at the stars that guided her as she sailed all over the deep blue sea. She again let her thoughts drift to Eleni, and what her hands would feel like as they reached her most sacred places.

She sat up with a start, looking for the source of the footsteps she was sure she heard. No one was there, and suddenly she realized how foolish it was to be alone in a place without lights, especially since she knew the kind of ghoulies that prowled the night.

"Well, hello," said the woman at the bottom of the stairs, her long blonde hair floating in windswept strands around her face, even though there was no breeze. "Why is a lovely creature like you here all alone?"

"Hi. I'm not. Alone, I mean. My friend..."

"Just left. And in rather a hurry, it seems. Sadly, I don't believe she'll be reaching her destination, since my friends decided she would be delightful company this evening."

Jayne winced, thinking of the somewhat sexy butch as some vampire's snack. "Oh, I didn't mean her. I meant my other friend..."

"Your vampire friend, you mean? No, she left as well. And rather angry, I think, as she didn't even bother to notice me as she left you and your paramour to enjoy one another. No, *amor*, you are alone. And you are going to be fine company for me tonight."

With a flourish, and barely a movement, the woman was suddenly beside her, bending over her, the low-cut dress showing ample cleavage. "I know you need me. You need release, don't you, *bonita*? You need someone to make you feel special? You are broadcasting your desire and hunger so that anyone can hear it. I can take care of your need, and so much more. Make this easy, sweet girl, and I promise to send you back to your vampire in the morning."

Her hand was like soft marble as it caressed Jayne's cheek and slid over her neck, the blood-red nails lightly grazing a trail over her collarbone. Her eyes glowed an unearthly green, the pupils a strange maroon color.

Jayne whimpered quietly, knowing from her time among them that fighting would only lead to a miserable death, while playing nice might let her keep her life, if not her sanity.

Eleni, she screamed in her head as the woman's mouth came down on her own, crushing her lips as the woman's tongue slid into her mouth and a rough hand clasped her breast, fingers pinching her nipple into a hard bud. Her T-shirt ripped down the front as the woman slowly tore it away.

"If you were my human, I would have marked you. You're simply divine. Such beautiful breasts," she said, cupping a breast in each hand and squeezing Jayne's nipples before lowering her mouth to take one between sharp teeth. "And such perfect white skin. I can hear your heart pounding for me. I can smell your desire."

She whispered the words almost reverently, and Jayne wanted her to keep going, to put out the heat between her legs, to suck her nipples and make her cry out. Deep within, she knew these thoughts weren't her own, but it didn't matter. She *needed*.

She nearly screamed when the woman vanished from above her, and could only curl into a fetal position as the intense desire, the unquenchable need to be deeply fucked rocked her to her soul. Managing to raise her head from the stone bench, she saw Eleni facing the woman, both in a predatory stance, the blonde hissing as Eleni crouched in front of Jayne protectively.

"It's rude to mess with someone else's human," Eleni said quietly, her Greek accent thicker in the midst of danger.

"You haven't marked her. She was alone. She's mine for the night."

"You could smell me on her. There's no way you can deny that."

"You? I can smell at least seven others on her as well. That suggests to me that she's open game, and tonight, she's my game. Move."

Jayne whimpered again as the flood of desire swept through her in wave after wave, crushing her beneath its heat. She didn't care that they were arguing over her as if she were a coveted toy, just so long as someone fucked her senseless. Soon.

"No. She's mine. She's always been mine. I'll take her back

to the boat and mark her now. Leave."

The beautiful blonde vampire shifted, her position one of consideration rather than violence. "You've come to my country, to my territory, with unmarked humans. Your pirates have already robbed several of our richer humans, and have already feasted on some of our finest women. I knew you were here, but did nothing to hinder you, as you have clearly come and will clearly go again by ship. But you insult me by denying me my meal for the evening."

Eleni, who had seemed calm, clearly tensed, and glanced at Jayne, still curled in the fetal position, her body trembling.

"What have you done to her?"

"I'm a vampire succubus. I've forced her sex hormones into overdrive. Only sex with me will make it better."

"Why should I believe you?"

"Touch her, fondle her, make her come. See if it relieves her. By all means, try. I like to watch." She sat down and crossed her legs, carefully arranging the dress and smoothing it around her.

Eleni crouched next to Jayne, gently moving her hair from her face. "Jayne, baby, can you hear me?"

Jayne nodded, pressing her face against Eleni's hand. *So good, it feels so good.*

"Baby, I'm sorry to do it this way, but I need to see if she's lying. I need to see if I can take you away from here without doing you harm. Do you trust me?"

Instead of answering, Jayne sucked one of Eleni's fingers into her mouth, sucking it hard and then biting the tip as Eleni withdrew it.

Jayne moaned and began to beg. "Please, god, please Eleni make it stop. Make it go away. Fuck me, please." She could hear herself begging as though from a distance, but the fire between her legs kept her from any rational thought.

She choked back a sob as Eleni slid a hand down her pants and palmed her throbbing crotch, pressing her soaked panties against her. Eleni pressed the heel of her palm against Jayne's clit and moved quickly, but had barely started when an orgasm rocked through Jayne, nearly lifting her entire body off the stone slab. Jayne collapsed back to the stone, only to start riding Eleni's hand again and Eleni saw the pain in her face as the desire only intensified.

She pulled her hand from Jayne's pants, trying to sooth her when she started crying.

"What do you want?" Eleni asked tersely.

"Perhaps we can go back to your little boat and enjoy her together? You are one of the nicest looking vampires I have seen for a very long time, and she is one of the most beautiful mortals. I think it would make for a lovely evening. And then her desire will go, and I will come back to my territory. We all win."

Eleni glanced at Jayne, worried that she had gone still, her body tense. "No death. You leave."

"Excellent. Shall we?" The woman motioned toward the sea.

Gingerly Eleni scooped Jayne into her arms, moaning out loud at the heat and desire emanating from her soft body.

Together the three of them moved through the city at lightning speed, and once at Jayne's boat the succubus took the wheel while Eleni cradled Jayne's trembling, sweat covered body against her own.

Eleni pulled Jayne tighter against her. Although this wasn't the way she wanted it to happen, she would have Jayne tonight, and every night, after this. The thought, mixed with the undeniable intensity of Jayne's desire, sent a flood of wetness through her center.

When the other vampire laughed in delight, clearly scenting Eleni's own arousal, she grimaced. She hated being forced into anything, and the Spanish vamp was forcing her hand with Jayne. But then, there were worse things than having sex with a beautiful vampire and a beautiful mortal at the same time.

They docked the little speedboat against the yacht and Eleni carried Jayne to the salon, where she laid her gently on the thick rug in front of the fireplace. The torn T-shirt fell open, exposing Jayne's amazing breasts and creamy skin.

"Boss? Everything okay?" Anna stepped into the room and stopped abruptly. "I wondered if I would see you here, Maria." She crossed her arms over her chest and shot a nasty grin at the blonde vampire.

"Indeed. It's been a hundred years, Anna. I've missed our fun. Perhaps you would like to join our little party?"

Anna raised an eyebrow at Eleni, who shook her head, and moved to hold Jayne's hands against the rug since she was trying desperately to get Eleni to touch her.

"She's used her powers to turn Jayne into a sex dinner. She says the only way to make it stop is for her to fuck Jayne. Is that true, Skinner?"

"Not exactly. She could make it stop if she wanted to, just by removing the magic. But if she goes away without taking away the magic, Jayne will exist in this state until it kills her. But yes, sex with the one who cast the spell will also cure it, assuming the spell isn't recast."

"Oh, how I've missed you, Anna. We used to have such good times. Come back to Spain, *querida*. Come back and have fun with me," Maria whispered, pushing her body tightly against Anna's, who remained as still as stone with her arms crossed.

"Your type of fun isn't for me, Maria. And if you hurt Jayne, you'll have everyone on this yacht to answer to." Looking past her at Eleni, she said, "If you need me, boss, call me. I'm finished feeding for the night, so I'll hear you. Keep your shields up, and you'll be fine." With that she pushed Maria away from her, none too gently, and slammed the door behind her.

"Let's begin, shall we? Her need is overwhelming, isn't it?" Maria slid her dress from her shoulders, revealing a black leather corset. The dress pooled at her feet like a puddle of rich blood, leaving her in black garters and thigh high stockings, her polished knee-high boots showing her shapely legs.

Eleni grunted in appreciation before letting go of Jayne's hands. "Jayne, I'm going to undress you, love. I'm going to make love to you so this pain goes away. Do you understand?"

"Please, Eleni, Please fuck me. Please make me come. I want you inside me. Please make the pain stop."

Unable to resist any longer, Eleni quickly took the rest of Jayne's clothing off, and then felt her own desire treble at the sight of Jayne's naked body glowing in the firelight. She watched as Maria knelt down next to Jayne and took a nipple in her mouth. Jayne's body arched and one hand tangled in Maria's hair while the other fisted in the rug. Eleni knelt on the other side and took the other nipple in her mouth, groaning when Jayne's hand tangled in her hair, pulling her closer, forcing her mouth down harder.

She slid her hand over Jayne's stomach, and lacing her fingers through Maria's, together they slid their fingers over Jayne's drenched pussy. Jayne was held down only by their mouths continuing to suck and bite at her breasts.

Eleni lead the way, pushing their entwined forefingers inside Jayne, where they set a rocking rhythm that made Jayne orgasm over and over again, her moans and pleas for more echoing through the room. They pressed a second set of fingers inside her and for a moment she was quiet as the pressure filled her.

Maria pushed hard, driving their fingers inside Jayne and moaning along with her as the orgasm ripped through her body, starting low inside her and spinning throughout her soul.

"Now."

Eleni moaned before sinking her teeth into Jayne's breast, drinking blood infused with the aphrodisiac of orgasm, and felt her own orgasm start as she watched Maria do the same thing to Jayne's other breast. They both pulled away at the same time as Jayne's orgasm started to fade and their own orgasms subsided.

Licking her lips and removing the small spatter of Jayne's blood, Maria said, "I'm not done. I want to make use of that beautiful mouth. And I want to watch you fuck her. Make her come. I want to feel her screaming inside me." She straddled Jayne's face, spreading herself open over her mouth and grinding down when Jayne's tongue slid inside her. "Fuck her, Eleni. Now."

Watching as Jayne eagerly licked the vampire's wet center, Eleni moved between Jayne's legs and licked her clit, sucking at it, biting it and then driving her tongue inside her in the same way she was driving her tongue into Maria. Adding three fingers she pushed hard inside Jayne, marveling that the feeling was better than anything she had imagined over the last two years. She was hot, tight, so wet, so deep.

Maria ground down faster and harder on Jayne's mouth, and suddenly she was coming, a deep howl flowing from her as she let go.

Letting go as well, Eleni growled and twisted her fingers inside Jayne, pressing hard against her G-spot and sinking her teeth lightly into Jayne's clit as she orgasmed.

Jayne screamed against the pussy on her mouth, the pleasure nearly ripping her in half, the body over her pumping in the same rhythm as the hand pumping inside her.

The body over her moved away, and as suddenly as it had

hit her, the painful hunger that devoured her was gone, leaving her body aching, sated and sore. She gently placed her hand on Eleni's head, where it was resting against her thigh.

Maria lounged back on her elbows. "That was exactly as good as I thought it would be. If you wanted to stay, you would both be welcome in my home. I think we could have a lovely time of it."

"Thanks, but no. It's time for us to move on. And the sun will be up soon. Perhaps it's time for you to go?" Eleni said pointedly.

"Ah, well. I tried. If you come back to Cartagena, do find me. I haven't had this kind of fun in quite some time." She laughed, and straightening her dress, left the room. The last Jayne saw of her, she had stepped off the deck of the yacht and was walking across the water toward shore.

"Are you okay, love?" Eleni moved to lie next to her, gently caressing her stomach.

"More than okay. That was intense, although I have to say I don't ever want to feel that kind of pain again. I can get horny all on my own, thanks. But the way you touched me...god, Eleni. That was amazing. How was the take tonight?"

Eleni laughed, her crystal-blue eyes lighting up. "Yes, you can get horny on your own. You've been on edge for ages now. Why didn't you come to me? Why go for that silly little human tonight when it's me you want? My touch you need? And the take was truly plentiful tonight. Why?"

"Arrogant, much?" Jayne grinned and moaned when Eleni tweaked her nipple in response. "You told me when you hired me that no one on this boat would touch me, that I was off limits. I figured that meant approaching you was out of the question."

"No, love. I said no one would touch you against your will,

or force you to do anything you didn't want to do. I wasn't dictating your actions—I was dictating theirs."

"You mean I could have gotten laid at any time on this goddamned trip?"

"Yes. But only by me, since the rest of the crew know that I have claimed you. And it's what you want, isn't it? To belong to me, and only me? To have me make love to you whenever you want me?"

"Yes," Jayne whispered as Eleni's hand stroked her slowly. "But that means no more women in your bed, except to feed. Unless I'm invited too. And I asked about the take because I don't want to go to port for a few days. I want you all to myself."

Eleni laughed again, delighted. Jayne was hers, her human companion, and one she would never let go, no matter what port they sailed to, no matter what desires she needed filled. Bending close to Jayne's ear, she slid a finger deep inside her and whispered, "You, and only you, love. That's all I need, forever."

IMPUNDULU

Regina Jamison

It was summer. I remember because I'd had the top down on the car. It was night and very dark in the woods. I wasn't driving. I'd sat in the car with the stars laid out above me. The vastness of the dark sky along with the twinkling abundance soothed me. I'd felt connected, somehow, to that deep void filled with gaseous matter that encircled planets creating fictitious halos and black holes that captured and sucked in one's soul. I felt as if my soul were an asteroid; floating, drifting in the darkness, searching for some force to bring it into the light. I wanted a celestial hand to caress me while spreading moon dust like salve upon my heart.

These were my thoughts when a bolt of lightning blazed in the field to the right of me. There was no sound, only a light so bright the air continued to glow after it had dissipated. I left my car and walked toward it. Before me there was what appeared to be millions of fireflies swarming a wide swath of land. Or maybe it was pieces of burnt paper that resembled butterflies fluttering about on the wind: one half blackened and cold like a dead star, the other half a bright, warm, beautiful ember. I stood there watching and grew warmer. Sweat bubbled up on my brow. The tips of my hair glowed and rushed about my face. There was so much movement and heat. The fireflies swirled and swirled then settled, forming an oval shape like a flame above a wick.

The egg-like shape sparkled and popped with anger. I couldn't believe my eyes. I glanced at the space around me and when I looked back the egg was still there. I walked its circumference wanting to touch it. I felt as if something were calling me, wanting me to burn in its iridescence. But I shoved my hands into my pants pockets and stepped back, then back again. I found the safety of darkness. My knees trembled. My legs shook as the ground gave way around me. I bent over slightly for balance but my legs collapsed, pitching me forward into the high grass. The rumbling continued as the ground shook and buckled around me.

With dirt on my chin, I stood. I looked up, whipped around and looked behind me. Nothing! No light. No fireflies. No glowing egg. I walked to where the egg had been and found a great hole. A path of crumbled dirt, like something had burrowed underground, stretched out from it and made its way toward the lake. I could have followed, but I ran back to my car, turned the key, and jettisoned myself into that black hole called night.

I couldn't sleep so I paced. I grew tired so I sat. I became weary of sitting, so I painted. Large, looming eggs filled the canvases like disembodied pupils probing; fiery eyes whose centers burned. I had to get it down. I closed my eyes and it was before me again—the egg from the field. It shimmered and pulsated to a beat whose rhythm spoke my name—*Li-lith, Li-lith*. I heard it moan in a deep and terrible bass that rattled my bones.

Quickly, I opened my eyes. *This means something*, I thought. I didn't know what, but I had to get it down. The egg was more than an egg; it was a life. I had felt it, could still feel it burrowing inside of me. I had to get it down, get it right. I could feel it growing; it wanted something. More paint. I needed more paint!

I created picture after picture and with each I felt as if I were nourishing a life. Each stroke was a placental strand connecting me to it. My hands shook; my vision blurred; I was tired but I couldn't stop. A hand, perhaps a foot was being formed within a shell. Now a leg. Now an arm. Its eyes opened, then its mouth. Again, it moaned my name and my throat filled with metallic bile.

The urge to create had passed. I'd given it life; my job was complete. My brush dropped to the floor. I took a canvas from the stand and cradled it. Something that loved me was born.

Once again the waters are upon me. My shell softens, collapses, then shrivels up like sugar in a warm glass. She has summoned me again—not with incantations and spells this time, but with her mind; dreaming me into existence so I can be with her. The colors she uses, they guide me. Each stroke is matched to the beat of her heart; the sound of a drum from long ago. Each stroke forms the path.

I am growing rapidly; shedding the membrane that once encased me. I begin to feel warm as the down of my feathers envelops me like the blanket that it is. My claws harden and grow sharp, quickly securing me further upon this tree from which I hang.

Finally, I open my eyes to the night. I can see crickets and cicadas running through the grass below me. I hear a faint rustle and spot a bird rushing late to his nest. I can smell the fish that swim in the lake from which I was born. I spread my wings, casting great shadows that darken the ground further. All becomes quiet for they know; they can feel my great strength.

I am Impundulu; the one who remembers. I open my mouth and a sound like no other is set forth. Maybe she will hear it and this time she will recognize her name. But perhaps she has, again, taken another as her lover.

Many days have passed since I first saw the egg, and as the week closes, I begin to wonder if I ever saw such a thing at all. Perhaps my longing for a difference in my life and a desire for change had overpowered me. Perhaps it was only a dream. Ingrid says dreams can creep into our reality, making our hearts race and our legs part. This I know, but still, what I felt was different.

"You seem bored, perhaps a glass of wine to begin your fantasy?"

I turned toward the voice and it turned into a vision of beauty. Lips full, as if pouting, filled a small yet strong angular face. Her brow ran straight across her almond-shaped eyes like a cliff above raging pools. Her hair had been shorn from her head leaving only a smooth reminder of it in its place. And while her eyes blazed like lightning, her skin gleamed as if polished and darkened to the deepest depths of blackness, and then smoothed and smoothed again until it was like the finest silky velvet clinging to the sharp bones of her face. She held a tall glass in her hand and her eyes to mine.

I had no choice but to accept.

"Thank you." I looked around to see if Ingrid, my friend and host of the party, was anywhere about. I saw her across the room leaning into the arms of a woman I did not know. The woman whispered in Ingrid's ear and she laughed.

"What else may I do for you?"

I smiled at Ingrid's joy and at this woman's insistence. "You've done too much already."

"Nonsense, my servitude has only begun. I am called Impundulu." She bowed deeply at the waist then stood straight. She was very tall and lean.

"Impundulu?"

"That is correct."

"It's an odd name, no?"

"Quite, here in the states, but back home it is widely known."

"And home is?"

"South Africa. Have you been?"

"No, I haven't."

"A pity, but the future is wide and full."

She smiled, and the fire in her eyes grew larger, forming tiny golden egg shapes like the giant one I had seen. I was captured by their glow.

"They call you?"

"Lilith." I put out my hand for her to shake. She turned it and placed a small kiss on the pulse of my wrist leaving her imprint behind.

I touched this brand upon my skin, traced the mark of those lips, and it felt hot. My wrist burned, but with a contained heat that knew its goal. It spread out from my hand to the fingers that caressed it, then made its way up to my heart. I was momentarily frightened when a new feeling overtook me—desire.

"It is a pleasure...Lilith." And I saw the same passion that had seized me take shape in her eyes, then dance about her face like so many little fires burning.

When she said my name it was...it was as if I couldn't breathe from being thrown into too much oxygen. There was abundance with deprivation crowding its corners. I couldn't speak.

"Tell me, Lilith, have you ever swum in the sea at night?"

"No, I haven't."

"Have you ever plunged through a cloud while it wept?"

My gaze had been on her face but now I *really* looked at her. Who *was* this woman? And what was she doing to me? "You play with me with your silly questions. Surely, no one has done the latter."

"Oh, but someone has."

"And I suppose that someone is you?"

She smiled and reached for me. "Come, we are at a party and yet only occupy a corner. What will the host think? We should dance." She linked her arm around mine as we turned toward the main room. Her long cape arched and swooshed just as the music began.

It was a Brazilian piece with deep sobbing drums that pounded my heart into submission. I had never before been enamored by a woman, but she was more than a woman. Impundulu was an entity, a force. I don't know how I knew this, but I did. I was so thoroughly mesmerized I fell into her arms and she held me. Her cape swaddled me, softening the blows from the rhythm.

She held me around my waist as we seemingly floated around the room. Her chin rested near my ear, and the dampness of her neck amplified her scent. It was a smell I knew. A familiar yet disturbing scent that begged me to remember something more but I could not. A warm, metallic scent rose up like a wall before me then it spilled into my throat, and I recalled this same taste from the day I painted the egg with fury. Suddenly, I felt great hunger and great pain. I gulped it down, all of it.

"You move with such ease," I said.

"It is you who moves me." She spun me around, then plunged

me toward the ground into a terrifying dip. I held on tight, clasping her hands as if they were a ledge and my salvation. But it was her eyes that saved me. They showed no fear, only promise and hope as she gazed down at me. It was this that I held on to.

Like a whip I was snapped back up into her arms. She held me close, her lips next to mine—mocking me. Do I dare? Would she? She leaned in closer. I turned my head, pretending to glance about the room. From the corner of my eye I saw her smile.

She pressed deeper into me. I felt her body aligned with mine and with great speed and dexterity she parted my legs with one of her own, lifted me, and rubbed me across the span of her thigh.

A great heat began to build there that was so innate and self-directed I found my hips tracing that same path up and down, over and over on their own. When I realized what was happening, I lost control over myself once again. But by then my face was as hot as the rest of me. I turned my head the other way so Impundulu could not see my wantonness.

She threw her head back and laughed as she lowered me down then twirled me away. "To dance with you is divine; exactly what I had imagined, but now we should take our leave. Tell me that you will accompany me."

"I'm not sure that I should. I...I don't really know you." I was still embarrassed by my former actions.

"You know me, Lilith."

"I...I feel as if I do, but..."

"You *know me*, Lilith." She said this firmly, with much conviction and a hint of impatience.

Before I could protest her lips were on mine, then our tongues did meet. I tried to pull away but she held me in a deep embrace, and the world around us began to spin. We twirled and twirled smashing through centuries. The outside world was a blur until finally it simply fell away. We had spun into another time, another world, a different party.

I looked around me. Nothing was as it once was; the people were different, their clothing and hair different. The women were draped in gowns that pushed their breasts out on top and cinched their waists tightly. And their behinds seemed to billow out like those tremendous growths one sees upon a tree.

"What...what have you done? Where am I?"

"We are where we were."

"Impossible! Look at this place, this room, the music, the people. Oh, my god, where's Ingrid? We were at her party."

"Do not fear, Lilith. We are where we were. We have only traveled back to a time where once you knew me; where, once, I was foremost in your mind. Do you remember, Lilith? Look around and try to remember."

I looked about the place. Chandeliers filled with candles hung low from the ceiling. On the tables, placed here and there, were candelabras. A small orchestra of violins, flutes and harps played on a small stage by a window, and the floor was filled with women—women dancing arm in arm and cheek to cheek to the music. There were women huddled in corners kissing the soft flesh of others that spilled out from the tops of low-cut dresses. Some women wore hats, pants and topcoats. They walked with the hard stride of a man but the softness of their faces marked them as women. There was a lady who looked like Ingrid, and she too was leaning into the arms of another woman while smiling.

"I do not know this place," I said.

"Do not use your mind but your senses; you must try to feel this place, this time. Hold my hand, close your eyes and search your heart."

I did as she asked.

"We lived here once, you and I. This house belonged to us. We had many parties like this where we danced and fell, continually, in love. We walked along the bayous at night and made love during the day. I held you in my arms, felt the flood of your desire and fed you when you were too tired to feed. We'd spent centuries together here. We were happy and in love. You must try to remember, Lilith. I've come to you in many places, many regions, many moments in time wanting to extend our love through the centuries and each time you must be made to remember. I wish you would not forget."

As she spoke I imagined her words. I saw us as we swept across the dance floor—me in a purple velvet gown folded into Impundulu's arms. I saw us in a huge room, on a huge bed with an elaborately draped canopy. There were many shadows on the walls. I was naked, on all fours, and calling out. Impundulu was positioned behind me; there was a woman under me and another on the bed beside her. There was a warm metallic smell. Iron, I believe. I was drawn to it. I needed it. Then...I saw it...blood. My mouth was filled with its slippery warmth. It spilled out and spattered on the collarbone of the woman below me, creating a large array of freckles. The woman's mouth was twisted and grotesque, but it didn't matter. It was the blood that was important.

Impundulu stopped talking and I was ripped from my reverie. Tears marked my cheeks.

"Is it true? Are you, we, the monsters that you've shown me?"

"I have only shown you your true nature, Lilith."

"No! That is not me! Was not me!"

"It is who I am. It is who you are, and it was you who summoned me. I am but one thing, Lilith, but you...you are much more and so when you have called me through the years, I came."

"I don't believe you!" A sob so great it shook me escaped from my chest. I covered my face with my hands as if to block out the shame.

"Why do you cry, Lilith?" She stroked my hair like a child. I let her.

"The blood...the blood...was everywhere. And that woman..."

"She had given herself freely. She knew her role."

"I don't care! That is not me! That is not who I am!"

"Oh, but it is. Come, let's go back farther." She took my hand gently in hers, pulled my head into her chest and kissed the hair on top of it.

There is tenderness in abomination, I thought.

A flute trilled a high ghostly command as Impundulu pulled at her cape and threw it over us like the great lid of a coffin.

When she released me, we stepped carefully into the night as if it were alive, stalking us. Unseen eyes and claws scurried about the darkness filling the wind with their desires. I shivered. She pulled me closer.

A great darkness loomed before us like the shoulder of hell. "Where are we now? And what is this deep void before me?"

"Feel it, Lilith. Open yourself up to it. Listen to the sounds around you; hear, taste and smell the beauty of the night as it is in this place."

I tried, but the darkness was like an evil pressing down upon me. It bruised me to simply stand before it.

"I can't," I said. "I can't."

Impundulu lifted her hand and we rose up toward the stars. I clung to her while looking down to where we once had been. We landed on a jagged rock that jutted out from a cliff.

"This is Drakensberg or the great Dragon's Mountain. We are in South Africa where you and I began."

There was a clap of thunder and nearby a lion roared. The valley seemed to swell with fog. Impundulu lifted her hand again. We plunged through the swell of the milky whiteness and landed in a village. A great darkness crouched about us; its shoulders hunched angrily about its ears. Women, their faces covered by masks but their breasts bare, danced about in a circle close to a fire kicking up dust with their feet. The children held sticks that, when shaken, rattled and hissed at the night. Farthest from the fire, playing drums, were men, covered in dark mud to match their dark skin.

They blended so thoroughly with the night that it was as if the drums beat out a rhythm on their own.

In the center, surrounded by the village and closest to the flame, stood a woman with glowing eyes. On her head she wore a crown of feathers. Her arms, too, were covered in feathers that caught the firelight. I saw colors ripple across them. Reds, blues, purples, greens—they were all injected and punctuated by the light. The woman danced out the beat from the drums while flapping her wings, which fanned the flames that grew higher. She yelled some words in a language that pierced me, and the villagers responded. She yelled more words, moved her feet in a staggering fashion, and the villagers answered back. The men beat their drums faster, clouds of dust hovered above the women's feet, and the children shook their sticks with vigor. The air grew thick around us. It darted and moved about like a blind man. I held on tightly to Impundulu's hand while ducking my head.

"What is it? What has happened to the air?"

"It has sent forth bats to do what it cannot—dance to the rhythm of the diviner, the witch. It is she who commands the sky. Look upon her, Lilith. Does she not seem familiar?"

The woman's body shook and her feathers ruffled and fell, ruffled and fell, like a wave. The drummers sped up, the women's legs moved faster, the children threw their bodies around because their arms were no longer enough.

This new speed moved me. It unlocked something inside; I dropped Impundulu's hand.

The diviner slowly turned her back to the night and toward me. Her eyes were flames that burned into mine and through the heat I indeed saw something familiar...an essence, a spirit, a glimpse of my soul. I knew then that this witch was me many centuries ago when I first sought out Impundulu, when I first called her to my side.

I warmed to the heat of her dancing and felt engulfed in the flames from the fire before me. She strutted around the fire toward me, then she came closer still. I readied myself to move, but Impundulu held me.

"Stay and remember. Know thyself."

My soul was before me. She spread her wings and with this movement came a metallic dust siphoned from planets and thrown into the air. It swirled about then settled on me.

Instantly, I became lightheaded. I moved to fall but it was as if the sound of the drums pulled me up. I leaned on and into the beat. My feet began to move first in the intricate patterns of the circled women, then more like the staggered strut of the diviner. She danced toward the fire and I followed. It was the remembering that connected us. Her arms swayed, her hips bucked, as did mine. We were reflections or moments within the same beat. I felt a freedom, a knowing that I hadn't experienced in a very long time.

One by one the women came up to us and flung themselves on the ground. Now I knew what to do.

The witch stood behind me calling out and fanning the flames while I lay upon each woman who writhed and moaned along with me. I sucked their breasts, inserted fingers between their legs, feeling the sea that lay within; the sea that held the golden egg. I put my lips to their fountains and drank. They opened up for me, offering their divine elixir, and I ate from every one of them. My face glistened. My tongue was numb, but I remembered.

I turned and walked to Impundulu. "You have united me with my soul."

"Yes."

"You have shown me memories of you and I."

"Yes."

"Once, I had given you life and now you repay me."

"We give birth to each other, Lilith, over and over again."

"Yes." I looked into her eyes. I longed to touch her. Her smooth, dark skin caught and played with the firelight. I ran my fingers over her sharp cheekbones hoping to be cut.

She grabbed my hand, kissed the wrist until the flesh singed and flaked away. I was filled with a great desire for her. I pulled her mouth to mine and our tongues met creating small sparks that blazed. The beat of the drum grew faster still, but it was farther away now.

Impundulu tore at my dress revealing my nakedness beneath. I slipped her cape to the ground and pulled at the buttons on her shirt. They popped and squealed when they met with the flames. I was presented with her breasts. They were small but full and sharp like her lips and cheeks. Her nipples were large dark moons cast over a black night. I licked them; they seemed to sparkle, and Impundulu pulled me closer.

Breast upon breast she held me, tracing the small of my back with her soft hands, following the curve of my ass as it reached out into the night. I shivered and lowered her pants in a single movement. She stepped out of them. Her legs were long like slender trees with a silky bush between. She pulled me down onto her cape, laid me flat and looked upon me as I looked upon her.

"I am so glad to have you with me again...fully, Lilith. So glad."

"Yes, Impundulu." I pulled her mouth onto mine; deeper and deeper our tongues searched. I felt as if I could not breathe.

She lay on top of me, parted my legs, and pushed her hips between. I felt her bush hot, wet and dripping into mine. I pushed down on her ass. Her lower lips spread and I felt her clit as it pushed against mine. Like puffed-up swords they battered against each other causing me to rock and moan with immense pleasure.

The drums beat faster still; Impundulu knew the rhythm. She pushed and ground her hips into mine, and I did the same to her. A great volcano was being built between us. I wrapped my legs around her waist; with three fingers she entered me. My back arched. I bit her neck. She growled and entered me with increased pressure. I met each thrust with my hips lifted far from the ground. She was so deep inside of me, it was as if she were grabbing at my heart.

I bit her again. She growled louder, then bit me; her teeth and hands sank into softness. I thrust higher into the air both wanting more and wanting to explode into a million stars, wanting to fill that black hole with the results of desire.

"Oh, Impundulu!" I yelled into the night. "I'm going to explode!"

"Then we will do so together."

Her hand pressed deeper into the surrounding walls and I spread my legs wider, reaching them higher onto her back.

Her hips moved against mine with such wanting, such desire, I couldn't hold back any longer, neither could she.

"I am yours forever," I said.

"As you have been, my love, as long as one of us remembers."

NIGHT AT THE WAX MUSEUM

Delilah Devlin

12:02 A.M.—Remind V. H. to call the exterminators. Rats, again, in the vicinity of the freak show exhibit!

Krista Pike clicked the end of her ballpoint pen, slid the small spiral notebook into her pocket and clipped the pen in her uniform lapel. Then she slipped her Mag light from its holster, picked up a sturdy broom and went in search of the rodent.

For the third night in a row her nerves were wired tighter than an M-16's recoil spring. They shouldn't have been. The security company that'd hired her told her that other than some minor vandalism to the museum's windows and door, this shift should be a cakewalk.

"Tell that to the fucking rats."

A skittering sounded behind her. She spun and aimed her light toward the floor. Nothing. As she raised the beam, it caught the exhibit. Light flickered in the eyes of the wax figure lying in the open coffin—a scene straight out of a horror movie, created especially for the Halloween crowd.

She shivered at the tableau: a raven-haired vampire with red glassy eyes and milky-white skin; the tops of her breasts exposed above the black, corseted gown; not a hint of color in her or the white-satin-lined coffin other than blood-red paint on her full lips. Above her, the vampire hunter stood with arms raised, a hammer and a wooden stake in his hands, ready to puncture her chest. The setting surrounding the two figures was straight Hollywood kitsch—a gnarled tree, an open pit readied for the coffin and a tall Celtic cross knocked at an angle.

The overhead track light beamed directly on the vampire's face, and her glass eyes appeared to be fixed right on Krista.

She shivered, and aimed the beam back to the ground, unsure which creeped her out more now, the rats or the red glowing lights the artist had placed behind the wax figure's eye sockets.

She moved along, scuffing her feet to make enough noise to scare away any critters looking for discarded scraps of popcorn or candy bars that patrons of the wax museum had tossed.

Damn nerves. She needed to make an appointment with her VA shrink to up her meds. Problem solved.

It was a total pisser she still needed those damn happy pills. Until she had a clean bill of health, the PD wouldn't clear her for duty again. And there was no way she wanted to return full-time to the force without being whole. Eighteen months in Afghanistan had left her in little broken bits. Shattered hip. Shattered mind.

A year of therapy—for the bones and her mushed brain— and she still wasn't one hundred percent. Not when a goddamn rat could spook her like this.

She was tempted to hit the utility closet and turn on all the lights just as she had last night, but the manager had chewed her ass for wasting electricity. She was stuck with the thin beams illuminating the exhibits, making the surrounding darkness feel dense and alive.

Another shiver shook her. "Fuck this," she bit out, pissed at herself for letting the place get to her. Maybe she should move on to the presidents. Nothing scary there other than the looming height and craggy face of Honest Abe.

The skittering sounded again, behind her. She spun and crouched, flashlight held like a nightstick, the broom like a sword, blood pumping every bit as hard as when her squad had come under fire in Kandahar. She'd shimmied under a burned-out van only to discover she didn't have enough room between the road and the vehicle's undercarriage to effectively return fire. She'd scooted back the way she'd come, but the battle was already over. Or so she'd thought. Kneeling beside Randy Hays's body, she'd caught a round in her ass, another in her torso, which the Kevlar ate, but the impact had still been strong enough to knock the breath out of her.

"Fuck this," she repeated, her voice sounding every bit as hollow as her resolve. Her beam caught the edge of the coffin, glared on the white lining of the lid. She moved on—then swung her light back to the bed of the casket. It was empty.

Not a goddamn rat. Someone else was inside the museum and playing a nasty trick.

"Not fucking funny," she said, straightening and aiming her voice around the room.

Soft laughter came from right behind her, and Krista punched her elbow backward and whirled, but again saw nothing except for a blur of gray.

Her breath caught. Nothing moved that fast.

Straightening, she tossed down the broom. "I know you're here," she said, deepening her voice, hoping whoever or whatever it was couldn't tell how freaked she was.

"I've been watching you," came a feminine, singsong voice.

Krista jerked, then cursed herself for giving away her fear. "Come out of the shadows. I'll walk you to the door and let you leave. I won't call it in."

"How sweet." The voice was girlish, almost childlike, but with an undertone of menace that chilled Krista to the bone. "Why do you limp?"

Krista breathed deeply, calming her heart. The voice had come from near the door leading to the Marilyn exhibit. Krista didn't know if the woman had a weapon or was just a thrill seeker. There wasn't anything of value inside the museum other than big wax dolls. Nothing irreplaceable. The cash box was cleaned out every night after closing. "Why'd you move the vampire?"

Another laugh. This one so close the hairs on the back of her neck stirred.

"Pretty boy, I didn't take it."

"I'm not a boy," Krista said, more to keep the conversation going than because she'd been offended.

"But you act like one. Even walk like one."

"I was a soldier."

"And they made you walk that way?"

"I don't have girly hips."

A hand cupped one notch of her uninjured hip from behind. A citrusy-floral scent tickled her nose. Something wet slid down the side of her neck. A tongue. Panic shivered down her spine.

"Not boy's hips." A hand trailed down the front of her pants, and fingers traced her split. "Not a boy's anything at all."

Krista didn't know why she stayed so still. She wasn't a superstitious person; didn't believe in ghosts or God. But she knew in her gut whatever was behind her wasn't human. As fast as the thing had moved, she couldn't outrun it. "You're that woman in the coffin, aren't you?"

"Not stupid like a boy either. Not like the last one."

"The last guard?"

"They didn't tell you?"

Krista shook her head. "I wasn't told why he had to be replaced." Fingers walked across the top of her shoulder and up her neck, pads skimming over her thudding pulse. Krista swayed, her eyelids dipped.

"Poor thing couldn't hold his bladder. All I had to do was blow in his ear and he'd shriek—"

"Like a girl?"

The laugh this time sounded more natural. Hands drew away.

She blinked and the raven-haired creature stood in front of her, her gaze studying Krista's face. "You're different."

"Than what? There are other female guards employed by Security Systems."

"Not what I meant. You're not frightened of me."

"Sure I am, but the rats creeped me out more."

"Rats won't kill you."

"I'm not afraid of dying."

The woman stepped closer, tilting her head to gaze up into Krista's eyes. "I can see that. But why?"

Krista felt her throat close up and cleared it. "Dying's easy."

The woman lifted her lips in a snarl, exposing the twin points of her upper canines. "For some, perhaps." She turned toward the windows at the front of the museum. "It's morning."

"It's just after midnight," Krista said, raising her arm to glance at her watch, but it was 6:30 A.M. "What the...?"

When she glanced back up, the woman was gone. Krista darted a glance at the exhibit. The woman was falling back into the coffin, as though in slow motion, her hair and gown billowing, then settling around her.

Krista dipped beneath the velvet ropes surrounding the exhibit, ignoring the twinge in her hip, and climbed onto the platform. She bent over the woman as she clasped her hands over her stomach. Their gazes locked for a moment, and then life left the vampire's eyes.

She lay still. Silent.

Krista cupped her fingers beneath the woman's nose. No breath. Her chest lay unmoving. She touched her lips. Hard and cold.

Drawing back, she gazed down. "But you didn't tell me your name."

The next night, Krista arrived at 6:15 P.M. "You're late," the manager said, frowning.

"Sorry about that. Got caught in traffic." A lie, but she didn't want to admit she'd fought a battle with herself that she'd lost. When she'd rolled out of bed, her hand had gone to the phone, ready to quit. She'd even punched the numbers to the office, but she'd hesitated.

She'd convinced herself she'd imagined the whole thing. A drug-induced dream. Then she'd dumped her meds into the toilet. Last night couldn't be real.

Still, once the door closed behind her, she headed straight to the horror exhibits. Everything was just as it had been. The woman stretched out in the coffin, unmoving, looking as waxy pale as any other life-sized wax figure.

However, this wax doll was different. Every detail perfect from the fine, feminine down on her cheeks and sparse nose hairs to the girly parts no visitor to the museum would ever see.

She'd cupped the front of the vampire hunter's crotch and found it smooth. The artist hadn't bothered to create genitalia where it would be hidden beneath clothing. When she'd played with the vampire's silk bodice, plucking it to peer beneath the fabric, she'd found perfectly rendered nipples—painted a lovely, rosy pink. Feeling like a perv, she'd backed off the platform before she'd given into the urge to check beneath the figure's skirt.

Hours rolled by and nothing happened. Disappointment weighed down her shoulders. Part of her had wanted last night's experience to be real. Not just because she didn't want to be crazy, but because she wanted to see the woman again. She glanced at her watch. It was almost midnight. Krista had a thought and pulled her notepad from her pocket. She'd heard the "rats" for the first time just after midnight.

Maybe that was it.

Afraid and anxious, she climbed onto the platform and approached the coffin. She knelt beside it, glancing up at the figure of the vampire hunter with the stake clutched in his hand. "What's it feel like to wake every night staring up at that?"

"Frightening."

Krista shot a glance to the woman whose eyes were open, red light flashing in her pupils before it faded.

"You came back," the woman said, her voice soft and lyrical.

"I'm not some guy who pees his pants over a little thing like talking to a vampire."

The woman stretched her arms high and sighed. "It was nice. Waking up to see you instead of him," she said, wrinkling her nose at the figure poised above them both.

"What's your name?" Krista blurted, then felt heat creep across her cheeks.

"Mina. Yours?"

"Krista."

Mina held out her hand and Krista grasped it. The hand was cold, but warming fast inside hers. "Let me help you up."

Feeling clumsy, Krista straightened, then reached out to help Mina from the coffin.

Their gazes locked for a long moment. Then with her cheeks flushing a delicate rose, Mina stepped over the edge and hopped over the ropes to the floor.

Not nearly as graceful, Krista followed. "I don't understand something."

Mina's chin lifted. "What do you want to know?"

"Last night. Time passed quick. One minute it's just after midnight. But then it's morning."

Mina walked around her, then leaned in from behind, her hands cupping Krista's shoulders. Her hair brushed the side of Krista's neck. Lips caressed her there.

"When I stood behind you yesterday," Mina whispered, "it wasn't just for a moment. I drank from you."

"Drank. As in you sucked my blood? Why didn't I feel it?"

"I wanted to linger. I bespelled you."

"Bespelled? As in, you cast a spell?"

"Not like a witch's chant, but more of a suggestion as I fed."

"Five hours worth? You need a bigger straw."

Mina chuckled, her warm breath gusting against Krista's ear. "No. I did other things too."

"What other things?"

A gray blur whooshed around her.

Mina stood close to Krista's chest. Her gaze fell. "I was curious about you." When she looked up, amusement glinted in her eyes. "I took out your notebook with your scribbles about rats."

"Reading that wouldn't take hours."

"I opened your shirt."

Krista's breath caught.

"When I pushed up the binding—"

"It's called a sports bra."

"When I pushed up the sports bra to see your breasts, I had to play with them."

"Was I a zombie while you did this?"

"You stood still, but you moaned when I touched you here," she said, rubbing a finger against her shirt, right above her nipple.

The nipple sprang, beading tightly.

Mina plucked it with her fingers, then leaned closer and bit the tip poking through the cotton with her smaller, human-sized teeth.

Krista rocked on her heels, drawing a quick, sharp breath between pursed lips. "You couldn't have spent hours doing... that."

"There was more." Mina toyed with the waist of Krista's pants, tucking a finger inside the waistband and pulling her closer. "I pushed down your pants and your white panties. I tasted you there, then had to taste again and again. You came when I allowed it. Gasping. You cried when I finished. I bit you here," Mina said, rubbing a finger in the crease between thigh and labia.

"Now I know you're telling a story. I don't cry during sex."

Mina cocked her head and gave a wicked smile. "You did for me."

Krista caught the hand rubbing between her folds and pulled it away. She stepped back. "You can't do that again."

The vampire clasped her hands together over her narrow waist. She cleared her throat. "Which part?" she asked softly. "Feed?"

Krista dragged in a deep breath, decision already made. "You can't make me forget."

Mina's features tightened. "But you would feel pain."

"I won't mind."

Mina shook her head. "You say that now."

"Again, I'm not some boy who's gonna pee his pants."

Mina's gaze dropped away.

"How often do you have to do that?"

"Feed?"

"Yes."

"At least once a week, or I get cranky," she said, with a crooked smile.

"Which is why the guards only lasted a week."

A dark winged brow arched. "You checked?"

"Of course. Not that I was sure any of this was real. But if it was, I wanted to understand. And now, since you denied me that knowledge..."

"You want me to take you now? Do it again, so that you know what you missed?"

Krista swallowed hard. "I don't want blood on my clothes."

Mina's pinched expression eased. "I wish we had a bed."

"The Marilyn exhibit—"

"Is in another hall. I can't leave this one."

"Why?"

Mina shook her head. "I just can't."

Krista blew out a deep breath as she thought about the problem. "There's a recliner in the employees' lounge. I'll be right back. You'll still be here?"

"I won't go anywhere. I can't."

Krista sped through the museum, marveling at the spurt of energy and her ease of movement. Her injury, for once, didn't consume her thoughts. She wrestled the brown vinyl chair onto a handcart and rolled it into Mina's hall. "If we keep it on the cart..."

"I understand."

Krista blinked and Mina was already sitting on an arm of the chair. She grinned. "I could get used to that."

"Looks like you have already." Mina patted the seat. "After you've undressed."

Well, Mina had already checked her out while she was zombified. Must not have been too disappointed. Krista shucked her utility belt, hanging it on a branch of the gnarled tree. She toed off her shoes, unbuckled her uniform trousers, then stripped off her shirt and pants. Standing in her underwear, she blew out a deep breath, then unsnapped her bra and let it slide down her arms.

Mina's gaze dropped to her chest, then lifted. Again, she arched a delicate brow.

The white panties went faster. She knew what she looked like: tall, boyish athletic build with straight shoulders, a narrow waist and a small round bottom; a far cry from Mina's feminine curves.

Mina patted the seat again. "Sit that pretty little butt right here, Officer Pike."

The fake leather was cold under her cheeks, but the look in Mina's eyes as she slid over Krista's lap, straddling her thighs, melted her core. Hunger burned in her dark gaze.

Mina went to work, pulling at the petticoats bunched between them until the last thin cotton layer was removed. Steamy, naked pussies aligned.

Mina leaned closer, her mouth so close to Krista's that her breaths brushed Krista's lips like a caress. "Want something else to feel while I taste?"

Krista nodded, her tongue glued to the roof of her mouth.

Mina gave her a wicked smile and pulled the ruffled edge of her blouse below her breasts to tuck into the top of her corset.

Krista's mouth watered in an instant at the sight of her ample breasts with their perfect, pink areolas. The tips were just beginning to spike. Eagerly, Krista raised her hands and palmed them both, hefting the mounds, then sliding a thumb over the nubs. They were small, but growing harder.

Mina cupped the back of one Krista's hands, trapping it against her. "Want it?"

"Yeah, I do. Right here in my mouth."

Mina let go and leaned over Krista, her hands flattening on the cushion at either side of Krista's head. She aimed her breast, rubbing the tip along Krista's lower lip.

Krista snaked out her tongue and lapped the swollen bead. Then she latched on to it, sucking it, pulling with her lips until Mina thrust her hand into her hair and held her there. She feasted on that warm, hardening nub, rubbing it, teething it gently. Then she backed away, staring at the reddened tip. "I want something, before you take that bite."

"Anything, Krista." Mina gasped and arched her back, rubbing her pussy on Krista's mound. "I'm feeling generous."

Krista reached for the lever at the side of the chair, raised the foot, then clutched the arms and pushed the back until it lay nearly flat. She scooted down, sliding beneath Mina. "I want you to strip, then turn around and put your pussy on my mouth."

"But we'll topple the chair."

"Not if you don't move too much. Balance yourself." She helped Mina strip away the layers of fabric, then turn. She held her hips while her round ass lifted and Mina scooted clumsily back.

The chair rocked. They both held still. Then Mina giggled. "I'll have to move lower."

"Lie down over me. Spread your legs wide—hang them over

the sides if you have to. I want that cunt on my mouth."

The bottom in front of her face inched back. Mina's hands landed on Krista's knees, and she stretched out to distribute her weight. She spread her legs, and her pussy landed on Krista's chest.

Krista stuck her arms beneath Mina's thighs and tugged her higher. Mina was spread, at her mercy, her pussy on Krista's chin.

Krista slid her fingers in the creases between thighs and labia and rubbed up and down. The sex-slick lips parted, pulling the pink inner petals open, exposing her entrance.

Krista ducked her chin and rubbed her lips all over the thickened outer labia, smoothing kisses north and south, nuzzling into Mina's sex to draw in the vampire's fragrant musk.

Her own body was wound so tight, so hard. Her nipples ached and her sex was juicy and making lush, wet sounds. She scissored her thighs together, rubbing them and her labia. Then she eased them open beneath Mina, who was rubbing her cheek on her thigh.

"You can't bite. Not until I say so," Krista rasped.

"Who knew you'd be the mean one?" Mina dug her chin between her folds.

Krista curved two fingers and thrust them into Mina while she licked at the bottom of her folds, lapping over the tiny hood. She twisted the digits, tunneling them inside, then pulling away, digging in again and again until Mina's buttocks tightened, and she pumped her hips up and down, giving Krista more sensory delight than she could stand.

She grabbed a buttock and pinched it, then smacked it with her open palm while continuing to lick and suck and thrust.

Arousal seeped from Mina, and Krista licked it up, rubbing her tongue in the creamy film. She cupped four fingers together, curving them, then pushed them into Mina, who stiffened for a moment before undulating.

Mina's entire body shuddered. Her pussy gave moist, lewd caresses as it clenched around Krista's fingers. Mina sank deeper between Krista's legs to tongue her folds.

The sounds, the heavy scent of Mina's steamy cunt, the feel of her from the inside—hot and raw and lush—pushed Krista over the edge. She climaxed, giving a muffled cry. "Now, now, Mina!"

Sharp stings, like being gouged by an ice pick, halted Krista's orgasm. She bucked and writhed, trying to escape the bite, but Mina held firm, her hands pushing Krista's knees flat.

Krista dug in her heels, vibrating against the pain, her head digging into the upholstered squabs as she hissed between her teeth.

She'd sliced her, on either side of her cunt, digging her fangs into the creases as she squeezed her thighs together, her lower jaw biting her labia, not piercing, but clamping to hold her still.

Krista became aware of other sensations. Those lower teeth began to chew, gently. Lips suctioned against her, pulling her blood from other parts of her body, straight to her cunt in a thrilling, icy-hot rush. Her clit swelled, becoming achingly hard. A finger tapped it, then tapped it again—and just that quickly, Krista was there again, riding that rollercoaster, taking the deep bend then soaring high, pushing her pussy against Mina's mouth, begging her silently to take more and more.

But Mina disengaged, panting over her ravaged cunt.

Krista was breathing hard, her chest weighed down by Mina's ass, reminding her of the glorious gift parked an inch from her mouth. She licked her, cunt to asshole, a long wet slide of tongue that was followed by another and another until Mina keened and ground her pussy on Krista's mouth.

Krista suckled Mina's clit, pulling on the tiny erect nub, pulling hard enough to stretch it and get her lips around the base. Then she didn't let go, teething it, licking the tip with her tongue inside her mouth, until Mina sobbed and quivered, stiffened, then slowly collapsed in a wet puddle.

"Hey. C'mon over here," Krista whispered.

Mina lifted her head, turned. Her eyes glowed red and stayed that way.

Krista should have been frightened by the wild, feral glance. Instead she opened her arms.

When Mina snuggled against her chest, her nose nuzzling her neck, Krista didn't give a shit whether Mina took another bite to finish her or not.

There were worse things than dying.

Not having Mina again might be that one thing worse.

"So, explain why you can't leave this place," Krista asked Mina three days later.

Her lover stirred inside her arms, rubbing her cheek against her breast like a kitten rooting at her mother's teat. Her tongue gave the wet nipple beside her mouth another slippery swipe. "I'm trapped."

"By whom?"

"Your manager. Asshole has a grudge. And a terrible sense of humor."

Krista tugged a long lock of Mina's hair. "How can I help? How can I free you?"

"You've already done so much for me. I haven't been happier in forever." She sighed and slid her thighs to either side of Krista's hips, sliding deeper on the dildo Krista had strapped to the harness she'd worn beneath her uniform, a surprise that had delighted Mina to no end.

Mina's blissful expression as she rocked forward and back didn't end Krista's inquiry. They'd spent aimless nights in each other's arms, but this night before Mina had awoken, Krista had been taunted with thoughts of more. She bracketed Mina's naked hips to halt her gentle motions. "How are you trapped?

"I must sleep above the dirt I was buried in."

Krista's glance shot to the exhibit and the mound of dirt beside the deep grave.

"Not that dirt. He wouldn't make it that easy."

Krista forced Mina off her, ignoring the snarl and the flash of teeth. Mina liked to posture, and might well be vicious if provoked, but she liked it even better when Krista took charge.

Krista removed the dildo. "Sorry, babe. You're gonna have to do better than that. Show me."

They climbed onto the platform. Mina bent beside the pit and pointed toward the bottom. "Beneath that layer of dirt is a manhole. Beneath that is a welded grating. The dirt's under it, too deep to scoop it up."

Krista slid into the hole and tapped the bottom with her feet until she heard a hollow-sounding thud. She knelt and brushed away the dirt. The manhole was unremarkable. She lifted her chin to Mina. "I know you're strong. Get your ass down here and lift this."

Mina's mouth twisted, but she jumped over the edge, thrust a finger through the hole and pried open the heavy iron covering. Just as she'd said, a metal grate covered a deeper hole beneath it. Krista reached over the grave's edge for her utility belt, snagged her flashlight and shone it down into the hole. "It's about six feet down."

Mina's shoulders slumped. "I told you, I'm trapped."

"Do you need all the dirt?"

"I need enough to sprinkle beneath whatever I'm sleeping

on. Or I don't rest. And I can't move out of a twenty-five-foot radius of the dirt."

Krista nodded. "Put it back. We'd best clean up. It'll be dawn soon."

When they'd removed the traces of dirt from their bodies and dressed, Krista pulled Mina into her arms. "I'll figure something out."

The next night, Krista felt a tap on her shoulder.

"What are you doing?"

Krista pulled the long garden hose through the grating and sat back on her haunches to wrap the hose around her arm. Then she laid it aside. She straightened, easing the ache in her hip, then climbed off the platform to stand beside the shop vac she'd duct-taped to the hose. "Want to take a walk?"

Mina cocked her head to the side, her gaze going from the hose to the appliance. "Problem solved?"

Krista unscrewed the top of the vacuum and pulled out the bag holding the dirt from the bottom of the hole. "I have a bed. Will you mind so much if I sprinkle a little of this under it?"

Mina's lips parted. Her eyes misted. "You did this for me?"

"I did this for us both—whether or not you come with me." She folded over the top of the bag, then handed it to Mina. "But now you have choices. You're free."

Mina reached for the bag, then pushed it back toward Krista. "I like it when you're in charge."

They made their way through the museum. At the door, Mina paused to read the note Krista had already taped there. Her laughter trilled.

Mr. Van Helsing—the rat problem is solved.

SHE KNOWS I
AM WATCHING

Rebecca Buck

She knows I am watching. I am her comfort and what makes her thrill with fear. I know she thinks of me when she is alone in her little college room in the lingering dark hours of the night. She believes I am a figment, a dream or a shade, an idea given life by her imagination alone, a result of too much reading, too much solitary longing. She does not realize she knows my appearance because she has seen me, a glimpse in the periphery of her vision, every day for six months.

She's a clever woman, the one I watch, with her stacks of books and hours spent clicking away on her computer. Clever, but with a soul aching for release from the lure of printed words and the struggle to achieve, from success measured in numbers and percentages. Her intelligence is something beyond these limited assessments. She craves her freedom. I give her that release even now, a fantasy promise of what I could grant, if I chose it.

This city is inhabited by many souls like hers, the life being drawn from all of them. Oxford is a vampire city. The ancient honey-gold college buildings, the Gothic arches and gargoyles, the flagstones and sun-drenched quadrangles, the old brick and the worn statues. All of it is steeped in the souls and the stories of those who were here before. The very masonry draws on the life force of those who pass through this place, drinking in a little of their glory, taking a taste of their intellect, nourished by their inspiration. The city is beautiful and celebrated only because of them; a dream of a city, fed by hopes and aspirations, more insidiously glorious than any place on earth. A vampire greater than any who ever lived. And I have known many in my time.

Is it any wonder I was drawn here? A traveler from the New World, where to be what I am is suddenly to be noticed, to be desired and copied. I exist in shadows and dreams. To be exposed is a trauma I feel in every cell. The movies, the books, the fashions, they have all come just a little too close. I fled to a place where the shadows of history are long, and the minds are far too busy to pay me any real heed. The city drains its inhabitants so profoundly, feeding them only to feast again. They do not notice me. Oxford is my city now.

All of it made sense to me when I found her. I had to come here because she is here. All the currents and tides of time, and history, and fate brought me to her, to watch her like a guardian angel and breathe vitality into her fantasies. I am not a death-bringer as the movies would have you believe. I am a life-giver. I do not look like an angel or a demon. When you see me in the edge of your vision I am merely a woman, my pale skin only remarkable if you were to run your fingers over it. I am not cold like death, but I do not feel human to the touch. You would feel it as a tingling in your fingertips, as you made contact with something only half of your world. The human body has merely five limited senses. You would need far more to understand me.

I saw her first when the sky was blue but the leaves brown, the days rapidly sliding into winter. In a steady shadow close to the library I lurked, watching all of the world pass me by. And then all else lost its color and life and there was only her, a slender woman descending the library steps, clutching two heavy books. Casual jeans and a gray blazer, the blue college scarf, could not hide a Pre-Raphaelite beauty manifested in fiery hair with languorous natural curls, skin almost as pale as my own. Anastasia. Stacie to her friends, the few she has. I know all of her friends. I always watch.

My thirst is under control. I have lived too many years to be prey to irresistible urges. But I cannot deny the longing I feel to taste her. I anticipate the flavors of her essence, of her lifeblood, every time I am with her. I catch her scent in the air and my tongue throbs with want for her. Not merely the physical sensation, the nourishing goodness of the liquid in her veins, but the taste of every part of her, of her knowledge and her emotions, of her experiences and her desires. I would taste all of it.

Today she was reading Shakespeare, the sonnets. They make her heart ache at the same time as they expand her mind, her wisdom. Her blood would be sweet today, a long draught of mellow and overripe summer fruits, a hint of honeysuckle and rose. She will taste of old England and of love. Last week she was reading stale academic texts, the analysis of the already overanalyzed. Her blood was bitter like coffee then, pulsing with frustration and want, sharp and intense. I love her most at night when her taste is as ancient and sweet as the honey of mead, and yet spicy and hot like cinnamon and ginger: the taste of desire unfulfilled.

I know already, you see, how she will taste, though I have never approached her. I only watch and nourish her. The world would call me *vampire* and yet, for now, it is she who draws on me. I see the changes; I smell them when she is very close. Her skin is pinker, her body somehow more voluptuous, though she remains as slender as when I first laid eyes on her. Her eyes glisten with a secret she wants only for herself. She is cold no longer. I have made her warm.

I am a dream-giver, a fantasy-builder. I would not be welcomed by many. The people who have no need for me do not see me at all; I pass through their lives unnoticed. You may never see me or any of my kind. By an unspoken and wise consensus we rarely touch the humans we watch, the pleasure we derive being mostly vicarious. We are sensitive beings and to simply watch and feed a fantasy can be enough. Those who want us always know when we are near.

Anastasia could not articulate that she is being watched. She does not understand who drives her thoughts, but she knows I am there with her, and she no longer feels alone.

No doubt she wonders if the incessant studying has driven her imagination to seek refuge in an elaborate fantasy world. But she only knows her way to that world because of me. I am her fantasy. I see her dreams because they are of me, the woman, the creature she believes she will never find. I am the darkness in her depths she is finally acknowledging. I am the edge of pain she craves with her pleasure. I am the place where she loses control and gives herself. I will take her.

I have loved many women in my long and undefined life, some of my kind and scores of humans. But never have I been so consumed with the idea of what it will be like with one woman. Hers is such pale skin, I burn to see her exposed, an expanse of untouched whiteness. I will touch her. I will leave my livid mark on that skin as it flushes with pleasure, and she will welcome it, as I possess her.

My hands will be firm at her wrists as I taste the salt of the smooth skin of her throat. She will feel the graze of my teeth and she will know what I am with a thrill of fear. Desire will follow the fear and she will burn for me, the throb of her pulse a delicious tease on my lips. I could drink and she would welcome it. But I will not.

I will press my mouth to the heat of her kisses and taste her desire. My hand will slide over her warm skin, lingering on soft breasts, feeling the motion of every breath. Her body will relax and when my fingers reach her silky and soft, wet folds she will be open and so ready for me.

Inside her, I will find my own fulfillment, intimacy without blood, as her body yields to me and yet commands me to give her pleasure all at once. In the moment when all of the sensations merge into pure ecstasy and she cries out my name, the name she did not know until that instant, I will have found energy to drive me forward into the future. I take more than blood. I take wisdom and pleasure and heat and lust. This is why I am her guardian, the angel of her fantasies. I must give to her what I need her to return to me.

And she, knowing what I am, will want more. The beauty of it is almost ironic. I need blood to sustain me, and I yearn for hers with its spiced fruit flavors, but she need not be my victim. Her craving is as great as mine. I have made myself her fantasy, taken possession of the place in her heart that was dark and hollow before. She let me in and now, though I have the power, really she is in control. I will not hypnotize her or resort to violence to drink as I need to. She will beg me to do so.

And so another glorious tease will begin. I will taste her essence as it coats my fingers still, a diluted and sweetened version of what is in her blood. I will lick my pink lips and let her see my teeth. I will finally allow her to touch my body in her hope that bringing me pleasure will make me yield to her pleas.

She will gasp at how I feel beneath her hands. "Taste me," she will say in a breathy whisper. My teeth will stroke over her skin again: the inside of her wrist where the blood is purple at the surface, the soft intimacy of her inner thigh. My breath on her throat will make her head sag back in anticipation. She has seen the movies too.

The risk of piercing her jugular is too great. I could heal the wound, but I will not endanger her life. I am not a killer except when I have to be. I give life, I do not take it. Eventually I will find the right place on her trembling body. The crease of her elbow, the flesh of her breast, the place where the cheek of her ass meets the back of her thigh. So many places I could choose. As she still pants for more I will allow my teeth to penetrate her skin, and I will taste honey and ripe fruit.

Filled with desire she will be like summer wine, intoxicating with the first lap of my tongue. I will be infused with wisdom and learning, with the fulfillment of desire and the longing for more. She will gasp and sigh with the pain and then be lost to the pleasure. She will be mine.

That is my fantasy. I wonder, watching her in her sleep, who is really the fantasy-giver. She dreams of me, as her hand creeps between her soft thighs under her cotton sheets in the night, because I have made it so. I have taken her emptiness and filled it with myself. And yet as I gaze upon her, I am as compelled to fantasy as she is. Unconscious though it is, she is just the same as me. Vampires and victims both, nourishing only to feed and, in the feeding, finding strength again. A cycle we are both locked in, each a reflection of the other.

But it is a fantasy only. I am only the ghost at the edge of her vision, the dream figure she does not understand. I watch still, because I fear shattering the fantasy into mirror shards. I could take her. I might take her. She wants it, I am certain. But we are meant to be dreams, or nightmares. We are meant to be part illusion, shrouded in mystery, only half-seen, half-known. That is why there are so many myths and movies. You know we are there, and you are fascinated, entranced. You want us and you fear us. But if we step into the light, what will you do then?

The eternal dilemma our kind face: to be a fantasy or a reality? If she sees me fully, will she still long for me? Or does she crave me because she believes she cannot have me? I could offer her freedom. In my bite I could make her mine forever. I could give that trapped soul wings and we could fly together. But I will be her fantasy no longer and she will not be mine. Could I give that up?

And so I still watch. She walks from her cramped room to the hallowed library, consumes the wisdom that will give flavor to her very blood. She passes through the throngs of the oblivious, separate from them all because she has me in her head and her heart. She lies in her bed and with frantic movements and fierce caresses finds a temporary release for the desires I have given her. I watch everything and absorb every intoxicating detail: from the blush that spreads over her cheeks and her breasts with their rosy hard nipples—as she thrusts the thin sheets from her sweating body—to the rhythm of her hand between her spread thighs. I see the glistening of her arousal, as her flesh swells and her breathing grows ragged, her hips rising as if begging for my intimate touch, her back arching as she offers herself to me.

As I watch, I cannot help but slip my own hand lower, to relieve the ache she creates in me, more insatiable than the blood thirst. Beneath the leather of my pants I find myself as swollen and soaked as she is. Powerless to resist, my fingers mirror hers, rubbing and pinching, circling. I am touching myself, but also her. When she finds her shuddering and gasping release—and the night is filled with the ripe, moist, scent of her—I am with her, falling over that precipice, the two of us locked together in that transient satisfaction. It is never quite enough. Desire compels me to finally reach for her. The need is biting and sharp. In every moment I want her. But I hesitate. Perhaps I want to be her fantasy more.

Do you feel us? In those moments in the dark when your desires are for the most forbidden fulfillment? When you crave the relief of losing yourself? When your passion is so strong only pain will give you release? Those moments where connection is everything, and you are so thirsty for more you feel you can never get enough? We know what is inside your yearning heart. We feed on that need and we make it stronger. We are your fantasies, always there, where you can almost glimpse us but are afraid to look.

Maybe you should look, and maybe you should be afraid when you see I speak the truth. Feel the thrill of the fear; it adds spice to your blood. At the point where fear and fantasy merge, that is when you are hardest to resist and where you draw from us with a hunger to equal our own for you.

Anastasia is mine, and I am hers. Vampires both. She knows I am watching.

ABOUT THE
AUTHORS

VIVI ANNA, a 2008 *Romantic Times* Reviewer Choice Winner and Canadian, likes to burn up the pages with her unique brand of fantasy fiction. Whether it's in the Amazon jungle, an apocalyptic future or the otherworld city of Necropolis, Vivi always writes fast-paced action-adventure with strong independent women who can kick some butt.

REBECCA BUCK is from Nottingham, England and the author of the novels *Truths and Ghosts of Winter.* An English graduate, Rebecca spends every free moment writing, the best outlet she knows for an overactive imagination.

ANGELA CAPERTON writes eclectic erotica that challenges genre conventions. Look for her stories published with Black Lace and eBury Publishing, Cleis, Circlet, Coming Together, Drollerie, eXtasy Books, Renaissance and in the indie magazine *Out of the Gutter.*

CHRISTINE d'ABO loves the world of science fiction, fantasy and romance. By combining the elements of those genres into tales of adventure and love, Christine creates the types of stories she loves to read.

ADELE DUBOIS is a former newspaper and magazine columnist, features writer, and foreign correspondent published in the Caribbean, the United Kingdom and the United States. When not on the beach by the ocean, or walking along the quiet shores of a Delaware bay, she enjoys her rural eastern Pennsylvania home where she is currently working on her next novel.

DELPHINE DRYDEN ditched a career in public education and an earlier stint as a lawyer to write smart, kinky, erotic romance novels. She also writes science fiction. Sometimes, she even writes kinky, erotic science fiction!

A. E. GRACE is a writer of horror and nonfiction, currently studying for a degree in creative and media writing at Middlesex University, England. In her spare time she is a DVD and book reviewer and enjoys reading both mainstream and genre fiction.

MYLA JACKSON pens wildly sexy adventures of all genres including historical westerns, medieval tales, romantic suspense, contemporary romance and paranormal romances with beasties of all shapes and sizes. When not wrangling words from her computer with the help of her canine muses, she's snow-skiing, boating or riding her ATV.

REGINA JAMISON enjoys writing fiction, erotica and poetry. Her poetry has appeared in *Clamour* and more recently in

Off the Rocks: An Anthology of GLBT Writing. Her erotica can be found in *Zane's Purple Panties.* She is currently pursuing her MFA in creative writing at City College in New York.

SHAYLA KERSTEN believes everyone deserves a little romance. Her published works include gay, straight and bisexual romances with one common thread—heat and passion. Shayla currently divides her time between writing, her mother, the evil day job and her spoiled rotten critters.

ANNA MEADOWS is a part-time executive assistant, part-time lesbian housewife. Her work appears in *Best Lesbian Romance 2010* and *2011.*

VICTORIA OLDHAM lives in England with her partner of more than seven years. She has published erotica in various anthologies, and is currently an editor for Bold Strokes Books, as well as a freelance writer with more than sixty published articles.

PAISLEY SMITH is a full-time freelance writer and can usually be found in front of her computer either writing, chatting, promoting or plotting. A true Southern belle, Paisley enjoys all things feminine such as the perfect shade of lipstick, a pair of killer heels and a sexy, confident woman.

KARIS WALSH is a horseback-riding instructor from the Pacific Northwest and the author of the romance novel *Harmony.*

ABOUT
THE EDITOR

DELILAH DEVLIN is a prolific and award-winning author of erotica and erotic romance with a rapidly expanding reputation for writing deliciously edgy stories with complex characters, creating both dark, erotically charged paranormal worlds and richly descriptive historical stories that ring with authenticity. Ms. Devlin has published over eighty erotic stories in multiple genres and lengths.

Her published print titles include *Into the Darkness*, *Seduced by Darkness*, *Darkness Burning*, *Darkness Captured*, *Down in Texas*, *Texas Men* and *Ravished by a Viking*. She has appeared in Cleis Press's *Lesbian Cowboys*, *Girl Crush*, *Lesbian Lust*, *Passion*, *Carnal Machines*, *Lesbian Cops* and *Dream Lover*. She is published by Avon, Black Lace, Harlequin, Kensington, Atria/Strebor, Cleis Press, Ellora's Cave, Samhain Publishing, and in 2011, Berkley.

To learn more about Delilah and her stories, visit DelilahDevlin.com.

More of the Best Lesbian Erotica

Sometimes She Lets Me
Best Butch/Femme Erotica
Edited by Tristan Taormino

Does the swagger of a confident butch make you swoon? Do your knees go weak when you see a femme straighten her stockings? In *Sometimes She Lets Me*, Tristan Taormino chooses her favorite butch/femme stories from the *Best Lesbian Erotica* series.
ISBN 978-1-57344-382-1 $14.95

Lesbian Lust
Erotic Stories
Edited by Sacchi Green

Lust: It's the engine that drives us wild on the way to getting us off, and lesbian lust is the heart, soul and red-hot core of this anthology.
ISBN 978-1-57344-403-3 $14.95

Girl Crush
Women's Erotic Fantasies
Edited by R. Gay

In the steamy stories of *Girl Crush*, women satisfy their curiosity about the erotic possibilities of their infatuations.
ISBN 978-1-57344-394-4 $14.95

Girl Crazy
Coming Out Erotica
Edited by Sacchi Green

These irresistible stories of first times of all kinds invite the reader to savor that delicious, dizzy feeling known as "girl crazy."
ISBN 978-1-57344-352-4 $14.95

Lesbian Cowboys
Erotic Adventures
Edited by Sacchi Green and Rakelle Valencia

With stories that are edgy as shiny spurs and tender as broken-in leather, fifteen first-rate writers share their take on an iconic fantasy.
ISBN 978-1-57344-361-6 $14.95

Out of This World Romance

Steamlust
Steampunk Erotic Romance
Edited by Kristina Wright

Shiny brass and crushed velvet; mechanical inventions and
romantic conventions; sexual fantasy and kinky fetish: this
is a lush and fantastical world of women-centered stories
and romantic scenarios, a first for steampunk fiction.
ISBN 978-1-57344-721-8 $14.95

The Sweetest Kiss
Ravishing Vampire Erotica
Edited by D.L. King

These sanguine tales give new meaning
to the term "dead sexy" and feature
beautiful bloodsuckers whose desires go
far beyond blood.
ISBN 978-1-57344-371-5 $15.95

Dream Lover
Paranormal Tales of Erotic Romance
Edited by Kristina Wright

A potent potion of fun and sexy tales
filled with male fairies and clairvoyant
scientists, as well as darkly erotic tales of
ghosts, shapeshifters and possession.
ISBN 978-1-57344-655-6 $14.95

Fairy Tale Lust
Erotic Fantasies for Women
Edited by Kristina Wright

Award-winning novelist and erotica
writer Kristina Wright goes over the
river and through the woods to find the
sexiest fairy tales ever written.
ISBN 978-1-57344-397-5 $14.95

In Sleeping Beauty's Bed
Erotic Fairy Tales
By Mitzi Szereto

"Who can resist the erotic origins of fairy
tales from Little Red to Rapunzel's long
braid? Szereto knows her way around
the mythic scholarship and the most
outrageous sexual deviations in Pandora's
Box." —Susie Bright
ISBN 978-1-57344-367-8 $16.95

Red Hot Erotic Romance

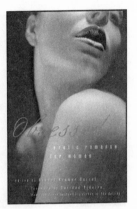

Obsessed
Erotic Romance for Women
Edited by Rachel Kramer Bussel

These stories sizzle with the kind of obsession that is fueled by our deepest desires, the ones that hold couples together, the ones that haunt us and don't let go. Whether just-blooming passions, rekindled sparks or reinvented relationships, these lovers put the object of their obsession first.
ISBN 978-1-57344-718-8 $14.95

Passion
Erotic Romance for Women
Edited by Rachel Kramer Bussel

Love and sex have always been intimately intertwined—and *Passion* shows just how delicious the possibilities are when they mingle in this sensual collection edited by award-winning author Rachel Kramer Bussel.
ISBN 978-1-57344-415-6 $14.95

Girls Who Bite
Lesbian Vampire Erotica
Edited by Delilah Devlin

Bestselling romance writer Delilah Devlin and her contributors add fresh girl-on-girl blood to the pantheon of the paranormal. The stories in *Girls Who Bite* are varied, un-expected, and soul-scorching.
ISBN 978-1-57344-715-7 $14.95

Carnal Machines
Steampunk Erotica
Edited by D. L. King

In this decadent fusing of technology and romance, outstanding contemporary erotica writers use the enthralling possibilities of the 19th-century steam age to tease and titillate.
ISBN 978-1-57344-654-9 $14.95

Heat Wave
Hot, Hot, Hot Erotica
Edited by Alison Tyler

What could be sexier or more seductive than bare, sun-warmed skin? Bestselling erotica author Alison Tyler gathers explicit stories of summer sex bursting with the sweet eroticism of swimsuits, sprinklers, and ripe strawberries.
ISBN 978-1-57344-710-2 $15.95

Erotica for Every Kink

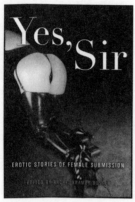

Yes, Sir
Erotic Stories of Female Submission
Edited by Rachel Kramer Bussel

The lucky women in Yes, Sir give up control to irresistibly powerful men who understand that dominance is about exulting in power that is freely yielded.
ISBN 978-1-57344-310-4 $15.95

Best Bondage Erotica
Edited by Alison Tyler

Always playful and dangerously explicit, these arresting fantasies grab you, tie you down, and never let you go.
ISBN 978-1-57344-173-5 $15.95

Best Bondage Erotica 2
Edited by Alison Tyler

From start to finish, these stories of women and men in the throes of pleasurable restraint will have you bound to your chair and begging for more!
ISBN 978-1-57344-214-5 $16.95

Spanked
Red Cheeked Erotica
Edited by Rachel Kramer Bussel

"Editrix extraordinaire Rachel Kramer Bussel has rounded up twenty brisk and stinging tales that reveal the many sides of spanking, from playful erotic accent to punishing payback for a long ago wrong."—Clean Sheets
ISBN 978-1-57344-319-7 $14.95

Rubber Sex
Edited by Rachel Kramer Bussel

Rachel Kramer Bussel showcases a world where skin gets slipped on tightly, then polished, stroked, and caressed—while the bodies inside heat up with lust.
ISBN 978-1-57344-313-5 $14.95

Ordering is easy! Call us toll free or fax us to place your MC/VISA order.
You can also mail the order form below with payment to:
Cleis Press, 2246 Sixth St., Berkeley, CA 94710.

ORDER FORM

QTY	TITLE	PRICE
____	_____	____
____	_____	____
____	_____	____
____	_____	____
____	_____	____
____	_____	____
____	_____	____
____	_____	____

SUBTOTAL _____

SHIPPING _____

SALES TAX _____

TOTAL _____

Add $3.95 postage/handling for the first book ordered and $1.00 for each additional book. Outside North America, please contact us for shipping rates. California residents add 8.75% sales tax. Payment in U.S. dollars only.

* Free book of equal or lesser value. Shipping and applicable sales tax extra.

**Cleis Press • Phone: (800) 780-2279 • Fax: (510) 845-8001
orders@cleispress.com • www.cleispress.com
You'll find more great books on our website**

Follow us on Twitter @cleispress • Friend/fan us on Facebook

Best Erotica Series

"Gets racier every year."—San Francisco Bay Guardian